S0-BNR-839

S
L
A
M

Acm Komal Kare
KGK3

Tres. Ted Vaik TFVØ

Books by Lewis Shiner

FRONTERA
DESERTED CITIES OF THE HEART
SLAM

SLAM

LEWIS SHINER

BANTAM BOOKS
NEW YORK · TORONTO · LONDON · SYDNEY · AUCKLAND

*This edition contains the complete text
of the original hardcover edition.*
NOT ONE WORD HAS BEEN OMITTED.

SLAM

*A Bantam Book / published by arrangement with
Doubleday*

PRINTING HISTORY

*Doubleday edition published July 1990
Bantam edition / November 1991*

*A portion of this book appeared, in much different form,
in* RE:AL, *Spring/Fall, 1988.*

Library of Congress Cataloging-in-Publication Data

Shiner, Lewis.
   Slam / Lewis Shiner.
     p. cm.
   ISBN 0-553-35449-3
   I. Title.
   PS3569.H496S55   1991
   813'.54—dc20   91-16644
                      CIP

Published simultaneously in the United States and Canada

*Bantam Books are published by Bantam Books, a division of Bantam Doubleday Dell
Publishing Group, Inc. Its trademark, consisting of the words "Bantam Books" and
the portrayal of a rooster, is Registered in U.S. Patent and Trademark Office and in
other countries. Marca Registrada. Bantam Books, 666 Fifth Avenue, New York, New
York 10103.*

PRINTED IN THE UNITED STATES OF AMERICA

CWO   0 9 8 7 6 5 4 3 2 1

FOR JIM BLAYLOCK
WHO GAVE ME FONTHILL, BRAINSTORMS, AND A HOME AWAY FROM HOME

My wife, Edith, read all the drafts of this book and helped immeasurably. I also owe thanks to: Martha Millard and Chris Priest, my faithful agents; Pat LoBrutto, my editor, for his inspiration and insight; Lou Aronica, for moral support; Bill Alberts, for legal advice; Allison Joyce, for parole counseling; Don Webb, for UFO mythography; and the many other friends who offered valuable suggestions, including: Neal Barrett, Joe Lansdale, Pat Murphy, Bud Simons, Nancy Sterling, and especially Terry Matz.

SLAM

D A V E had been through Bastrop a dozen times on his way from Austin to Houston. Just outside town the land suddenly rose up and there were pine trees everywhere. The red dirt turned brown with fallen needles and the air became cool and sweet. The Lost Pines, they were called, because there was nothing else like them for a hundred miles in any direction.

He'd spent a weekend with a girlfriend in Bastrop State Park. They'd rented a log cabin and had sweaty sex in front of a fireplace with the inscription "Clever men are good but not best."

He didn't know about the federal prison there until he ended up inside it.

T H E Bastrop Federal Correctional Institute was a few miles north of the main highway, surrounded by forest. There were no signs until the last turnoff. During his six months there Dave learned a number of things. He found out that the prison's main products were military helmets and life rafts. The government paid for them with surplus khaki uniforms for the inmates. He learned not to make eye contact in the yard, and how to sleep no matter what went on around him.

He also learned that his life, or anybody's, was like a piece of soft wood. He could shape it to a certain extent, but it could also get dented or even broken beyond repair.

Most of the people Dave got to know there were drug

dealers. Some were high enough up in the business to wear tinted gold-rimmed glasses and have manicured nails. They ate better than Dave and they landed the trusty jobs. Then there were the repeat offenders, with slurred voices and eyes that didn't quite focus. Not to mention the prisoners waiting for trial at the federal courthouse in Austin. They were thrown in with the general population, regardless of what they'd done. It was hard for Dave not to feel sorry for some of them. It was also dangerous to feel very sorry for anybody, himself included. Dave seemed to be the only tax dodger in there, among the pushers and kidnappers and serial killers. The IRS had, in short, hung Dave out to dry.

His parole came through on October 15, 1988. It was a Saturday, nine days before his fortieth birthday. There was a prison bus headed for Elgin, Bastrop, and Austin later in the day. Dave had elected not to wait around.

"Who's picking you up?" the gate guard asked him.

"My ex-girlfriend." Dave sat on one of the blue plastic chairs in the waiting room. From there he could see out into the parking lot and the surrounding hills. The grass was still a parched yellow from the last days of summer. He could see the road all the way out to the perimeter fence where it curved to the right and met Highway 95. "Haven't seen her since we split up. That was back before I got busted, more than a year ago." Dave looked at his watch again, like he'd told himself he wouldn't do. On the phone she'd said she would be there by ten-thirty. Here it was nearly eleven o'clock.

"Maybe she's got fond memories," the guard said.

"Yeah," Dave said. "You got to have hope."

He'd thought about being free so long he'd milked all the emotion out of it. There was nothing left but nerves. If he turned around he would see the twin chain-link fences,

woven with razor wire, that surrounded the prison yard.
He didn't want to ever see them again.

A red Camaro roared into the visitors' lot. Dave felt like
the guardhouse floor had dropped a couple of stories. He
grabbed his cardboard suitcase and headed for the door.

"Good luck," the guard said.

That was when Dave saw the man sitting next to Patsy
in the front seat.

"Thanks," he said. "I may need it."

T H E Camaro squealed to a stop in front of the building,
rocking slightly on its shocks. Patsy had never been intimi-
dated by the presence of the law. Dave walked up to the
passenger window. Inside he saw a lanky cowboy in a straw
hat that was stained and creased from too much han-
dling. The man wore a black Jack Daniel's T-shirt and jeans
with no knees left. He hadn't shaved in a couple of days.
The hat was pulled low over his eyes and one hand held a
Budweiser peeking out of a can-sized paper sack.

Patsy got out of the far side of the car. She looked the
same as ever. Her blonde hair swept back in wings from
the sides of her face and curled down her shoulders. She
had on a red T-shirt stretched tight over her breasts and
jeans scuffed white across the rump. "Dave, this here is Marc
with a *C*."

"Mucho gusto," Marc said with a Texas accent, and poked
his hand out the window.

Dave shook it. Apparently Patsy was not going to say that
he was just her younger brother, in town for a surprise
visit, or that he was just her mechanic and would be taking
the car on into the shop. Instead Marc said, "Honey, get

your ass back in the car and let's get this old boy where he needs to go. I'm horny as a three-peckered billy goat."

Patsy shrugged at Dave and said, "Love is blind, don't you know?"

Marc seemed disinclined to move, so Dave got in on Patsy's side. He could smell her perfume and the sun on her skin and the hot vinyl upholstery.

"How long was you in for?" Marc asked. Patsy hit the gas and the car took off on smoking tires.

"Six months," Dave said. The acceleration pinned him to his seat.

"So tell me. Did big black guys fuck you up the ass in there or what?"

"Now Marcus," Patsy said. "You behave yourself."

"No offense," Marc said. "I did a little time in the slam myself. Just a couple weeks in county jail. They had to no-bill me. Wouldn't have been there at all except I couldn't make bail."

"What did they get you for?"

"Arson. Hell, they should of give me a medal. Sumbitch went straight up, burned to the slab in seven and a half minutes, didn't touch a damned thing on either side. Took every bit of evidence with it."

Dave turned to watch the prison recede behind him. The grass, he had to admit, looked good. A nice, even green. He'd spent seven hours and fifteen minutes a day, five days a week, working on it. He didn't think he'd miss it.

"So what's this job you said you got?" Patsy asked. She slowed briefly for the stop sign at Highway 95 then spun the wheel hard over and hit the gas. Dave's suitcase slid the length of the seat and tumbled to the floor.

"It's in Surfside," Dave said. "On the coast, just down from Galveston. I'm going to be caretaker."

"We ain't driving you all that way, are we?" Marc asked.

"No," Dave said. Patsy was clearly a lost cause. "In fact you could let me off just up the road, where the Greyhound stops."

They passed the first houses Dave had seen in months, tiny one-bedroom shacks. A couple of them had red storage buildings shaped like miniature barns. Dave saw a toy tractor and a Chihuahua not much bigger than his hand. It was like the entire world had shrunk while he was in prison.

"Caretaker," Patsy said. "I can't feature you going all the way to Surfside just for a job."

"This is not your everyday kind of job. You ever hear about those rich old ladies that leave their money to their cats? Fred's got one down there that just died. I mean, I never thought about it before, but somebody's got to feed the little bastards and clean up after them and all that."

"I can't feature you with all those cats," Patsy said. "How many are we talking about here?"

"Twenty-three," Dave said.

"Lord. You never liked them one at a time."

"Maybe I'll get used to it."

"You mean they're going to pay you for that?" Marc asked.

"Marc here isn't a big believer in jobs himself," Patsy said.

"Work ain't natural," Marc said.

"Amen to that," Dave said.

T H E Y turned east on 21, away from the main part of Bastrop, away from the HEB grocery and the Wal-Mart and the road to Austin. They climbed past an old white frame church with a high steeple. A moment later they were in the trees and Dave could smell pine sap and fallen needles. Patsy pulled in to the Hilltop Express Lane Grocery and Exxon. She put the car in park but didn't turn the motor off.

"I'll just walk him in," she told Marc.

Dave bought a ticket to Galveston for $23. It was nearly half the fifty he got when he left prison. Patsy kissed him on the cheek and then dabbed the lipstick off with a crumpled Kleenex from her purse. "I still think about you, you know . . . every now and again."

Marc, waiting in the Camaro, tapped lightly on the horn.

Dave waved goodbye as they drove off, then bought himself a sandwich and a 7-Up. "I can't sell you no beer," the woman at the counter said. She was in her fifties, with long, dirty red-brown hair, and she barely came up past the top of the counter. "Not if you're on parole."

"That's okay," Dave said, alarmed that it was so obvious. "Just this stuff."

"Fine," she said. "I just can't sell you no beer, that's all."

He sat outside under a stand of pines near the old lady's trailer and waited for the bus. Inside his cardboard suitcase was a Walkman they hadn't let him have in prison. Some of the more resourceful convicts, it seemed, had learned to sharpen the capstan posts and convert them into tattoo machines. In a minute he would take it out and put the headphones on. For the time being it was enough to listen to the wind move through the trees.

D A V E had spent a lot of time in the prison library. It reminded him of primary school: the long Formica tables, the dark green metal shelves, either against the wall or no more than waist-high, the expressions of fierce concentration focused on Dr. Seuss. For some reason there were dozens of travel books. They'd left Dave with a powerful urge for motion. One of them had quoted Pascal, saying that human restlessness was a result of innate human misery. That if human beings weren't constantly distracted they would sink inevitably into despair.

Dave found this hard to swallow. It seemed to him that there were important pieces of knowledge, things that he needed to complete himself, scattered all over the planet. It was his sovereign duty to go around and pick them up. His parents, misreading the same impulse, worked endless jigsaw puzzles, settling for a less emphatic click.

When they did travel they were armored with cameras and baggage and suntan lotion. They never made it through the membrane. Behind the membrane was where the locals lived, where the good stuff was hidden.

Greyhound buses went to the other side. They were full of men with sideburns and shirts buttoned to the throat, and fat young mothers with squalling kids. They stopped at the Hilltop Grocery instead of the Hilton. Dave was satisfied to be where he was, making good time down I-45 out of Houston, nearly forty but on the verge of a fresh start, a free man, open to possibility.

Out the right-hand window he got his first glimpse of the Gulf of Mexico. It had crept slowly in toward the highway from the southeast. First there were boats parked in the driveways, then canals between the houses. Then, in the distance, the ocean itself. After that came Tiki Island, on Jones Bay, with its A-frames and condos on stilts, then, over the next rise, the mile-and-a-half-long causeway to Galveston.

From there Dave could see Galveston itself in the distance, a cluster of marinas, a red-and-white checked water tower, a multi-story hotel. Off to his left was the old causeway from the turn of the century, low arches of concrete that barely cleared the water, with a permanently raised drawbridge in the middle.

As soon as the bus was on solid ground again the median sprouted palm trees and oaks and shrubs that looked like eucalyptus. Palm trees had nothing but good associations for Dave. They were a universal visual code for beaches and good weather and no work.

Fred wasn't at the bus station, even though Dave had called ahead from Houston. There was no answer at the office or his apartment. He was about to try the phones again when he saw the faded yellow Porsche jockey toward him through the traffic. It swung out in front of a semi and skidded past him to a stop. Thin white smoke chugged out of the tailpipe under a bumper sticker that said "Shit happens."

Dave opened the door and got in.

"*Ça que c'est, homme?*" Fred said. He was six three, well over two hundred and still gaining. He was big all over but deceptively light on his feet. He had a thick mustache to compensate for the front half of his hair being gone. He wore expensive Italian sunglasses with a safety pin through one of the hinges.

"You hear they've quit using rats for experimental animals?" he asked, burning rubber as they pulled away. Dave tried to remember if he had any friends that drove at normal speed. No names came to mind. "They're using lawyers instead. Three reasons. One, they're easier to come by. Two, you don't get so attached to them. Three, there's some things a rat just won't do."

Dave put his hand on Fred's shoulder and squeezed it hard. "Man," he said, "I am so glad to see you." He had to blink the sudden moisture out of his eyes.

"Yeah, well, we all missed you too. Listen, that's too bad about Patsy, what you were saying on the phone. I always liked her."

"Sure you did."

"She was cute. Fabulous magumbas. But if what you need is to get laid, I could maybe set something up. There's a massage parlor pretty close to here where I got three or four clients. I can get you a discount."

"Later, maybe."

"Whatever. I guess we should go see your parole officer, anyway. She's staying late just for you."

F R E D parked at a meter in front of the main post office. They were on Rosenberg, a block south of Post Office Street. Also known as 25th Street and Avenue E, respectively. Fred had tried to explain. The grid system had come first, dating back to the Galveston City Company in 1838. People got tired of it and subverted it. Eventually the common names went up on the street signs alongside the letters and numbers.

The old post office had actually been on Post Office Street. The new one was built in the 1930s from carved yellow stone, with brooding eagles over each of the two entrances. As Dave walked under the eagles he saw they had started to crack. He and Fred rode an ancient elevator up to Room 504.

Dave's stomach hurt. "Do we have to do this now?"

"C'mon, Dave. It's the law. You got to check in within twenty-four hours, and she didn't want to have to come down here tomorrow."

The office was empty and dark except for shafts of orange light from the setting sun. "Mizz Cook?" Fred said.

A gray-haired woman in her fifties appeared next to the maze of cubicles in the middle of the room. She wore a gray polyester pant suit, gray shoes, and a gray satin blouse with a bow. Her silver cat's eye glasses glinted as she looked Dave up and down slowly. Finally she nodded and held out her hand. "David," she said.

"Call me Dave. Please."

"Very well. I'm Mrs. Cook."

"Hi," Dave said.

"I understand from Fred that we shouldn't have any trouble with you."

"No ma'am."

"Come on back to the office."

The room was barely large enough for a gray metal desk and a pair of filing cabinets. She had a cat calendar on one wall, and, behind her, a poster of a cat clinging to a horizontal wooden pole. Puffy letters across the bottom read, "Help me hang in there Jesus." Dave caught Fred's eye and tilted his head at the poster. Fred shut his eyes and gritted his teeth. Dave sat down. Fred stood in the doorway with his arms folded, looking off into the hallway. He had his lips pursed, feigning a nonchalant whistle.

"You have a job waiting for you, is that correct?" Mrs. Cook asked.

"That's right," Dave said.

"Is something funny, David?"

"No ma'am."

"I see. Well, we won't go into details today. I'll stop off Monday and take a look at your place of employment, and then we'll have you in, let's see, how about Thursday? During the day?"

"Uh, that would be fine, I guess."

"Let's say Thursday at eleven. In the meantime, let me remind you of the conditions of your parole. You are re-

quired to not associate with criminals, or anyone on probation or parole. You are required to not frequent places of
a disreputable character, or places where alcoholic bever-
ages are sold and consumed, or places where illegal drugs
are sold or consumed. You are required to report any criminal offense in which you are involved, even a traffic ticket,
within forty-eight hours to me personally. Do you understand?"

The poster didn't seem very funny anymore. Dave nodded.

"I expect this seems very harsh to you. Experience has
taught us that we cannot allow any leeway in the enforce-
ment of these rules. You have to understand that the law
has made us responsible for your well-being. We intend
to take care of you and keep you on the straight and narrow. Is that clear?"

Dave nodded again.

"We'll get to the rest on Thursday. Mostly I wanted to
take a look at you, make sure I could count on you to do
your part. I *can* count on you, can't I?"

"Yes ma'am," Dave said.

"Could you speak up?"

"Yes ma'am."

"Very good. The address I show here is 403 North Beach
Front, Surfside, 77541. Is that home or business?"

"Both. I'm going to be caretaker there."

"Caretaker." She made a note on her page. Dave thought
she looked skeptical. "I'll see you there on Monday."

"Yes ma'am. What time on Monday?"

She looked up slowly. Dave couldn't see her eyes behind
the glasses. "We'll just let that be a surprise."

' '   .   .   .   S 0 the lawyer jumps over the side of the life-
boat and starts swimming for land. The priest can barely

stand to watch. The two sharks head right for the lawyer
and then, at the last minute, they veer off, like this, one on
each side, and away they go. The priest says, 'Praise the
Lord! It's a miracle!' But the doctor shakes his head and
says, 'Just professional courtesy.' "

"That fucking poster," Dave said. "Can you believe it?"

"Well," Fred said, "at least it shows she's got a heart. Of
some kind or other."

They were on Seawall Boulevard, headed south. The
streetlights had come on even though it wasn't fully dark
yet. Off to the left was the Gulf of Mexico, as far as the eye
could see. At the moment the water was dirty brown, but
in bright sunshine it would reflect the sky in shades of deep
crystalline blue. They passed the Pleasure Pier, with its
shell shops and fast food, and the traffic started to thin out.

"It's not that big a deal," Fred said. "You convince her
you're a good boy, then it's down to once a month, a one-
hour meeting. How hard can it be?"

On the sidewalk Dave saw a middle-aged guy on a skateboard, being towed by a Labrador retriever in a bandanna and sunglasses. The guy wore nothing but white shorts
and carried a beer in a coozy cup. The top of his head
was sunburned bright pink.

"Did you see that?" Dave asked.

"See what?"

Dave shook his head. Another of the books he'd read in
prison said travel was the search for a magic place, where
the traveller would be transformed. This seemed too good
an omen to put into words. "Never mind," he said.

Dave watched the girls along the seawall. Six months. The
only women he'd seen in the flesh had been in the visitors' room, and they were there to see somebody else. Usually crawling all over them, too, doing everything two
people can do without taking their clothes off.

These women, though, looked like they didn't belong to anybody. It put Dave in the grip of powerful yearnings. There was something sexy about the town itself. It was the palm trees and the salt air, even the look of the houses. They reminded Dave of New Orleans, all the three-story brick buildings with wrought-iron balconies on every floor. There was a sense of history, of things having settled in. The convenience stores and fast-food joints were tucked in between nineteenth-century gingerbread houses. The city was like a blonde with dark roots, sitting on a barstool, a line of empty glasses in front of her and an afternoon to kill.

He absolutely had to stop thinking about sex.

"Listen," Fred said. "There's something I should tell you. It's no big deal or anything. It's just, there's a couple of other people interested in the house."

"What do you mean, interested?"

"Well, what it is, they're trying to break the will. Listen, calm down. They haven't either one got a chance in hell. The first one runs some kind of UFO church on the local cable. Strictly a nut. The old lady used to give him some money, is all."

"And the other one?"

"Even less of a problem. Her name is Nixon, widow, early fifties, thinks she's nineteen. Dyed blonde hair, tight clothes, it's ridiculous. Keeps coming up with these forged documents to prove she's related to the old lady. I mean real pieces of shit. Looks like she got kindergartners to finger-paint them."

"If it gets to be something I should worry about, though, you'll tell me. Right?"

"Oh, sure. Absolutely."

They passed a short brunette in a red two-piece bathing suit and matching high heels and sunglasses. The sunglasses were pushed up onto the top of her head, California style. She had a dog too, a shaggy gray poodle on a red leash. The dog robot-marched along, head down, the collar pulling its ears forward at an angle. "This is nice, here," Dave said.

Fred checked the rearview mirror. "Easy, bro. You're just a little pussy-crazy right now. These here are mostly a bunch of college assholes that drink themselves stupid and throw up on their shoes. Galveston is a wonderful town, but they aren't the reason, okay?"

"Whatever you say."

The right side of the highway was an endless row of condos. They were lined up like dominoes, with sliding glass doors and balconies full of furniture that faced the ocean. "What happens," Dave asked, "if a hurricane comes through here?"

"Some insurance companies take a beating. The seawall works, though. It's thick at the bottom and then curves, turns the big waves up when they hit. And hell, people got to live somewhere. You got any idea what those babies sell for? About a hundred grand per bedroom, that's what."

Dave looked at him. "You've got money in some of these, don't you?"

"Is that a crime? You're going to have some money left over with what you're making now. Maybe you should put it to work for you. I can set something up, whenever you're ready."

"I don't mean to sound ungrateful," Dave said. "But you know you're wasting your time."

"Listen, compadre. You're forty years old."

"Thirty-nine. But who's counting?"

"I'm worried about you, okay? Not just me. Anson and Mad Dog were up here the other week and they're worried too. I'm only saying this because I love you, man."

"I know, I know. I wish you'd relax. I'll be fine."

"You always say that. And look at you. You ended up in Bastrop FCI."

"An oversight."

"My ass. IRS went after you because you wouldn't play ball. You cheated on your taxes, for Christ's sake. It wasn't like you actually hurt anybody. It was your attitude."

"My dad used to ground me for my attitude. It was because he couldn't think up any other excuse. Look, I'm sorry. You guys came to see me in the slam, and that means a lot to me. You guys and my mom were the only ones. I love all of you. But don't ask me to start buying real estate or playing the market. Have a little respect."

"Okay. But have a little respect for me too. This caretaker gig is a sweet deal. Don't get so proud you feel like you have to fuck it up."

T H E frenzied overbuilding ended where the island did, at Red Fish Cove: a fully planned and zoned community (under development). A toll bridge led back to the mainland, followed by a rough stretch of two-lane blacktop that passed through the Brazoria National Wildlife Refuge. Most of the west side of the road was salt marsh, full of razor-edged grass that was never quite the right shade of green. What houses there were all sat up on stilts.

Fred opened the Porsche up once they got off the bridge. They covered the twenty miles to Surfside in less than fifteen minutes. Fred had already started to brake when the headlights caught something off to the right. It looked like a cross between a French chateau and a fairy castle made of melting ice cream.

"What the hell was that?" Dave said.

"It's called Fonthill. Some old guy built it back around 1910. You get a lot of nuts in this part of the world. The entire thing is made out of cast concrete. I mean stairs, desks, ceilings, everything. Had to put pilings down to bedrock to keep the thing from sinking. Forty-two rooms. It's condemned now. Nobody can afford to fix it up."

"I thought I saw somebody on the roof."

"Skateboarder, probably."

"In the dark?"

"They're crazy. You can't keep them out. Every couple of months they cart another one off to the hospital, all busted to shit from falling off."

They were coming into something like civilization. In the distance was a high bridge over a barge canal. On the left they passed a bar with a handpainted sign that said BCI #2. The parking lot was full of Harleys. Down the street was Beth's Surfside Inn, a motel done up in weathered gray lumber and stucco. They all had yellow portable signs out in front. Fred hit the brakes again and the Porsche fishtailed as it slowed. "Here we go," he said. He pulled into a rutted dirt road that led toward the ocean. At the corner was a frame building painted bright purple, one of the few not on stilts. The portable sign in front said "Kitty's Purple Cow" and "Burgers." Coming up in the headlights was the Cedar Sands Motel, two stories of whitewashed cinderblock.

Fred turned left into the driveway of a beach house across from the motel. It was up on wooden six-by-sixes, with a double carport underneath. The house itself was two stories, approximately square, with a balcony that faced the Gulf. Fred parked next to a late-model band-aid-colored Dodge K-Car. As soon as he shut the engine off, Dave heard cats yowling. He looked at Fred. Fred shrugged.

They got out of the car. A strong breeze blew off the water, making Dave's short prison haircut stand on end. A
set of wooden stairs led up the inland side of the carport.
Fred went up first. The cats seemed to hear him and
screamed even louder. Dave hung back, the heart suddenly
gone out of him.

Fred looked down. "What's the deal? You said you liked
cats."

"I lied," Dave said.

"What?"

"I'm not phobic or anything. I just never liked the little
bastards, is all."

"This is a hell of a time to tell me."

"If I'd told you any earlier I'd still be in jail."

"Can you handle this or not? I mean, late as it is,
I'm going to need some kind of final decision from you
here."

Dave grabbed the two-by-four banister and pulled himself up the steps. "I can handle it. Like you always say,
how hard can it be?"

Fred worked the deadbolt then put a second key into the
handle. "Careful," he said. "They're supposed to stay inside. It's in the will."

He opened the door.

"Oh Christ," Dave said, gagging. Fred shoved him through
and slammed the door behind them.

"Clean-up man hasn't been here in a couple of days,"
Fred said.

"No kidding."

"Let me get a window."

"Oh, man."

Fred got a window open and they stood in it together.
Dave inhaled the aroma of salt and dead fish and marsh
grass and thought it fine as imported perfume. He filled

his lungs and turned around and blinked the tears from his eyes.

Across the room from him was a six-foot round window that looked east onto the Gulf. The living room was open for the full two stories. Stairs on the south wall led up to a walkway and closed doors. Cats sprawled everywhere. Dave counted a half-dozen on the living room furniture. Two more circled his shoes, sniffing at them and then hissing at each other. One sat on the black-and-white linoleum in the kitchen doorway, one dozed on the breakfast bar, and he could hear another crunch dry food inside the kitchen itself.

"The sooner we get started," Fred said, "the sooner that smell goes away."

"Right."

"Hey," Fred said. "How hard can it be?"

They opened every window in the house and cleaned all ten litter boxes, one for each room plus an extra on the second floor landing. The used litter was black and greasy and filled two Hefty Steel-Saks. It took three 25-pound bags of Tidy Cat 3 to refill the boxes. When they were done Dave put the garbage sacks on the porch and washed his hands in the kitchen sink. He could see the waves come in from where he stood and they nearly hypnotized him. Finally he went back into the living room. Fred sat on the edge of the bureau under the big round window.

Dave threw a chubby gray kitten off the couch and sat down. All the furniture was covered in bright blue cotton and the walls looked freshly painted. "Nice place," he said. "Even before you compare it to where I've been."

"It's worth a quarter mill easy," Fred said. "You got a screened-in front porch and a second bath upstairs—hell, you could put four or five couples in here every weekend, no sweat."

There were doilies on every flat surface and framed photos on the doilies. Dave picked one up. It showed a plain young woman with a 1940s hairdo. "I thought you said the old lady didn't have any relatives."

"She didn't. She cut all those pictures out of magazines."

"Weird. Well, nothing says I have to keep them around, right?"

"Wrong, Dave. The will says everything is to be kept exactly as it is. *Exactly* as it is. If the lawyers for the saucer nut or the widow Nixon find a picture frame or a cat out of place, we're in probate court the next day. I get fired, they become trustee, their client gets the house and salary."

The small gray cat jumped back on the couch and got in Dave's lap. It began to knead his crotch, lifting its front feet head-high with each stroke. It purred audibly. A black cat with some kind of skin problem on its nose got up on the back of the couch and sniffed at Dave's ear. He fought not to react to its cool, damp touch.

"That striped one over there is called Greaseball. The one looks like he's got nothing in him but sand? I don't know too many of the others' names . . ."

"Does the will say I have to call them by name?"

"No," Fred said. "But it might help your attitude, you know?"

Dave held up his hands. "I'll try. Okay?"

"That black one is called Morpheus. He's got a fungus on his nose there that you need to medicate every couple days. The salve's in the kitchen with a copy of the will. Everything you're supposed to do is written down in there."

A huge black and silver tabby wandered over to look at Dave's shoes. It butted them with its forehead and rubbed them with the sides of its face. Then it rolled onto its back and grabbed at Dave's ankles. Dave could feel the ends of its claws like tiny tweezers picking at his skin. He sat perfectly still, uncomfortably aware of his hands as they lay at his sides.

He caught Fred sneaking a look at his counterfeit Mexican Rolex. "Hey," Dave said. "You don't have to babysit me, for God's sake. If you've got a date or something, go ahead on."

Fred stood up. "As a matter of fact . . ."

"Anybody I know?"

Fred shook his head. "I barely know her myself. All I know is . . ." His hands turned palm up, fingers bent. He looked from one of them to the other. "She's got . . . such . . ."

"Yeah," Dave said. "I know. I know."

"Listen, Mad Dog brought up all the clothes and stuff you left at his place. I put them in the guest room upstairs."

"You got everything I own in one closet?" It struck him as a little sad.

"Most of it was cassettes. What the hell, at least he didn't have to rent a U-Haul. You can even move the stuff up there around if you want. You should do okay. It's not so flowery as the old lady's room, which she didn't want anybody sleeping in anyway. The car downstairs goes with the place. It's got maybe a hundred miles on it. Here's the keys to everything." He set them on the coffee table, in the narrow space between two of the pictures. "Oh yeah. You probably need a little capital to get started." He took out a money clip. There was a twenty on top and a thick wad underneath. "How much you need?"

Dave's eyes bulged. "Forty or fifty would probably be fine."

Fred pulled the clip off. The other bills were all singles.

"Twenty's fine," Dave said.

"Sorry. I'll have the checks for you in a day or two. Can you think of anything else?"

"Not a thing," Dave said. He tried to shove the cat out of his lap. It hooked its claws into his pants and he had to pry one leg off at a time. He stood up, holding the cat awkwardly around the middle.

"Listen," Fred said. "Let me call and cancel that date. This is ridiculous. I can't just go off and leave you on your first night back."

"I swear to you it's not a problem."

"It could be. This is a crisis node for you."

"A what?"

"Forget I said anything. We'll go into Freeport, get a couple burgers, take in a movie or something."

"Fred, goddammit, I'm fine. I'll bring home a few groceries, kind of putter around for a while. It'll be good."

"You're sure?"

"Positive."

"Well. All right. But tomorrow night we cruise for burgers."

"Absolutely."

I T was after eight-thirty. When he checked the refrigerator Dave found a very old carton of yogurt and something that had once been an apple. The other shelves were empty except for nine mason jars containing homemade jam, jelly, and preserves. Dave waded through the cats and went out the kitchen door and down the stairs. The air was still warm, though the last of the sunlight was gone.

He crossed a low rise and there was the ocean. He took off his shoes and socks. The sand at the waterline was the same dark khaki color as his trousers, drying to perfect cream in the dunes where he stood. The water was murky green and it flashed blue in the starlight as the waves curled into the land. Out to sea the drilling platforms made islands of harsh white light. Closer in, Dave saw the running lights of a barge headed for Freeport.

There were a few cars parked by the water, no more than six or eight between where he stood and the pier a mile to the north. Somebody had a jam box playing rap. All Dave could hear of it was the thud of the drum machine and an occasional raspy cry. He stood and watched for a while. Then he closed his eyes and listened to the tide rumble toward him and hiss slowly away.

A six-pack, he thought. Maybe a can of Planters cocktail peanuts and a hot dog with mustard and relish. A couple of cream-filled chocolate cupcakes with white squiggles on top for dessert. The thought of it almost made him pass out. And a *Playboy* and a *Penthouse* that he could read without anybody looking over his shoulder.

He walked to the highway and put his shoes back on. Off to his left, two blocks away, it intersected a second highway that came from the general direction of Freeport. The second highway had just come down off a high bridge. Red and green lights hung underneath the bridge and, below it, squares of light shone in the windows of the A-frames and stilt houses that lined the barge canal.

There was a 7-Eleven on one corner of the intersection and a much older grocery across from it. Dave headed that way, keeping to the gravel along the edge of the road. The town of Surfside, such as it was, seemed on the verge of drying up. Next to Kitty's was Evelyn's Seafood and Steaks, now closed. The block after it was empty except for an abandoned white stucco convenience store.

Dave cut across the highway to the Surfside Grocery. It was a long, low, frame building, light blue, with a couple of gas pumps in front. The inside smelled of yeast and sugar. It was a smell 7-Elevens never had. The counter

ran along the front wall to the right of the door. An old
wooden magazine rack stood in the left-hand corner and
from the doorway Dave could see they had an extensive se-
lection of off-brand skin magazines. It didn't matter,
though, because the woman at the register was so young
and good-looking he was embarrassed to buy them from
her.

Dave got a twelve-pack of Bud and some 7-Ups and looked
through the junk food rack in the middle of the store.
Gimme caps and bandannas hung from a clothesline overhead. Dave pretended to examine a bandanna with a skull-
faced biker and flaming letters that read "Highway to Hell."

The girl leaned into the counter, talking to a man in a
volunteer fireman's cap. Her hair was black and cut so
that it stuck straight out all over. She wore a black T-shirt
with the sleeves ripped out. The front of the shirt showed
a skull between the words "Suicidal" and "Tendencies." It
was the name of a thrash band that Anson had talked
about. Her lipstick was the color of arterial blood and her
eyes were outlined heavily in black. A single black tear
was either painted or tattooed below her right eye. A toy
dagger hung from the opposite ear. She might have been
five or ten pounds overweight. Dave was not inclined to
criticize.

"Got to go," the fireman said.

"See ya," the girl said. The fireman eased out the door
in a Texas walk, big steps taken very slowly.

Dave put the drinks and junk food on the counter and
asked for a hot dog. She rang up the rest of the groceries
while it cycled through the microwave. "Can I see some ID
for the beer?"

She had a soft voice with no discernible accent. Now that
he was closer he could see her hair had grown out light
brown at the roots. It gave her an odd, half-finished look.

Dave nodded and got out his wallet. He already had the license on the counter before the absurdity of it hit him. Jailhouse reflexes, he thought. He still did what anybody told him to.

"This license is expired," she said.

"Oh come on. I'm forty years old, for God's sake. Are you seriously not going to sell me that beer?"

"Maybe I just wanted to see what your name was." She showed him the edge of a smile, then rang up the beer, five beeps and a whir. "And it says there you're only thirty-nine."

"Okay, I confess," Dave said. He put his elbows on the counter and leaned closer. "I'm fourteen. The license is a fake."

Her eyes cooled. "Radical," she said. The microwave chimed. She put the hot dog in a bun and the bun in a foil bag. "That'll be nine eighty-three."

Dave paid her. As he put his hand on the door she said, "I bet they call you Dave."

He hesitated. "That's right."

"Goodnight, Dave."

He was outside before he realized he hadn't asked for her name. What a moron. But then she was just a kid. Much too young for him. And some kind of punk besides. Did they even *have* a minimum age for selling beer in Texas?

Drop it, he thought.

O N the northeast corner of the intersection, across from the 7-Eleven, was the tourist information center. It was a beige portable building that looked long abandoned.

Beyond it the road dipped down to the beach. The wind
had come up and Dave could hear the waves going off
like muffled explosions. The spray glinted briefly as it hung
in the air. West of the building, lined up along a rutted
dirt lot, were four historical markers. There was nothing
else but low marsh grass anywhere around.

Dave stopped to read the markers by the light of the
7-Eleven. They talked about the city of Old Velasco. The
first battle between Texas and Mexico had been fought there.
He found himself oddly moved. He'd let himself forget
about history. Places, like people, were the sum of the things
that had happened to them. Surfside hadn't always been
there, and it hadn't appeared out of nowhere.

The same could be said for Dave. Once he'd been a high
school student, on scholarship at St. Mark's School of
Texas in Dallas. It was where he'd first met Fred and Anson.
Mad Dog had come later. Steve Miller and Boz Scaggs,
soon to become rock stars, were only two grades ahead of
him. Their band, the Marksmen, had played at his sophomore dance. His senior year he'd been in love with a girl
named Alice. Her image—short, dark, head cocked at an
angle—had become the symbol of all his adolescent longing.

They didn't teach Texas history at St. Mark's. The stu-
dents were expected to already know it. Dave had trans-
ferred from out of state and had never picked it up. Standing
there at the edge of the highway, listening to the tide,
smelling the salt flats, Dave felt disconnected. Like he was
just visiting. The brown cast-iron markers told him that
the love of the land, like any other kind of love, was something he would have to earn.

He took his dinner home and sat on the front porch to
eat it. The cats got in the windows and rubbed their entire bodies against the glass and screamed. The hot dog was
mostly cold and tasted long dead. The Budweiser was sour

and gave him an immediate headache. By that time he'd
lost interest in the cupcakes so he put them in the refrigerator with the rest of the beer.

He stood for a second and looked at the red-and-white
cans against the bare metal shelves. Mrs. Cook had said
no booze. Surely, he told himself, she wouldn't care if he
kept a few beers around for visitors. And if she did, well,
to hell with her.

The thought of this day, of being out of prison and by
himself again, with a comfortable place to live and enough
money to get by, was the only thing that had kept him going
for the last six months. Now he wanted somebody to blame
for the way it was turning out.

He went upstairs to look through his stuff. Most of it reflected the useless knowledge he'd spent his life accumu-
lating: books on neurology and Japanese calligraphy, the table
from his homemade animation stand. A decent turntable
and tape deck, a crummy amp, some headphones, no speakers. Enough clothes to go a couple of weeks without doing
laundry, plus a suit for weddings and funerals. A couple of
hundred homemade tapes.

He took a handful of cassettes downstairs. The shelves
under the staircase held a 24-inch TV, a VCR, and a
stereo with surprisingly hip components: Akai, Kenwood,
big Advents, even an equalizer. He put on Burning Spear's
Marcus Garvey and cranked it up to where he could feel
the backbeat move against the out-of-key horns. That was
better already. He picked Greaseball up under the armpits
and danced him around the room. The cat stared at him
with mild contempt as he hung limply from Dave's hands.
"Relax," Dave said. He decided he would have a 7-Up.

On the way back from the kitchen he turned the TV on
with no sound. In Bastrop FCI the TV had been on constantly. The prison officials knew the true opiate of the peo-

ple when they saw it. Dave had learned to tune it out, but it really got under some people's skin. One of the guys Dave knew used to talk about fucking a TV set. Say a black-and-white portable that he could carry around with one hand. He wanted to go to a sex shop for an artificial vagina and have a TV man install it directly into the picture tube. Then the next time one of those models got up there and started to come on to him he could put it right in her mouth.

Dave knew how the guy felt. So many heart-stoppingly beautiful women, and all they wanted was to sell him minipads or cars or mutual funds. It could get the idea of sex all twisted around in somebody's head. Especially with no real women there to straighten him out again.

The old lady had the full package of cable, including movie channels. Dave went through them all without finding anything to hold his attention. He looked through the video tapes on the shelf under the TV. None of them had labels. Dave put one in the machine and fired it up.

The Army recruitment ad on the screen went blank and a grainy, taped image fluttered into place. It showed a young man with brown hair past his shoulders, a mustache, and tinted fighter-pilot glasses. He stood behind a stainless-steel pulpit engraved with two concentric circles inside a square. The same symbol had been painted on the wall behind him, below three-foot-high letters that read AASK. The letters looked to be made of Styrofoam covered with Reynolds Wrap.

Dave turned the stereo down and the TV up. "—st potent of all the unconscious symbols," the man said. Dave leaned closer to see the man's tie. It was not just the unusual pinspot lighting. The tie was clear plastic and had red lights that blinked on and off. "It is also a symbol of the unconscious itself in Jung's work, representing the psyche. Thus when combined with the square, representing earthbound matter, we have the image of wholeness."

The man had a nice voice, Dave thought, deep and smooth, like a late-night FM DJ. He also had remarkable eyes. They seemed to focus, in turn, on specific people in the audience and burn into them. He was clearly getting worked up. "And is this wholeness not the very thing that spiritualists have always sought? Have not mediums throughout history been greeted with the same words, 'Adonai Vasu,' that the Visitors use to greet us? And have not spiritual seekers through the ages met with the same repression when they got close to the truth? Madame Blavatsky encountered Men In Black—whom she called 'Brothers of the Shadow'—just as Albert Bender or Morris Jessup did."

The camera turned to pan across the audience. They seemed to be exclusively women, few of them below fifty. Their eyes were unfocused, as if the content of the lecture had failed to penetrate.

"Their weapons are always the same. Whether they are the telaugs of the deros or the white sound produced by Auralgesiac devices, their end is repression, withdrawal, denial."

Dave's own eyes had started to glaze. He hit FAST FORWARD on the remote. The man on-screen waved his arms furiously. There was another shot of the audience. Dave slowed the tape. "—page 82 of *Man and His Symbols*, and I quote, 'In order to sustain his creed, contemporary man pays the price in a remarkable lack of introspection . . . His gods and demons have not disappeared at all; they have merely got new names. They keep him on the run with restlessness, vague apprehensions, psychological complications, an insatiable need for pills, alcohol, tobacco, food—and above all, a large array of neuroses.'"

Dave skipped ahead again. "—through the healing powers of the Visitors. For they can bring our conscious and unconscious selves together. And we can bring the Visitors to us through the power of our belief, the power of our desire for wholeness, for cosmic vision." He pointed to the letters on the wall behind him. "Americans Awaiting Saucer Kidnap. AASK. Ask and it shall be given you! Wishing does make it so! Adonai Vasu!" The audience burst into applause. Superimposed letters appeared on the screen, reading "Make checks payable to Bryant C. Whitney," followed by a Freeport PO box number. Dave hit STOP.

So this was the saucer nut that wanted to crack the will. A little flaky, especially in his choice of ties. Still he was more widely read than necessary to please his audience of lonely, aging women.

Dave turned off the TV and finished his 7-Up. Now that the litter boxes were clean the house had a lilac-and-face-powder smell that seemed to come out of the very walls. It told him on an animal level that he was not on his own ground. He changed into an old pair of jeans, a clean white T-shirt, and moccasins. He was, after all, a free man. Anything could happen. Adventure might be just around the corner.

He switched off the stereo and went out into the night.

H E walked along the edge of the water, carrying his moccasins in his left hand. His feet sank into the wet sand and waves splashed his ankles where he'd rolled up his jeans. The moon rolled slowly up out of the Gulf.

There was a bonfire up the beach, at the edge of the dunes. Three couples, young black kids, sat around it. One of the boys shouted at Dave as he walked by. "Hey, man!"

Dave stopped.

"Yeah, you, man. C'mere a minute."

There was nobody else on the beach. Dave had a moment of nerves. He flashed on his first few days at Bastrop, where every walk around the exercise yard was another challenge, as he was worked into the social order. That order was presided over by a huge black man named Terrell, with a shaved head and his own name tattooed on his forearm. Dave reminded himself that this wasn't Bastrop. The boys had their dates there and everything. He walked over to the fire.

"Say, man," the kid said, "how you doin' tonight?"

"All right," Dave said.

"Listen, brother, you wouldn't know where we could score a little weed, would you?"

Dave shook his head. "Sorry, man. I'm new around here myself."

"You sure, man? Like, if I had some money, could you take me where I could get some?"

"Sorry, man." He held out his hands. "There's nothing I can do."

They looked at each other for a couple of seconds. Dave didn't show him any of what he was feeling. The kid said, "Okay, brother. You be cool now, you hear?"

"Oh yeah," Dave said.

He walked on toward the pier. He was a little paranoid, that was all. This was the free world, where most people were pretty decent.

Up ahead was some kind of bar, with an outdoor stage that backed up onto the beach. The stage was surrounded by a chicken-wire fence laced with wooden slats. There was a van parked next to it. Some kids in sleeveless shirts and ripped jeans sat in back, smoking. Just then, loud enough that Dave felt it inside his skull, somebody checked the tuning on an electric guitar, four notes up and three down. It stopped Dave in his tracks. He hadn't heard live music in years. Patsy had once offered to take him to Country Music Night at the Austin AquaFest and he'd turned her down. Fred and Mad Dog didn't seem to care about music at all anymore and Anson only liked it on CD.

He rolled down his pants legs and put on his moccasins. At the edge of the dirt road was a yellow portable sign that said "Shove It Inn" and "Random Axe" and "$2 Cover." About thirty kids milled around in front. Dave was the oldest there by fifteen years. Some of the kids going in got their hands stamped for booze. The ones outside looked like they planned to stay there. A lot of them had dressed for it, with spiked hair and leather and eyeliner.

Dave paid and went in. The band had started. The drummer played a basic one-two beat, loud and fast. The singer had a T-shirt wrapped around his head and a bare chest. Nobody else seemed to think it looked silly so Dave let it go.

Almost everybody had their hair dyed black or bleached white or both. There were T-shirts with skulls and dripping red letters, leather vests and studded wristbands and belts. Nobody danced, but nobody seemed ready to sit down either, even though there were picnic tables scattered around in the gravel.

Dave bought a 7-Up at the bar and found a section of fence to lean on. He liked the singer's voice. It had a lot of character. The music was like a wall that held Dave in the present. It didn't leave room to think about anything else.

A half hour into the set people started to turn and look back toward the door. Dave turned too. Five kids came in together and sat at one of the benches. The girl from the Surfside Grocery was with them. She made no sign that she'd noticed him. She was with a boy who looked like a surfer, lean and athletic, with blond hair to his shoulders. He could have been as old as twenty-three or -four. The others were younger, all boys, and the youngest couldn't have been more than fifteen. He had brown hair with a long forelock and a patch gone from one side of his head. Matching cuts on his face had almost healed. He walked with a limp and his left forearm was wrapped in a lightweight partial cast. He carried a beat-up skateboard in his right hand. The bottom was covered with stickers for products that Dave had never heard of—Thrasher, Vision, Kryptonics, Indy, Santa Cruz—all plastered over a psychedelic checkered pattern.

They changed the flow of energy in the club. Everyone had an eye on them, like they were local celebrities. The blond kid brought two pitchers of beer to the table and everyone took a glass, even the fifteen-year-old with the cast. The woman behind the bar watched him drink and didn't interfere.

A couple of girls started to dance in front of the stage. They made Dave's heart ache. They were both high-school age, lean and tan and impossibly limber. One wore a T-shirt slashed off below her breasts. Dave was childishly grateful to see her stomach muscles ripple as she danced. When the song finished, the girls went to stand by the blond kid. They shifted their weight from foot to foot and pushed their hair back from their faces. They took glasses of beer and giggled at each other over the tops of them. They talked to the blond kid all through the next song and then left with him.

The girl from the Surfside Grocery had her back to Dave. Her shoulders hunched and she drank a couple of beers without coming up for air. The three younger kids didn't know how to cheer her up. They were already feeling the beer. The girl shook her head at them and finally went to sit at the bar.

It was time for Dave to go. The girl's problems were none of his business. He had problems of his own. For one thing, he was in violation of his parole just by being there. He started for the door and then hesitated. "Hey," he said. He was only a few feet from her. She didn't seem to hear. "Hey!" he said again.

She looked around. "It's Dave," she said. "What are *you* doing here, Dave?"

"I wanted to hear the band."

"*This* band? You don't listen to this kind of shit, Dave." She squinted and leaned toward him. "Do you?"

"You never know," Dave said.

She swayed back again. "Radical." She reached for her beer.

"Are you okay? Have you got a way home and everything?"

"Yeah, Dave. I'm fine." Her eyes were red and the eye-liner in the corners glistened. As she turned away she said, just loud enough for Dave to hear, "But thanks for asking."

He shouldered through the kids in front of the club and made for the beach. He hadn't remembered to ask her name this time, either. At this rate it could be years before he even managed a date with a woman again. Sex seemed hopelessly distant.

The moon was well up and the tide had run out. The Gulf lay quietly, saving its strength. The band was on break and Dave couldn't hear anything past the ringing in his ears.

Then, suddenly, a girl laughed. The voice came from a black Nissan ZX parked by the beach. Through the open window Dave could see the back of the blond kid's head. Kneeling on the passenger seat, facing him, was the girl with the slashed T-shirt. She peeled the T-shirt off while Dave watched. He could see her adolescent breasts and the small, dark shadows of her nipples. She looked up and their eyes locked. She was really quite beautiful. Dave knew he should look away but he wasn't physically able. Instead he felt himself start to smile. She looked right at Dave and smiled back. Then, as he turned toward home, he saw her head go back and heard her laughter echo out over the water.

H E woke up once in the night. He didn't know where he was, had only the conviction that he didn't belong there. He stared at a lace curtain fluttering in the light from the motel across the road. The lightness of the walls, the eerie silence, the very proportions of the room were wrong. Finally the sound of a cat crying outside his door brought it all back to him.

He got up to use the bathroom, still expecting somebody to shout at him.

Terrell had explained prison to him. There were only two kinds of prisoners. The ones that cracked—that stopped fighting back, that learned the rules, that made the adjustment—got paroled. Then they found out they couldn't live outside. They didn't have enough aggression left to look for work, to fend for themselves. So they always blew it, one way or another, and ended up back in prison.

The ones prison couldn't break, the ones like Terrell, never got out. They got thrown in the hole and had their release dates taken away. Terrell came in on a government payroll robbery and inside a year had assaulted a guard and killed a fellow inmate. They would never let him out alive.

Terrell said that Dave was lucky. Six months would hurt him. It didn't have to break him.

Dave padded back into the bedroom. The night air was cold so he stopped to close the windows, standing there for a while to watch the endless, indifferent sea.

I N the morning he fed the cats and changed the litter and ran for a mile or two along the beach. Exercise was a habit he'd picked up in prison. At first it was a channel for his hostility toward the guards, toward the IRS, toward the other inmates, toward the things that tried to bend him into someone else's shape. Finally it was a way to mark his body as his own. Running was easier than tattooing himself with a safety pin or pumping iron until his veins stood out in high relief.

Afterwards he showered and walked down to the Surfside Grocery. The black-haired girl wasn't there. He came home with a sack full of food and a Sunday paper. He got a lot of pans and skillets out and cooked enough breakfast for two or three people: bacon, eggs, toast, jelly, grits, hash-browns, orange juice, coffee. He used the flesh-colored depression glassware from the cabinets and even kept the toast wrapped in a cloth napkin so it wouldn't get cold. All in all it would have been pretty swank if he hadn't had to keep throwing cats off the dining room table.

The newspaper was full of the upcoming elections. Dave was unable to finish any of the stories. The stretch in prison had hurt his interest in who was really tougher on crime, who was more against drugs. For the first time, with a twinge of guilt, he considered the possibility of not voting at all. Who would know?

Finally he put the paper aside, brushed his teeth, and stacked the dirty dishes in the sink. It was ten in the morning. He thought about all the dishes he'd washed at Patsy's house. And the times he'd ended up cleaning the entire kitchen while he was at it. Patsy was sweet, but not much of a housekeeper. The memory of the nights he'd spent with her suddenly left him weak. He could see her face above a white pillowcase, smiling, her naked body wrapped in rumpled white sheets. He put the plate he'd been scrubbing back into the water and stood there with his head down until the worst of it passed.

When the dishes were done he stacked the newspaper neatly on the counter. He realized he was putting off the inevitable. He shuffled reluctantly into the living room and dialed his parents' number in Dallas.

His father picked up the phone and said, "It's your nickel."

"Hi, Pop. It's me."

"Are you out?"

"Yeah, Pop, I'm out."

"Did you escape or did they let you go?"

"They let me go."

"I hope they knew what they were doing. Talk to your mother."

Dave's father was recovering from his third cancer operation. He'd had lung, colon, and now liver cancer, plus a quadruple bypass for his heart. He looked like Frankenstein's monster from the neck down. The last time Dave had seen him he'd aged terribly. His eyebrows had run wild, like brown-and-white kudzu. It seemed strange to Dave that the last part of the body to give up was the hair in the nose and ears and eyebrows. These days his father always looked as if he just woke up. In fact that was often the case.

He muttered something Dave couldn't hear and then his mother came on the line. She chuckled without conviction. "You know your father's sense of humor, dear," she said. "Where are you?"

"In Surfside, Mom. Taking care of all those cats, remember?"

"I thought you didn't like cats."

"I'll be okay. Do you still have the phone number I gave you?"

"Better give it to me again. I'll write it down."

Dave read her the phone number. He'd gone through all of this the week before, but she didn't remember. There was a lot she didn't remember anymore. For the moment his father was satisfied to let her wander around in a daze, then make cruel fun of her for it. Before long Dave would have to do something with them—a live-in nurse, a rest home, an apartment closer to Surfside, where he could take care of them himself.

"Have you got a girlfriend yet?" his mother asked.

"I just got out of prison yesterday. Give me a chance."

"What about money? How much money are you making?"

"To tell you the truth I haven't asked yet. Enough. I've got room and board with the job."

"You need more than just 'enough.' You're forty years old. You can't play around in the sunshine forever. You need to start thinking about those rainy days ahead. Believe me, I know."

"Thirty-nine," Dave said.

"What's that, dear?"

"Nothing. Is sis okay?"

"She's fine, darling. She called yesterday. She got that senior partnership. She and Bob bought one of those cute little Mercedes cars to celebrate, though I do have to say it doesn't seem very practical, since you can't get more than two people inside—"

Someone knocked at the door. "I have to go, Mom. There's somebody here."

"You could call her yourself, you know. She'd love to hear from you."

"Sure she would. I'll call you soon. I love you, Mom."

"Dear? What's your phone number there?"

"I just gave it to you, Mom. I got to go. I'll call you."
He hung up and sprinted for the door.

T H E woman on the landing had one hand up, shading
her eyes. She was trying to see through the glass panes of the
door. Dave recognized her instantly as the widow Nixon.
Her blonde hair was pulled back with a powder blue band,
matching her jogging suit and her eye shadow. She had a
gold mesh purse under her arm and a single strand of
pearls around her neck.

Dave opened the door.

"Oh," she said. "Hi." Fine lines softened her eyes and
mouth. Her eyes were deep blue, the lashes built up to
incredible lengths with mascara. She was the sexiest fifty-
year-old Dave had ever seen. He wished he could see her
without all the makeup. "I hope I'm not . . . I was just driving by and . . . oh, bother." She stuck out her hand. "Mary
Nixon." Her voice was husky, with a Texas accent that added
a tiny squeak to her words.

"Dave," he said. He took her hand and she held on to it
longer than he expected.

"Yes, you certainly are. I've heard so much about you.
Most of it good, of course." She laughed easily and said,
"Are you going to keep me waiting on the porch all morning?"

"Oh, uh, no, of course not. Watch the cats." Dave stepped
back to let her by. Her shoulder brushed Dave's chest as
she passed and he caught the faint odor of peroxide behind her perfume. It stirred up erotic memories of slow
dances in the St. Mark's gym.

"Oh my," she said. "It's really lovely in here, isn't it?" She bent over and scooped Morpheus up as Dave shut the door. "Do you know," she said, "this is the first time I've actually been inside?"

Great, Dave thought. Now I've done it.

"You did know she was my aunt?" She pronounced aunt to rhyme with gaunt. "My great-aunt, actually."

"Fred told me about you, yes."

"Oh really?" She arched one carefully penciled eyebrow.

"Just that, uh, you were interested in the estate."

She looked Dave in the eye and smiled again. "Oh yes. Very interested." The cat leaped out of her arms and she patted her hands together cheerfully. "Fred can be such a spoilsport. I can tell you'll be a lot more fun."

Dave felt his face get hot and he looked away. Was he imagining things, or was this woman coming on to him? A woman he'd never seen before? A woman at least ten years older than he was? A woman Fred had already warned him about?

She headed for the stairs, as if she roamed around in other people's houses every day. Dave cleared his throat. "Would you maybe like a cup of coffee?"

She hesitated, with her hand on the banister, and then said, "Sure."

Dave poured coffee and they went out onto the porch. Dave left the door open and a Siamese chased the chubby gray kitten around and around the white metal lawn furniture. Finally the kitten ran up the screen wire next to Dave and hung there, howling in a small, plaintive voice.

"So," Mary Nixon said. "Tell me about yourself. Tell me everything." She cupped her chin in her hand and leaned toward him.

"Not much to say," Dave said awkwardly. "I'm just a regular guy."

"Married?"

"Afraid not."

"Not ever?"

Dave shook his head.

"That's so old-fashioned of you, darling. It's not like marriage is forever. Take me, for instance. As Henny Youngman would say. Widowed once, divorced twice. I'm an incurable romantic. Of course husbands can have a practical value too. If a girl wants to see a little of the world, have a little excitement, and not work her pretty tail to the bone to pay for it."

Dave said, "The word 'adventuress' might have come up."

"But what's wrong with adventure? I've had a wonderful life. Photographing wildebeest in Africa. Scuba diving on the Barrier Reef. I've seen the Great Wall of China and the Cape of Good Hope. I've flown airplanes and helicopters, driven race cars and eighteen-wheelers."

Her tone was so casual Dave was not sure he believed her. "How did you end up here?"

"Cash flow, darling. And I'm not quite sure what's next. Waiting for the impulse to strike, I suppose. And when it does, look out. There's just no telling what love might make me do."

She fed him another inquiring look. No doubt about it, Dave thought. She was coming on to him.

"You don't like to talk about yourself, do you?" she said.

"I don't know you. I mean, I never laid eyes on you before ten minutes ago."

"Can't you trust your impulses? I always do." She waved one hand. "That's okay. Take your time. George—my second husband?—took a long time to come around. He was a character. Absolutely wild for Chinese fortune cookies. Used to carry his favorite fortunes around in his coat pocket. I can still quote most of them. There was one that said, let me see, 'He who is the most slow in making a promise is the most faithful in the performance of it.' Finally I told him how you were supposed to add the words 'in bed' to those things, and that did it. Pushed him right over the edge."

That did it for Dave as well. He got up, heart thumping, and stood in front of her. He grabbed the arms of her chair. She looked up with an expectant smile. Dave kissed her, tasting lipstick and coffee. He thought he could feel her mouth smile under his.

Dave was breathing hard. He lifted one shaking hand and put it on her breast. It was bare under the sweatshirt and he felt the nipple rise quickly to meet his fingers.

She pushed him away with one hand on his chest. "Now Dave," she said. "It's not that I'm not flattered—but isn't this kind of sudden?"

Dave backed slowly away from her, his face burning.

"Sit down, sit down," she said. "Don't get all upset. I'm sorry if I gave you the wrong idea."

Dave sat. "What idea," he said, getting his breath, "did you mean to give me?"

"Believe me, I sympathize. You just out of prison and all. It must have been a long time for you. This whole sex business gets really confusing, doesn't it?"

Dave looked at the ocean and tried not to think about the softness of her flesh. "I'm what you could call confused at the moment, yeah."

"It took me the longest time to understand that as soon as a man even begins to like you he wants to go to bed with you. You'd be surprised how many women don't know this. I even forget it myself, especially when I meet somebody I really like."

"There you go again."

"I'm sorry. Maybe I should go. I know this is difficult

for you." She stood up and tugged at the front of her
sweatshirt.

"No," Dave said, "really. I didn't mean to . . ."

"Run me off? You're not, darling, really." Dave followed
her into the kitchen. She took a card out of her purse
and put it on the dining room table. "Here's my phone number. Call me sometime." She kissed him quickly on the
lips and was gone.

D A V E ran upstairs, masturbated, then lay for a while
listening to the ocean. As his intellect gradually reasserted
itself, he tried to look on the bright side. He had, after
all, just kissed a woman for the first time in six months.
That had to count as progress.

Eventually he got up and wandered into the other upstairs bedroom. It was the only room in the house he
hadn't seen. Apparently the old lady had used it as her study.
There were bookcases along the back wall and file cabinets and metal storage shelves everywhere else. There was
a desk under a window that faced the Gulf, and on the
desk was a personal computer and a stack of typed pages.
Dave stopped to look at the underlined phrases in an article torn out of *Omni*: ". . . artifacts that accidentally
dispose the culture toward anarchy. The skateboard is one
. . . and so . . . is the microcomputer."

Anarchy? Dave thought. It seemed an odd concern for
an old lady with a house full of doilies and cats. The book-
shelf was stacked with titles like *Guerrilla Capitalism* and
God and the State and *The Abolition of Work*. Most of the
boxes on the metal shelves had books and papers in them
too.

Next to the computer were four slipcased manuals and a small beige paperback. The paperback was an introduction to the computer, complete with a cartoon bird and lots of color pictures. Now here was something, Dave thought. Maybe he could come out of this able to use a computer.

What Fred and Patsy and Mad Dog had never understood was that he didn't object to work per se. He just didn't see the point in doing something he didn't enjoy merely to make money. He'd always been willing to consider a job, as long as it was fun and he'd get something more than money out of it. In other words, as long as it was something he'd do even if he didn't get paid. The whole idea seemed obvious. Who could argue about it?

Dave paged through the book for a few minutes and then decided to hell with it and switched the thing on. A motor started to hum. Lights flashed on the front by the diskette slots. It clicked and beeped and then words appeared on the screen.

"Hot damn," Dave said.

He played around for an hour or so before he got to the point where he had to read some more of the manual. He took it downstairs and worked through it while he drank his cold coffee and watched the traffic.

F R O M the porch Dave could see the dried Christmas trees that the city laid out every January, end to end, along the dunes. They were nearly buried in the sand they'd trapped over the year. Between the dunes and the Gulf was a broad, flat plain of sand packed hard enough to support cars and trucks. A steady stream of them had rumbled past all afternoon.

This late in the year, Dave knew, the weather could turn ugly and stay that way. The kids from Houston knew it too and they were out in their flowered jams and visors and plastic lawn chairs, drinking beer and turning red in the sun. The cars were predictable—oversized pickups, Japanese compacts with a Z in the model number, and a few beat-up local Ramblers and Fords. The only car Dave couldn't account for was a bright red '56 Thunderbird, the kind with the portholes and the "continental" spare tire mounted on the back of the trunk.

The third time it drove by, Dave leaned forward for a look at the driver. It turned out to be a young guy with long hair, a mustache, tinted glasses, and a tie that reflected too much sunlight. Bryant C. Whitney, the UFO nut.

The big black-and-silver tabby jumped on Dave's lap and said something that sounded like "Burke." Dave threw him down and paced back and forth across the porch. His mood had soured. What did these people want from him? Why were they hanging around? Why couldn't they leave him alone? He felt the pressure of their greed like a tight rubber suit, squeezing off his air. He wanted to go downstairs and get in the car and drive. Maybe to Mexico.

Sure, he thought. Jump your parole. That's smart.

Instead he put on a pair of cutoffs and went for a swim. The water was warm and brown and full of mullets, fish the size of his hand that would leap straight out of the water, a foot or so into the air, shaking their tails and straining for every inch of height. "Settle down," Dave told them. "You wouldn't like it out here anyway."

He swam out to where the water was over his head and decided to take his own advice. Maybe he was eating too much sugar. He was giving himself fits over imaginary problems. All Mary Nixon had done was flirt with him, and all he'd done was kiss her. Which she hadn't seemed to mind, particularly. And if Bryant C. Whitney wanted to drive around and look at the house, then let him.

Dave had read somewhere that after the Civil War, Texas had been a refuge for all kinds of outlaws. Confederate soldiers escaping the Reconstruction, bandits and killers, men whose farms had been taken by the bank. They left their homes all across the country with no other message than "Gone To Texas." Dave was no different. Surfside was a clean start for him. He could hurl himself out of the water until he drowned, or he could relax and make the best of it.

He swam until he burned off the worst of his nerves, then walked back to the house. He had a shower and sat back on the porch. There were a hundred things he'd always meant to do if he had time. Learn to play piano, make animated cartoons, write a screenplay, build fine furniture. None of them seemed immediately attractive. He was about to pick up the computer manual again when he saw the girl from the grocery walking up the beach.

She was headed north, obviously just off work. She had a paper sack in one hand instead of a purse. Today's T-shirt said "Meat Puppets" and had childish drawings on the front. Her black hair was pulled tight off to one side and tied with what looked like a plastic fastener from a trash bag. "It's Dave," she said. "How ya doing, Dave?"

"I'm okay," he said.

She climbed onto the dune below the porch. "You didn't tell me you lived in Mizz Johnson's house."

"Was that her name?"

"That's right. Marguerite Johnson."

"I didn't even know it. Everybody always calls her the old lady."

"She used to come in for cat food and donuts every morning. She was pretty cool."

"Yeah?"

"Most old people are pretty down on skateboards. You can feel it, the way they look at you. She wanted to ride one. You own this place now or what?"

"Caretaker," Dave said. "I'm watching the cats. Where do you live?"

"Down the road." Her eyes got vague and Dave saw she didn't want him to know. "Gotta go. See ya around." She started to walk away.

"Hey," Dave said. "I still don't know your name."

"I guess not," she said. She looked over her shoulder at him. "I guess that puts me one up on you."

F R E D showed up at seven. Dave gave him a beer and Fred said, "Pope John Paul gets to heaven same time as this lawyer. Saint Peter shows them where they're going to live. Shows the lawyer this beautiful three-story job, columns, landscaping, swimming pool, the works. John Paul thinks, wow, if a lawyer gets a nice place like this, I'm going to get a palace. But they keep walking and the neighborhood goes to shit. They end up at this shack. The Pope goes, 'You're giving a lawyer that mansion and me this shack?' and St. Pete goes, 'Hey, popes we got. That was our first lawyer.'"

Dave said, "You've got real estate on the brain."

"To hell with it. Let's blow this cheap hotel."

From the top of the Surfside bridge, looking south, Dow Chemical's Oyster Creek Plant covered the horizon. Dave remembered summer trips to Padre Island with Fred and

Anson. From Houston south, the Texas Coast swarmed
with refineries and chemical plants, with vast spherical holding tanks, lattices of columns and pipes and catwalks, towers that pumped out huge cylindrical clouds of off-white
smoke.

To Dave's right was a cluster of weathered frame houses,
near a boat ramp. Farther north was the Bridge Harbor
Yacht Club, a Spanish-mission-style development with tan
stucco walls and red tile roofs, all of it behind an eight-
foot wall with a guardhouse. Dave could see tennis courts
inside and a three-story tower, but not many cars.

"They just went under," Fred told him. "Complete
reorganization."

They passed a burned-out souvenir shop called the Black
Light. Just beyond it was a hamburger joint with plywood where the windows should have been. "Is this whole
town going broke?" Dave asked.

"It's tough right now. I guess it's like when the dinosaurs started to get all those comets. People in Texas lived
on oil money forever. Now the oil money's gone, it's a whole
different climate. The ones that can't change are going
toes up."

They came to a stoplight. Ernie's Texaco, souvenirs, swim-
suits, and fishing tackle was on the left. They turned south
onto Highway 523, another piece of two-lane blacktop that
ran through marsh grass and flat, swampy land. They went
over a barge canal and a set of railroad tracks, both leading
into the Dow Plant, and then finally crossed the Brazos
Turning Basin. The guttural sound of the Porsche's exhaust came back loud and flat from the water. The basin
was an old arm of the river that was now full of shrimpers
and sailboats. Murky green water reflected blue and white
from the boats. White gulls turned lazily overhead, shouting comments.

"This is all right," Dave said.

"It's a bit downscale. I guess it'll do. Listen, are you okay?"

Highway 523 was now Velasco Boulevard. They were in a business district of a sort, with one-story brick and stucco buildings, most of them empty or closed. "Sure," Dave said.

"It's just you seem kind of, I don't know, passive these days." They turned west onto Eighth Street and idled through a suburb of frame houses with cars in the yards.

"Yeah, well," Dave said. "That's what prison is all about. Taking the starch out of you."

"Was it really bad? I mean, if you don't want to talk about it . . ."

"No, I can talk about it."

"I mean, you know, is it really guys fucking each other up the ass and everything?"

Dave looked out the window. The thing to do was pretend like he was talking about somebody else. That way he didn't have to connect, emotionally, with the ugly stuff. "Yeah, I got fucked up the ass, if that's what you want to know. It was this guy Terrell. He was kind of the king there. He was pretty hardcore for Bastrop, I mean, murder and assault and all that. He only ended up there because they had to keep taking him into Austin for trial. The hell of it is, after it happened, he kind of took care of me. He kept the other guys away from me, and he left me alone too. Said he'd rather do it with somebody who liked it."

Eighth Street ended at Brazosport Boulevard. There was a strip center there with a big sign that said Four Corners. Dave read the comforting, everyday signs: Kroger, Weiner's, Eckerd Drugs, Video Super Stop. This is where I am now, Dave told himself. That other is over and done. It can't touch me anymore.

Fred parked in front of Red Top Texas Style Burgers,

next to a Pizza Inn. "Listen," Fred said. "I'm sorry I brought it up. I was just being nosy."

Dave shrugged. His throat had swollen and he didn't want to talk through it, afraid it might choke him. He got out of the car. There was a breeze off the Gulf, even here where he couldn't see the water. The sun was low in the sky and everything had a pinkish tinge. Dave got his breath and went inside. The smell of frying meat snapped him back to reality and reminded him how hungry he was.

"Let's eat," Dave said. "You're buying."

AFTER dinner Fred took a different route home, following Brazosport Boulevard north. They passed the library and the courthouse and the police station, all in a row, at the edge of Municipal Park. In the middle of the lawn was a marooned fishing boat with the word "Mystery" painted on the side.

"What the hell is that?" Dave asked.

"It's like a monument to the shrimp industry or something."

"Don't you find it the least bit weird? To have something in the middle of town with 'Mystery' painted on it in big red letters? Doesn't it make you want to know why?"

"It's not a big deal to me, man, no. You ask too many questions. You get all worked up over nothing at all."

When they got home Fred took a beer and they sat out on the porch in the darkness. Dave had the Doors on the tape deck. Phosphorescence sparkled on the water. "So how's Judy?" Dave asked.

"She's dead."

"What?"

"Okay, I lied, she's not dead. It's just something I tell myself. You've never been divorced, you wouldn't understand. Hell, you've never even been married. I still don't know how it happened to me. I'm a lawyer. What was I thinking?"

"You were in love. Trust me, I was there."

Fred shook his head. "They should let husbands and wives kill each other. It's so much cleaner and less painful."

"She still calls you?"

"Hell, sometimes I call her. It's the horrors of dating. It makes you think, God help you, your marriage couldn't have been that bad. I'm sorry. You don't need to hear this kind of shit."

Fred got up and came back with another beer. "We still fuck sometimes," he said. "What am I supposed to do? Sex with strangers is too weird at my age. But afterwards I'll want a beer and that pisses her off or she starts doing her nails in bed and that pisses me off. I tell you, the idea of spending the rest of my life with one woman—especially that woman—gives me the crawlies. But I get so goddamn lonely without her."

"It's the same with me. I've been living in garage apartments all my adult life. I mean, I've never lived anywhere where people's cars started on the first try. I've never had a house to myself before. I really like it. I could see myself staying here forever. And slowly getting buried under all this . . . *stuff*."

"Paradox," Fred said. He stood up and chugged the rest of his beer. "It's at the heart of everything. It's like reality was designed that way, so there would always be something you couldn't account for. It's what made Jim Morrison in there have to get up and sing. Me, it makes me thirsty." He went after another beer.

Something in the air, maybe a premonition of fall, had

the cats on edge. They paced in complicated patterns around the furniture and gave each other the fish-eye. Fred chased a cat out of his chair and sat down again. Suddenly a plate smashed in the kitchen and Dave heard claws skitter on linoleum. A second later came two moaning noises, like off-key ambulances.

Dave stood in the doorway and clapped his hands. "Break it up in there."

"I got just the thing," Fred said. "C'mon."

He took Dave down the back stairs and around the carport. He wasn't swaying, but he wasn't light on his feet either. Dave suspected he'd had at least three or four before dinner.

"Check it out," Fred said.

There were a dozen square yards under cultivation. Dave hadn't seen them because of the rear wall of the carport. There were cherry tomatoes and okra and a few withered pieces of lettuce. The old lady had apparently brought in soil from the mainland. It looked black next to the sand dunes.

"This here is what we're looking for." Fred bent over and pulled up some kind of weed.

"Dope?" Dave asked.

"No, man, look at the leaves. It's catnip."

"I never saw it in its, uh, natural state before. Does it work without drying and everything?"

"Wait and see." They went back upstairs and Fred tore off a handful of leaves and threw them up in the air. Five or six cats came over to look. The black-and-silver tabby sniffed at a piece, then lunged and bit it. It stuck to the top of his mouth and he turned his head sideways, smacking his lips, like an old man with peanut butter stuck to his dentures. One of the others pushed a piece around the floor, trying and failing to nibble at it. Greaseball knelt down and rubbed his neck and shoulders in it, then bumped it with the scent glands in the top of his head. The cats' pupils swelled up until their eyes seemed to bug out of their heads. They jumped sideways like skittish horses and swatted at ghosts.

"Wow," Dave said. "They're really fucked up."

Fred got another beer. He was laughing so hard that tears rolled down his face.

Within ten minutes half the cats in the house were stoned. The black-and-silver male lay on his side and licked at a piece of leaf, too wrecked even to crawl. Fred put the rest of the plant in a baggie in the refrigerator. "I got to get out of here," he said.

"You okay to drive?"

"What, are you kidding? Just a few beers. No big deal."

"I could make some coffee. Hell, you could stay here."

"I'm fine. A little tired, that's all."

Dave walked him to the car. Fred got in and rolled his window down. "I really envy you."

"Me?"

"You're free, man. You're the only person I know can say that. You got no ex-wives, no car payment, no mortgage, no job to go to. Christ, if I was in your shoes . . ."

"Yeah? What would you do? Tell me."

Fred shook his head. "I'd probably blow it," he said. "Get married and buy a house or something." He rolled up his window and drove away.

Dave put the empty beer cans in the kitchen trash. The house smelled like beer. The cats lay on their backs, paws in the air, or were strewn limply over the furniture. Dave was disgusted by the spectacle. He changed into an old pair of shorts and went running barefoot on the beach. He ran as far as the pier and back again. Everyone had gone home and he had the night and the surf and the moonlight to himself.

He showered when he finished. The exercise had him too pumped up to sleep, so he went up to play with the computer. With the gray kitten sitting on his lap he wrote up a batch file that changed his prompt command to read HI DAVE>. It seemed like a major triumph. He felt another complete world behind the screen, tugging at him.

WHEN he got up the next morning the '56 T-Bird was parked next to the Cedar Sands Motel. While Dave watched, the engine fired up and it roared away, the tires spraying damp sand in all directions.

Dave went down to pick a handful of the old lady's okra. There were a couple of cherry tomatoes that the birds hadn't gotten to and a bell pepper. He cut the okra into thin slices and rolled them in corn meal and fried them up. Then he cut up the pepper and tomatoes and mixed them into his scrambled eggs.

A half-dozen cats sat at his feet and yowled. "Piss off," he said. "You're a bunch of goddamn junkies. You want drugs, go out and shoplift for them, like everybody else."

The food was delicious. "Goddamn," Dave said. He pushed his chair back and nibbled on the last of the fried okra. An idea rose from the depths of his brain, breaching like a whale after a long dive. He did the dishes and then went through the upstairs bookshelves. Sure enough, there was a book called *Texas Gardening*. He took it out on the porch with him.

He'd barely started reading when the phone rang.

"Hello?" Dave said.

A familiar, well-modulated voice said, "Let's have lunch. We have a lot to talk about."

"Bryant C. Whitney," Dave said. "The UFO guy. What the hell's the idea of driving by my place all night and day?"

"I'm sorry," Whitney said carefully, "but I have no idea what you're talking about."

"Do you or don't you have a red 1956 Thunderbird with portholes and that funny spare tire that sticks up in the back?"

"Yes, I do."

"Well?"

"Well what?"

"I must have seen it half a dozen times yesterday. And you were parked outside my house this morning."

"Are you serious?"

"Of course I'm serious."

"This is amazing. A little frightening, in fact. Do you know what this means? Wait. Don't tell me. The man driving. He was dressed *completely in black*. Am I right?"

"I don't know what he had on. All I saw was the hair and mustache and glasses."

"Oh. Still. It's clear we have a great deal to talk about. Are we going to have lunch, or are you going to wait until *even stranger things* begin to happen?"

"Is that supposed to be a threat?"

"Heavens no. But I am concerned for your safety. If you're being watched by MIB, you could be in grave danger."

"MIB?"

"Men In Black. It's a generic term, actually. They don't always wear black. Clearly this is about the house. Things have gone further than I imagined."

"What things?"

"I'd rather not talk about this over the phone. Can I pick you up?"

"No," Dave said, resigned. "No, I'll meet you somewhere."

"Good. Excellent. How about the Pizza Inn on 288? Say, one o'clock?"

I T was odd to drive a car again. Even though it was only a Dodge compact, Dave couldn't get rid of a thin-ice feeling of impending disaster. Nobody else on the road seemed to have any sense of the vast power in their hands.

He found his way back to the Four Corners center with no problem. He parked in front of the Pizza Inn and waited. It was already one o'clock. He listened to KLOL for ten minutes on the car radio, then decided to take one quick look inside before he split. Whitney might, after all, have come in another car. Just as he got out, the red T-bird screamed into the parking lot on two wheels.

The car rocked to a stop next to Dave and Whitney leapt out. He wore black jeans, a black satin tour jacket, and a clear plastic tie with red and yellow toy dinosaurs inside. "You must be Dave," he said, and offered his hand.

Dave shook it and followed him in. The back of the tour jacket said AASK in red script. They found an empty table and a waitress took their drink orders. Dave got up to serve himself at the buffet.

"Be right with you," Whitney said.

Dave got a salad and four slices of pizza. They didn't serve pizza in the federal prison system. Dave had missed it. When he got back to the table the drinks had arrived. Whitney had one hand on his iced tea, staring down at the checkered plastic tablecloth, his eyes out of focus. "Aren't you going to eat?" Dave asked him.

"What?" Whitney said, jerking to attention. "Oh, yeah. Right." He left and came back with two slices of pizza.

"Look," Dave said. "I don't know what you could possibly want from me. I'm just the caretaker of the place. I got nothing to do with the execution of the will. I couldn't give you the old lady's money if I wanted to."

"It's not the money," Whitney said. "Do you know anything about orgone?"

"It's supposed to be, I don't know, some kind of sex energy or something, isn't it?"

"It's a universal energy, cosmic energy, the energy of life. Wilhelm Reich discovered it in the late thirties. And later he found out the UFOs—or Eas, as he called them—are drawn to concentrations of orgone energy."

7-Up
ns,
Sprite

Dave wolfed down a slice of pizza and took a swig of his Sprite. He'd always been a 7-Up man, himself. This particular Sprite had an odd, cloying flavor. He looked at it, rubbing his tongue against the roof of his mouth.

"Something wrong?" Whitney asked, glancing quickly around the room.

"Tastes like a diet drink or something. No big deal. So what does all this orgone stuff have to do with me?"

"There are four or five places along the coast that have unusual concentrations of orgone energy. Your house is one of them. What this means is you have a vastly improved chance of a visitation. Which may be why you've drawn the attention of the MIB."

"What is it they're supposed to do to me?"

"Well. I don't wish to frighten you unduly. No one knows exactly what they do. Their victims refuse to talk afterwards. The ones that are still alive, that is . . . are you all right?"

There was definitely something wrong with the drink. "I'm going to take this back," Dave said. He stood up.

His legs started to wobble. "Whoa," he said. "What's this?" He seemed to be on his knees. That was the last he remembered. *they dragged him.*

T H E floor was vibrating. Dave dragged his eyelids open. His head felt twice its normal size, like it was about to crack from internal pressure. Pain stabbed at the backs of his eyes. The blinking lights all around kept him off-balance.

He got onto his hands and knees. The floor had the hard, shiny look of an aluminum cookie sheet, but was slightly soft to the touch. The walls seemed to curve in on him. He blinked twice and determined that the walls actually did curve. He was in a donut-shaped room. The center was a slatted wall with muted lights inside. The outside wall was covered with instruments and padded swivel chairs. A monitor screen showed the Earth rapidly falling away. The camera tilted upward and the screen filled with thousands of bright, unwavering stars.

His heart lurched and his eyes bulged. What in god's name had Whitney done to him?

He slumped into the nearest swivel chair. In front of him was a computer keyboard, like the one in the old lady's study. The letters on the keys looked like Hebrew. He slapped his hands over his eyes. The vibration came right up through the chair. Over it he could hear a faint mechanical keening, almost like music.

He rubbed his eyes until they hurt and then slowly uncovered them. He couldn't get them to focus, as if they'd been dilated by an eye doctor. He reached up to touch the TV screen and noticed that the plywood around the edge had worked loose.

Plywood?

He got his fingers under it and pulled. Below the edge of the screen he could make out the letters S-O-N-Y. He took a long breath and started to calm down. The chairs, he could see now, were just office furniture, and none of them quite matched. The floor was made out of layers of duct tape.

"Whitney?" he said. "Whitney, you son of a bitch! Get me out of here!"

He got unsteadily to his feet and looked for a way out. There had to be one somewhere. "Whitney!" he shouted again. He pounded on the walls.

A Klaxon alarm went off. It sent cascades of pain through Dave's skull. He put his hands over his ears and staggered. Suddenly there was a hiss and the air tasted funny. He heard himself hit the floor.

Not again, he thought.

THIS time he came around to the sound of waves. He lifted his head two inches and saw that he was on the beach in front of the old lady's house. It was late afternoon. The damp sand stuck to his cheek and lips and eyelashes. He didn't have the strength to brush it away. He let his head fall back in the sand.

After a while he noticed that his right ankle seemed to be wet. The ocean noises were louder now. Get up, he told himself. The tide's coming in and you're going to drown.

"Dave?"

He opened his eyes. It was the girl from the grocery. "Unh," he said.

"Isn't it kind of early in the day to be this fucked up?

Are you some kind of degenerate or something?" Dave
believed she was making fun of him.

"Help," Dave said. "Me."

She stuck the toe of one shoe under his chest and rolled
him onto his back. "Are you okay?"

"No."

"Do you think you can stand up?"

"No."

"Let's try it anyway." She took his left arm and he managed to gather his feet under him. "I was just walking home
from work," she said, "and saw you there. What happened?"

"Long story," Dave said. With her taking most of his
weight he managed a couple of staggering steps toward
the house. "I was kidnapped. What day is it?"

"Monday. Who kidnapped you?"

"A guy that wants the house."

"People are crazy for real estate around here."

"No kidding."

She got him upstairs and inside without any cats escaping. He collapsed on the couch. "There's beer in the fridge
if you want." He had to close his eyes. He heard her move
around in the kitchen. It was a domestic, calming sound.

"You want me to call somebody for you? A doctor? The
cops?"

"I'll be okay."

"Here," she said. "The Mr. Coffee was still on."

The smell of it got his eyes open. He took a sip and then
another. The cats, he saw, had already swarmed the girl,
rubbing at her bare legs and her high-top tennis shoes. She
knelt down to pet them.

"What are their names?"

"I don't know."

"They should have names. You ought to be thinking about
that. What's upstairs?"

"Bedroom. The old lady's study. Computer room."

Her face lit up. "Cool. Has it got a modem?"

"A what?"

"Can I look at it?"

Dave waved vaguely at the stairs and she took them two at a time. That left him to struggle up to a sitting position by himself. He made it without losing any of the coffee. He drank half of it down, waited out a few shooting pains in his head and stomach, and carefully climbed the stairs.

The girl sat at the keyboard, typing furiously, the can of Bud sitting unnoticed to one side. The screen blanked out and then displayed a list of options. There was a click and then Dave heard a dial tone, followed by a flurry of beeps and a distant ringing. After two rings the girl said, "They're not answering. The board must be down."

Dave sat on the floor. A long-haired orange cat tried to crawl under his arm. "Board?" he said.

The girl stood up. "*Thrasher* magazine's got a bulletin board. Skaters call in and leave messages and stuff. Listen, I have to get back."

"Skateboarders on computers?"

"Sure, man, it's the end of the century. Where have you been? Everybody's got networks."

"Can you show me?"

"There's some numbers there by the CRT. Keep trying Thrasher, and Factsheet Five. They're pretty cool. Just follow the menu, you'll do okay." She stopped in the doorway. "You feeling any better?"

"Yeah. I'll make it. But thanks. I really mean it. I could have drowned without you."

"S'okay. You be careful now, hear?"

She'd left the program running. Dave studied the screen, rubbing at his eyes to get them to focus. A zero and an E got him out. He wrote down the message that came up after and turned the machine off. Then he carried the unfinished beer downstairs and got in the shower.

AFTERWARDS, his brain beginning to thaw, he put on a clean pair of jeans. He stood shirtless in front of the Brazosport phone book, rubbing his hair dry with a towel. AASK was in the white pages with the address 410 W. Broad Street. He was trying to find somewhere to write the address when he heard a knock. He thought it might be the girl from the grocery again. He shoved a cat out of the way and opened the door.

"Just getting up?" Mrs. Cook asked him.

Shards of sunlight glinted off her glasses and silver hair. She didn't look happy. "No," Dave said, "actually, I . . . uh, come on in." She looked at his outstretched hand with disdain. He stood aside and she walked past him, sniffing at the air.

"I would like to give you the benefit of the doubt," she said. "For all his failings, Fred is a decent person. I would hate to think his compassion is wasted on you. When I see you in this condition—the bloodshot eyes, the pale complexion, the lack of balance—"

"Condition?" Dave said.

"Oh, don't worry. I've seen it often enough. I'll wait here while you put some clothes on."

"But I haven't . . ." He let the sentence trail off. There were no words to convince her that Bryant C. Whitney had drugged him in order to put him in a plywood UFO. "I'll be right back," he said.

When he came back she had the lid off the kitchen trash

can and was stirring the contents with the handle of the broom. She turned slowly to face him. "Did you drink *all* of these yourself?"

"Actually I didn't drink any of it. Fred—"

"There's no use lying to me." She opened the refrigerator and took out the rest of the twelve-pack. "You left a half-finished can on the dining room table. It's still cold to the touch. Yes?"

Dave shook his head. Mentioning the girl would not help things.

"It's bad enough that you don't even get up until five in the afternoon. Then you immediately begin drinking again. The habits you create in these first days will decide whether or not you will be able to return to society. I have to say that at this moment your future does not look bright. Excuse me."

Dave got out of the way of the door. Mrs. Cook stopped suddenly, as if in the grip of an irresistible impulse. She picked up a bad-tempered Siamese with a white streak over one eye and held him upside down, like a baby. Dave held his breath, waiting for the cat to shred her face. Instead he began to purr.

"These poor animals," she said. "That's what truly offends me. These are God's innocents. When you fail in your duty as caretaker—as steward—to these creatures, you are not just hurting yourself anymore. You've become not just foolish, but cruel, and I warn you: I have little patience for cruelty."

She set the cat gently on his feet and he promptly began to pummel her shoes with his forehead. The whole business, Dave thought, did not speak well for cats as a species.

When she straightened up again, the hint of moisture Dave thought he'd detected in her eyes was gone. "I'll see you in my office Thursday morning," she said. "I advise you to be on time."

A F T E R he was sure she was gone, after the sound of
her car had faded completely away, he lay facing the back
of the couch, with his knees pulled up to his chin. The
worst thing they can do to you, he thought, is send you
back to jail. How hard can that be?

Hard, he answered himself. Very hard.

The Siamese jumped on the back of the couch and stared
at him. "You were a lot of help," Dave said. "You son of
a bitch. Why didn't you rip her throat out?"

His mind, drifting, suddenly registered the fact that the
Dodge had not been in the carport when he'd limped back
from the beach. Whitney must have left it at the Pizza Inn.
It might even have been towed by now. It was too much
for Dave to handle. He staggered to the door to look downstairs and make sure. The door was only open a crack
when the black-and-silver tabby shot through the opening
and disappeared.

"Wonderful," Dave said. "Just what I needed." He pictured the cat flattened by an eighteen-wheeler, pictured
himself in handcuffs, being hustled into a squad car. He
slammed the door behind him and dashed down the stairs.
The cat saw him coming and tore around the side of the
carport. Dave lost his footing in the dunes and fell on
his face. As he got up he felt sand trickle down into his
underwear. "I'll kill you myself," Dave said. They ran all
the way around the building twice. The third time Dave
cut through the carport. The cat saw him coming and
skidded away.

Dave pounded upstairs. There was nothing in the house
but dry food. He ran all the way to the grocery. An East

Indian clerk stood at the register and watched him grab a
can of tuna. His hand stayed under the counter, doubt-
less on a sawed-off shotgun, while Dave paid. Dave ran home
and opened the ring-pull top. The salty tang made his
stomach turn over. The cat stuck his head around the corner, eyeing Dave warily. Dave pried out an oily chunk of
tuna and threw it to the cat. The cat wolfed it down. "Nice
kitty," Dave said. "Nice goddamn kitty." It took five minutes for the cat to break down and come for another bite.
Dave had learned in prison how to turn anger into patience. When the cat was in range Dave lunged and got a
rear leg.

He carried the cat upstairs in one hand, the can of tuna
in the other. He put the tuna on a plate and made him
watch while the other cats finished it.

The whole business cost him forty-five minutes. He called
a taxi and went into town to get his car. It was still in
the parking lot. Dave had a brief instant of relief, then realized the cab was going to cost him all of the rest of his
money. He fired up the Dodge in the white heat of anger
and drove to Whitney's temple.

UFO place in old church

H E ' D expected something spectacular, a neon-and-
stucco building shaped like a flying saucer. Instead he found
a complex of geodesic domes, a medieval castle as designed by Buckminster Fuller. When he looked closer at the
marquee he could see where the original lettering for a
Baptist church had been painted over. A FOR SALE sign had
been stuck in the middle of the lawn; the area code on
the phone number was 713. Houston.

The front door was unlocked. Dave walked into the stage

set from the videotape, complete with steel pulpit and giant foil letters. Without the colored lights it looked pretty shabby.

A door behind the podium opened on a narrow hallway. A second door, locked, was located halfway down. Dave stopped and put his ear to it. He'd have bet money, if he had any, the fake UFO was on the other side. He didn't hear a sound. At the end of the hall was a third doorway that led into a carpeted living room. He could see a fireplace, a big-screen TV, a wet bar, a leather couch, and a couple of chairs. Whitney sat on the couch next to a woman who looked to be in her seventies. She wore jeans, a green flannel shirt, and a shower cap. Whitney had papers in one hand and the other arm up on the back of the couch behind the woman.

He looked up. "Dave! It's a pleasure to see you."

"We need to talk," Dave said.

"Mrs. Stevens, I'll call on you tomorrow, if that's all right. We can finish up the details then."

"All right," the woman said, standing up. "Come by any time. It's not like I have pressing engagements."

Dave watched the old lady out the door and then said, "You drugged me and kidnapped me, you son of a bitch."

Whitney stood up, smiled, held a finger to his lips. "Now Dave, keep your voice down. You don't want anybody to get the wrong idea."

"What idea is that?"

"The idea that you didn't just have a peak experience."

"Are you completely nuts? A bunch of old office chairs and plywood and duct tape?"

"Come on now, admit I had you going for a while. When you first woke up. Your heart jumped right up in your mouth, didn't it?"

Dave sat down. The energy of his anger had deserted him. "I should get the cops in here."

"And what would you tell them? If you meant that, you'd have already done it."

"So you're not even going to deny it?"

"When you were a kid, didn't you promise yourself that when you grew up you were going to live someplace really cool, not in some sterile tract house like your parents had? Maybe in a cave, or a tree house with all kinds of different levels? Or at least have secret tunnels under the floors and a room like a flying saucer and another room where all the furniture was glued to the ceiling? Remember? You've lost touch with that part of yourself. Where's your sense of wonder?"

"This doesn't make any sense. What did you think you were doing? What were you supposed to get out of it?"

"Nothing! I just tried to open you up, my friend. To make you see the possibilities. Flying saucer kidnap is not just a pipe dream. It's the most potent myth in our culture. Escape! Empowerment! Esoteric knowledge! You don't know how lucky you were just to have a brush with something like that."

"I suppose you go riding around in flying saucers all the time. You're secretly the Queen of Venus' consort, right?"

Whitney shook his head. "What I wouldn't give just to *see* a saucer. Just a scout ship. Anything." He turned his soulful eyes on Dave. "Don't you see how it makes me feel? All these years, and the MIB have never followed me or tapped my phones. I'm not worthy of their attention. I don't know enough to be silenced. And now . . ."

He sighed dramatically. "Now I've lost my lease. They're selling the place out from under me, some faceless developers from out of town. The church will go under. And I know I'm so *close*."

"Which is why you want the old lady's place so bad."

"What am I supposed to do?"

Dave got up. He had to put one hand on the back of the chair to steady himself. "Just stay away from me, okay? You're nuts. Don't drive by my house anymore. Don't lurk across the street. Just keep the hell away."

He turned, weaving just a little, and walked out.

H E turned in at Kitty's Purple Cow, slowed as he came up on the Cedar Sands, and then stomped on the brakes in horror.

There was a car parked in the carport. It was a 1972 pale green Chevy Impala. Along the driver's side, in dark green runny letters, was the name TERRELL.

"Oh my god," Dave said.

He pulled over and left the car next to the motel. His heart pounded and his eyes would not focus. Maybe it was a practical joke. Maybe it was Terrell's wife or something. He climbed the steps as if they led to the guillotine. The black-and-silver tabby sat outside the door, yowling to be let in. He turned his head to look at Dave and said, "Burke."

"Burke, is it?" Dave opened the door and nudged the cat in with his foot. "Fine. Later. Later I'll find some way to make you pay."

Terrell sat sprawled on the couch, both arms up along the back. An open Budweiser stood on the coffee table in front of him. He wore wheat jeans and a brown-and-orange western shirt with pointed pockets and pearl snaps. "One of them cats got out," Terrell said.

"Terrell," Dave said.

"Dave, sit down, uncork you a beer, get you breath. You sound all upset."

"What in God's name are you doing here?"

"I had me a escape. Looking to see am I on the news."

"Terrell, your name is painted on the side of your fuck-ing car."

After a second or two Terrell slowly turned to look at Dave. His hair had just started to grow back in, making odd clumps of black on his scalp. "Yeah, okay. Maybe I ought to do something about that. You got any spray paint?"

"You can't stay here. Do you understand? I'm on parole, for God's sake. If they find you here, it's all over for me."

"Calm yourself. They ain't going to catch nobody if we get that car painted. Now you got some paint or what?"

Dave found a can of black spray paint in a storeroom downstairs. Terrell covered over his name with a few broad strokes. "Put my name on the motherfucker last time I busted out," he said. "Supposed to keep the old lady from sell-ing it on me. Worked, too. She give it away instead. Give it to some boy she been giving pussy to. No way that boy could say it wasn't mine."

"You didn't kill him, did you?"

"Shit, over a car? That ain't no way to act."

Now there was a long, dripping black rectangle down the driver's door. Terrell turned his head to look at it side-ways, then painted a peace symbol on the trunk. A bumper sticker underneath said, "HARD WORK NEVER HURT ANYBODY/But why take chances?" Terrell painted waves along the pas-senger side and an *A* in a circle on the hood.

"Like it?"

"It's great, Terrell. I'm sure the cops won't look at it twice."

Terrell tossed him the paint can and said, "Sometimes I think I missed my calling. I should have been a artist, or a interior decorator."

Dave leaned against a six-by-six support and crossed his arms. "How did you get out?"

"They had a bunch of us up to Austin for some pre-trial shit. Put a couple new guards on us. I didn't answer my name when they called roll. Gave 'em some other name instead. They couldn't find no record for it so they cut me loose."

"I almost believe that."

"It happened, man. Pained me not to use my own name, too."

Upstairs the phone rang. Dave sprinted up to the kitchen and snatched the receiver.

"Hi, Dave. Mary Nixon here."

"Mary. Hi."

"I just wondered if you were free tonight. I thought I'd give you another chance. Maybe a romantic dinner, we could talk over old times."

"Mary, I'm in the middle of maybe the worst day of my life. I don't think I'm going to be up to it."

"You don't have to explain," she said. "It's the name, isn't it? You can't get romantic over a woman named Nixon. You find yourself thinking about ex-presidents with brow ridges and five o'clock jowls. Well, it's the name I was born with. God knows I had plenty of husbands' names to pick from, but I always kept my own. If that's a crime, then so be it."

"I've got your number. Maybe I can call you later."

"Don't lead me on, Dave. I can take a hint. I won't bother you anymore." She hung up before Dave could answer.

"Who was that?" Terrell asked. He had a fresh beer and had settled his feet on the coffee table, shoving the framed photos to one side. "She coming over?"

Dave shook his head.

"Call her back. Shit, see if she got a girlfriend. Better yet a boyfriend, a nice young one with a—"

"Terrell, you're an escaped convict. Try to get that into your head. We can't go around giving parties in your honor. My parole officer was here this afternoon, okay? She could come back at any time. She's already convinced I'm some kind of degenerate. If she even finds beer in the house I'm going back to jail. Is any of this getting through to you?"

"You really upset, ain't you?"

"Yes. I'm really upset."

"You ain't gonna cry again, are you? You know I can't stand that shit."

"It could happen. It could happen any second."

"Aw hell. All right. Tell you what. I'll just stay here for the night. I'll move along in the morning. That all right? I'll stay there in the old lady's room and not mess up a thing."

"Not the old lady's room. Take my bed, upstairs."

Terrell raised his eyebrows.

"No, goddammit, I'm not going to be in it. I'll sleep on the couch. I don't want anybody in the old lady's room."

"Suit yourself, man. Hey." Terrell pointed to the TV. "Look here at this shit."

Dave edged closer so he could see the screen. It was a pantyhose ad. A beautiful model with brown hair cut to her shoulders flirted with her boyfriend. At the end of the ad she tumbled over backward into his convertible.

"You see what they saying, there? They saying if you ain't got a Porsche you ain't shit. You want prime pussy like that, you got to have the bucks. People want to know what's wrong with this country, there the answer is. TV make you go fucking crazy."

"You don't have to watch it," Dave said. She seemed to

him like the perfect woman: independent, sensual, full of mischief. He wondered which station it was, if they ran the ad often. He wanted to see her again.

"You don't watch it, man, how you know what's happening?"

"Listen," Dave said, "I got to go out for a while."

"You not gonna call the cops? You know if you did, I could put you in the shit. Tell them you helped me break out."

"I know that."

"All right then. You go do what you have to do. Tear off a little piece for Terrell. I won't wait up."

Dave stopped with his hand on the doorknob. "Are you okay for money?"

"Yeah, I'm good. Nice of you to ask, though."

"No, I mean, can I borrow ten bucks?"

T H E same East Indian was in the Surfside Grocery when Dave drove up. He kept his hand under the counter again. Dave tried to smile.

"Hi," Dave said.

"Hello. How may I help you please?"

"You know the girl that works here afternoons? Black hair, lots of eye makeup, ugly T-shirts?"

"Mickey."

"Mickey?"

"Yes. Like the television program. You know? M-I-C, K-E-Y . . ."

"Do you know where she lives?"

"Why do you ask me this?" The muscles in his right arm tensed.

Dave held up his hands. "No reason. No reason at all."

H E drove into Freeport and bought some flowers at Gerland's Food Fair on North Gulf, half a dozen roses in a gnarled green vase. Then he sat in the parking lot for five minutes, feeling like an idiot. Roses? For a girl that liked bands named Suicidal Tendencies and Meat Puppets? She'd laugh in his face.

After a while he started the car. He listened to it idle and watched a gang of seagulls fight over the garbage in the dumpster. Finally he put it in drive. What the hell. He was only guessing where she lived. He was probably wrong. Then he could take the flowers home to Terrell, who would like them a lot.

He drove past the old lady's house and kept on toward Galveston. When he got to Fonthill he pulled onto the shoulder and killed the engine. There weren't any lights showing. He was sure the place was deserted. That gave him the nerve to walk up to the front door.

The door matched the fairy castle motif. It was made with varnished planks and had a green glass porthole at eye level. Dave knocked, then realized music was coming from inside, the muffled drone of heavy metal. The music stopped. It was suddenly quiet enough that Dave could hear the surf on the far side of the highway. He waited for a long time for somebody to come to the door. When nobody did, he tried the handle.

It opened on a dim anteroom. The walls were smooth concrete. On the far side of the room was another door. Light showed underneath. Dave cautiously pushed it open and stuck his head through.

He saw a cavernous room lit with candles and hanging

flashlights and Coleman lanterns. Three of the boys from the Shove It Inn were there, including the tall blond and the kid with his arm in a cast.

Dave stepped into the room, holding the flowers behind him. The space had no logic to it, full of odd corners and randomly spaced columns. The columns themselves were mismatched, square or round or hexagonal, some inset with pastel tiles. He could see three cast-concrete stairways from where he stood, doubling back on themselves and disappearing into the shadows. The stairs and the beams of the ceiling glittered with still more tile.

The walls were spray-painted with graffiti. NO RULES. A circle with an *A* inside, like Terrell had on his car. SKATE TOUGH. Rough gesture drawings of skaters and dragons and spaceships. FACE YOUR FEARS. What must have been signatures, too stylized to read.

A cast-concrete picnic table came up out of the floor. A jam box sat on the table, and the third kid had his hand on the controls. The air was cool and smelled faintly like a locker room. Dirty clothes, skateboards, and battered knee pads lay all over the place.

"I'm, uh, looking for Mickey," Dave said.

The blond kid squinted at Dave. "You her dad or something?"

"I'm a friend of hers. Is she here?"

The blond kid turned toward one of the staircases. "Oh *Miiii*ckey! There's a *boy* here to see you." The two younger kids laughed and looked at the floor. "What you got behind your back?"

"Nothing," Dave said.

The third kid turned the jam box on. Dave recognized Ozzy Osbourne's distinctive howl, the harsh, serrated lines of the lead guitar. The kid got up casually and sneaked a look behind Dave's back.

"Flowers!" the kid hooted. "The borf brought her flowers!"

"What an asshole," said the kid with the cast. Dave could barely hear him over the music.

"She turning tricks now or something?" the blond said. "Man, I hope you used a rubber."

"I'll wait outside," Dave said. "I'd appreciate it if you'd tell her I was here."

"Whom should I say is calling?" the blond asked sarcastically.

"My name's Dave. What's yours?"

The kid hesitated a second. "Steve," he said, as if admitting to something. It seemed to take the aggression out of him.

Dave saw Mickey come out of a shadowed balcony. Her eyes registered him, then looked at Steve. Dave went outside.

The night was clear and the day's heat had already leaked off into space. Dave replayed the scene a couple of times, thinking of smart-ass answers he could have made. He couldn't see that it would have helped. He walked around the back of the house. He found a drained swimming pool, perfectly dry and swept clean. The graffiti here was blunt and to the point: AGGRO, SKATE, FUCK YOU.

Behind the pool was a ruined greenhouse. The glass was all cracked or missing. The framework was intact, though, and there seemed to be benches and shelves still inside. He'd read somewhere that they used clear plastic pillows instead of glass these days. It wouldn't be hard to fix. He thought about the old lady's okra and remembered he hadn't finished lunch.

Apparently Mickey wasn't coming out. Dave headed back toward the car. Then the front door opened and a shadow broke away. Dave assumed it was Steve and there would be a fight. He'd rather have avoided it. He set the flowers down in the gravel behind him.

The shadow said, "Hi," in Mickey's voice.

"Hi," Dave said. It took him a second to calm down. Then he said, "I guess I fucked up by coming here. I hope I didn't make trouble for you with what's-his-name in there. Steve."

"Don't worry about Steve. He's pretty out of it." She wore jeans and an oversize pink sweatshirt with the neck ripped out. She stuck her hands in her back pockets, uncomfortable and very young-looking.

Dave handed her the flowers. "I just wanted to thank you for helping me this afternoon."

She looked at them like they were clothes she didn't think would fit. "It wasn't anything, really. Anybody would have done it." She glanced back at the house then cautiously sniffed one of the roses. "Shit, Dave. Nobody ever gave me flowers before."

"Well," Dave said.

"You want to walk down to the beach?"

"Sure."

They crossed the street. Mickey carried the flowers with her, holding the vase like a can of beer. The silence stretched awkwardly between them.

"The kid in the cast," Dave said. "What happened to him?"

"That's Bobby. He went off, like, an overpass."

"In a car?"

"On his skateboard. He slammed really hard. He was in the hospital and everything for a couple of weeks. He's only fifteen. That's why everybody's paranoid. Bobby's parents have cops looking for him and all."

A barbed-wire fence cut them off from the beach. Mickey pushed the bottom strand down with her foot and pulled the next one up so Dave could duck through. They went over a low dune and then they could see the moonlight sparkle off the water. The beach was empty. Dave sat in the dry sand and Mickey sat a few feet away.

"That's a really amazing house inside," Dave said.

"You wouldn't believe some of the shit that's in there. Little toys cast into the ceiling. All these tiny little rooms hidden away. Washbasins in the middle of the bedroom. It's nuts."

"How long have you been there?"

"Just this summer. Steve's been there for a year now, on and off. He figured a way to get the water turned on and stuff."

Dave sifted a handful of sand. "So," he said. "What's the story with you and Steve?"

Mickey looked out at the water. "No story. Not as far as he's concerned. I mean, I fucked him. He fucks a lot of people. I was just something else to fuck. Just a warm place to park his dick."

Dave didn't say anything.

After a while she said, "What about you, Dave? You'd like to fuck me too, wouldn't you?"

Dave took a turn looking at the ocean himself. "Yes," he said, finally.

"So what happens if I let you fuck me, Dave? What happens then?"

"I don't know."

"See? That's the trouble, isn't it?"

"It's hard to know how you're going to feel about somebody until . . . until you know them better."

"Until you fuck them, you mean. Some people think it means too much. Some people it doesn't mean enough. Which kind are you, Dave?"

"I don't know. I guess both. One time or another. Doesn't this seem weird at all to you? To talk about sex with somebody you barely know?"

"Hey. I'm used to *having* sex with people I barely know." She took one of the roses out of the vase. The night breeze made it flutter in her hand. "Okay, maybe I'm exaggerating." She took a deep breath from the bud of the flower, then squeezed it until her knuckles went pale. When she opened her hand two dark drops of blood swelled up on her palm. She smelled the rose again, closed her eyes, and put it back in the vase. For a second or two she sat perfectly still. Then she got quickly to her feet.

Dave made a move toward her.

"No," she said. "Stay there. I have to go back."

"I'll go with you."

"No," she said. She went down on one knee next to him. Her hair fell down over his face as she kissed him. It was less a kiss than a promise of one. Her lips were soft and warm and made him tingle where they touched. He reached out one hand to stroke her cheek and she scrambled away.

"See ya," she said. She ran up the hill, head bent forward, the vase in her left hand spilling dark drops of water into the sand.

D A V E snagged his shirt getting back through the barbed wire. It reminded him he'd been trespassing, violating his parole again. Of course that was small change compared to harboring an escaped felon.

He drove back to the house. He could hear the distant hum of the TV set as he got out of the car. For a second he could smell his cell at Bastrop FCI, the Pine Sol, the sweat, the bitter tang of metal. He couldn't face Terrell yet. He took the last of Terrell's money on foot with him to Kitty's Purple Cow. For $3.95 he got a shrimp sandwich consisting of four pieces of deep-fried shrimp, Texas toast, and fries. It tasted so good he wished he could afford another.

The guy who ran the place was tanned, maybe fifty years old, with a white crewcut and beard. Dave watched him handle a drunk who'd missed the last bus to Houston. Two fishermen at the bar, in ratty T-shirts and gimme caps, argued about TEDs. Dave wished he knew the bartender's name, that he knew what a TED was, that he could walk in and order "the usual" and not have anybody look at him funny.

Someday. Tonight if he got into much of a conversation he'd either have to admit he was on parole or lie.

When he got home the place was dark. The door was locked and Burke was on the wrong side of it. Dave and the cat looked at each other while Dave unlocked the door. "You know, of course," Dave said, "this means war." He nudged the cat in with the toe of his moccasin.

Terrell's snores drifted down from upstairs, eerily familiar. Dave put food in the cats' long trough and smeared medicine on Morpheus' nose. He carried Terrell's empty beer cans into the kitchen and took out the trash. Finally he tried to stretch out on the couch. It was too short for him, and the cats kept climbing onto him and shifting around.

At 2:09 a.m. he took some aspirin and shut himself in the old lady's room. Who was to know? He'd wash the sheets in the morning and put everything back the way he'd found it.

The cats yowled for a while outside the door. Dave put a pillow over his head and eventually melted into sleep.

T H E TV woke him up around eight. He'd dreamed
about Mickey. In the dream she was taller and thinner,
with longer hair, and her face was different. His body felt
stiff and his head still hurt. Otherwise he was all right.
He put on a pair of shorts and went straight out the kitchen
door without saying anything to Terrell. He ran a couple
of miles and then went back inside to shower and brush
his teeth. His reflection managed a weak smile in the
mirror.

All his clean clothes were upstairs. He wrapped a towel
around his waist and went into the living room. Terrell
had cats all over him. On TV Donahue asked five husky
young men about their sex lives.

"Strippers?" Dave asked.

"Centerfolds."

Dave nodded and went upstairs. Terrell had made the
bed and pulled the bedspread tight over the pillows. Dave
put on clean jeans and a fresh T-shirt. None of his T-shirts
said anything. This one was red and had a pocket.

There was coffee made downstairs. Dave sniffed at it
doubtfully. It turned out to taste just fine. Terrell's breakfast dishes soaked in the sink. The simple domesticity of it
warmed Dave's heart. How could he put Terrell back on
the street?

He shook his head and came back to reality. "Listen,"
he said, taking the chair next to the TV.

"Don't worry about it," Terrell said. "I be out of your
hair today."

The phone rang. Dave turned the TV down and answered it.

"What have you got when you've got six lawyers up to their necks in sand?"

"Morning, Fred."

"Not enough sand. How you doing?"

Dave retreated farther into the kitchen as Terrell turned the TV up with the remote control. "Fine, I'm fine."

"I got the account set up in your name, and some temporary checks, and a card for you to sign. I can run them by this morning if you want."

"No," Dave said. "I mean, that's great, I need to come in to town today anyway, I'll swing by your place and pick them up."

"Are you sure everything's okay?"

"Oh yeah. Coming right along."

"Good. That's good. I'll see you later, then, I guess."

Dave hung up. He was sweating. He was no good at this. He went back to the armchair.

"Someday," Terrell said, "everybody live like this."

"Like male centerfolds?"

"No, man, like this here. See, in a few years computers be doing all the bullshit work, making all the money. Everything be automated and shit. Then the government—or the companies, or the *zaibatsus*, or whoever—give everybody enough for a crib and food without they have to work. Then they do whatever they want. Just like you get to do now."

"Me?"

"Look at you. You the citizen of the future. Except you don't know what it is you want to do. Well child, you better figure it out, that's all I got to say. You what, forty?"

"Thirty-nine," Dave said.

"When your birthday is?"

Dave sighed, trapped. "Next week."

"I only say this cause I'm your friend. You need to get

cats on welfare

your shit together. This here is your big chance. Don't
fuck it up. Otherwise you end up like these fucking cats,
lie around and take handouts all day, like they on welfare
or some shit."

"Yeah, well, speaking of the cats, how many did you let
out yesterday?"

"I don't know, two or three, while I was fucking with
that door, you know. My B & E ain't what it used to be."

"Do you remember what they looked like?"

"These here white people's cats. They all look the same
to me. Hey, come on, Dave, that's a joke."

"That's it. I'm done for."

"Now look here. They got you brainwashed. This ain't
no way for a cat to live neither. It's like they in jail here.
And they got you acting like one of 'em. You afraid to poke
you own nose out the door."

"I don't want to lose this job. If I lose the cats, I lose
the job."

"You knuckling under, man. Change the rules. You got
to live by you own rules, not the ones they give you. Look
at these cats. You think they like this shit you feed them?
They could have what they wanted, they'd eat cockroach
flavor food, or rat flavor food, or bluejay flavor food. People don't want cats to act like cats so they give them people food. They don't want people to act like people so they
give them a lot of bullshit rules. They want everybody to
act the same so we don't scare each other."

"Yeah, okay, Terrell. I'll think about it. Right now I got
to go in to Galveston. I'll be a couple of hours."

"Maybe I be gone before you get back. I just got a couple things to do. Couple phone calls to make."

"Just do me one favor, okay? Use the pay phone down
at the 7-Eleven. They can give you change and everything."

"I don't need it. I got me a credit card number."

He shook Terrell's hand, not quite able to hide his relief. "Take care of yourself."

"You too, home. And remember what I told you."

H E took the first mile or so as slow as traffic would let him, expecting to find shattered cat bodies sprawled across the tarmac. There weren't any. That left him not knowing how many cats were gone. It was like an itch on the bottom of his foot, where he couldn't get at it.

It was another dazzling autumn day. The breeze was cool enough to take the sting out of the sun. As he came into Galveston along Seawall Boulevard he could see a line of surfers bobbing gently out in the swell. Three skateboarders slalomed through the crowd on the sidewalk. They had no waves to wait for. While Dave watched, one of them shifted his weight back and ran straight up the wall, grinding his axles against the concrete lip. Seagulls floated overhead, wings stretched out as far as they would go. The air was full of the sound of the sea.

' ' . . . S 0 the priest says to the hippie, 'You're young, you have your whole life ahead of you. Take the last parachute.' And the hippie says, 'That's okay, father, we've both got parachutes. The "world's smartest lawyer" jumped out of the plane with my knapsack.' "

"These here are the checks, right?"

"Checks. Oh, yeah. Sign that card and drop it off at the bank. Take a hundred a week for yourself and give me

85

receipts for everything else. Non-taxable food items you get reimbursed for. Booze and cigarettes and like that has to come out of your pay. Okay?"

"Hard to beat."

"Yeah, like the man said, nice work while you can get it."

"What's that supposed to mean?" Dave asked.

"Well, it ain't going to last forever, that's all. You did read the will, like I told you to."

"I kind of skimmed it. Hell, Fred, it's written in Lawyer. You didn't expect me to make any *sense* out of it?"

"What it says is, when the last cat kicks, you're out. Even if you don't fuck up in the meantime."

"Hell, that could be ten, fifteen years, right?"

"If you're lucky."

"What happens to the house then?"

"It gets auctioned off, proceeds to charity."

"Who picks the charity?"

"Well, she left that to me. Forget it, Dave, it has to be a *real* charity."

A white haired man in his sixties stuck his head in the door. "Oh! Sorry!" he said. His voice had a nasal quality Dave had heard before. He's deaf, he realized.

white haired man is deaf

"Come on in," Fred said, gesturing broadly.

"Let me get Barbara," the old man said. A second later he came back with a small, frowning woman. She wore dark glasses and held on fiercely to his arm.

"Charles and Barbara, two of my oldest clients. This here is Dave. He's looking after the Johnson place." He spoke slowly, with exaggerated lip motions and then did something with his fingers which Dave assumed was D-A-V-E in sign language.

Charles gave Barbara a significant look, which she could not see. Then he held out his hand. "Pleased to know you."

"Old?" Barbara said. "Did he say old?"

"Did you ask him about the map?" Charles asked Fred.

"Not yet. I will in a minute."

"Okay. Then you have to sue UTMB for Barbara. I think they left a sponge in her after they did her hemorrhoids. She can't stop drinking water ever since she came home."

"Okay, Charles. You wait here. I'm going to walk Dave out to his car, and then we'll talk about it."

"Don't forget to ask him about the map."

Out on the street Fred said, "They're really nice folks, just a little cracked. He's deaf, she's blind. He drives the car, she talks on the phone. I hardly ever charge them for anything. Mostly I just talk them out of stupid stuff."

"Don't tell me," Dave said. "They're after the house too."

"Well . . . not exactly. They think . . . well, they think there's a pirate treasure under the carport."

"Pirate treasure?"

"All the BOIs talk about it."

"BOIs?"

"The old timers. Stands for Born On the Island." Fred sat on the hood of the old lady's Dodge. "See, back in the early 1800s, back when this was still called Snake Island, Jean Lafitte had a pirate camp here. Campeachy, they called it. At one point they must have had over a thousand people here. Wives, kids, shipfitters, dogs, the whole bit. Then in 1821 the US ran him off. He burned the place to the ground and disappeared. Nobody knows for sure what happened to him. Some say he died in Mexico, some say he went off to join Karl Marx, some say he ended up with a wife and kids in Indiana. But he's supposed to have left treasure buried around here somewhere. Hell, it might *be* in Surfside. Charles says the old lady had a map and she promised they could have it."

"You sound halfway convinced yourself."

"You got to understand. Texas has always been a pretty lawless place. This part of it is the worst. Up until 1957 Galveston was a wide-open city. Gambling, prostitution, booze, anything you wanted, and the cops just looked the other way. Or were right there to sell it to you. Guy named Will Wilson broke it up. He was state Attorney General, out to grab some headlines. Just like a lawyer to screw up everybody else's fun. Lot of people around here would rather he'd left well enough alone."

The talk of outlaws made him think of Mickey and the skateboarders. "That concrete house—Fonthill? That must have some history too."

Fred shifted his weight, suddenly restless. "Not really. It's been empty as long as I've been here."

"Who owns it?"

"Why?"

"Just curious."

"It doesn't really make any difference," Fred said. "They're going to knock it down next month."

"Are you serious? Why?"

"Why else? Condos. The foundation on that place is amazing, got pilings halfway to China. They'll build on that."

"Isn't anybody trying to stop them?"

Fred shrugged. "Maybe some blue-haired old ladies. Most people would be glad to knock it down just to get rid of all the winos and vandals that hang out there. How come you're so interested?"

"No big thing. I stopped by the other day and looked inside. It's really beautiful in there."

"I wouldn't get too involved if I were you. You're an ex-con, fresh out of jail, and you've been a Surfside resident for all of three days. It's not like you've got a lot of clout."

"Yeah, right." Fred stood up and then Dave said, "What's a TED?"

"A what?"

"A TED. I heard some fishermen talking about it."

"I think it stands for Turtle Excluder Device or something. It's a hot topic around here."

"Are we for them or against them?"

"Fishermen don't like them. They're too expensive, and they exclude shrimp as well as turtles. Got any more questions?"

"I guess not."

"Good. My advice is go home, mind the cats, watch TV, stay out of trouble. How hard can it be?"

Burke out — wants in.

BURKE was on the porch again when Dave got home, crying to be let in. So was the chubby gray female. Terrell sat on the couch, watching TV. The only thing that had changed was the number of empty beer cans stacked on the coffee table.

"Terrell."

"Hi, Dave. We watching Heckle and Jeckle."

"Terrell."

"Yeah, Dave."

"How many cats did you let out, Terrell?"

"Two or three. I ain't sure. Hell, you the one made me go down the street to use the phone."

"You said you were leaving, Terrell. Because of my being on parole and all."

"I couldn't just leave without saying goodbye."

"We said goodbye this morning."

"Okay, okay. I can take a hint. Is it too much of a imposition if I stay to the end of the cartoons?"

"Terrell."

"Shit, okay, just this one, then."

Dave sat down, his head in his hands. Terrell, I am beaming my thoughts to your brain. Do you hear me? Terrell, I am scared shitless. I am watching my beautiful, soft gig turn to dust. I can hear police sirens coming for me, I can hear that solid, echoing slam of the prison gate . . .

There was a knock at the door.

Dave shot out of the chair like it was electrified. He gestured frantically at Terrell to pick up the beer cans and hide in the bathroom. His heart tried to crawl out of his throat.

He crept up to the door and peeked around the curtains. It was Mickey. He leaned against the wall as he opened the door, not sure his legs would hold him.

"You okay?" Mickey asked him. "You look like you're about to pass out."

"No. No, I'm fine. Really."

She glanced over his shoulder. "Hey, Terrell." She shoved one of the cats out of the way and shut the door.

"I, uh, didn't know you guys were acquainted."

"He bought some beer this afternoon," Mickey said.

"Bitch carded me, too. I couldn't believe it."

"Yeah," Dave said. "She's like that."

Nobody had anything else to say. Mechanical crashing noises came from the TV, followed by cartoon music, heavy on the clarinets. Mickey put her hands in her back pockets and looked at the door.

"Terrell," Dave said.

Mickey took a step toward the door. "I was just . . ." she said.

"Wait," Dave said. "Just a second."

Terrell got up and turned off the TV. "Yeah, okay, I hear you, man. I'm gone." He slowly edged past the two of them, shaking his head. Dave saw a wedge of sky as the door opened and closed. Clouds were blowing in off the Gulf and the air was cooler than it had been.

"So," Dave said. "Hi." He heard Terrell's footsteps all the way down the stairs, heard his car door open and shut. He heard the starter crank and the engine fail to catch, heard the starter crank again and the engine cough and spin and build to a rattling thunder. He heard the crunch of gravel as Terrell backed out of the driveway and smelled the last trace of his exhaust as it filtered up through the floor.

"Hi," Mickey said. She looked painfully young. It showed in her eyes. She didn't know what came next and it made Dave awkward too. She said, "I was just, you know. On my way home. Thought I'd stop and say thank you. For the flowers and all."

"Sure," Dave said.

The man was supposed to be the aggressor in these things. It was expected of him. The woman could then be the voice of reason. The responsibility seemed crushingly heavy to Dave. How old was this girl, anyway? What if she was really as crazy as she said? Maybe they could just neck a little and see how they liked it.

She knelt suddenly and petted one of the cats. She put all her attention into it, so much so that the cat looked over its shoulder to see what she was doing.

"You want a beer or something?" Dave asked.

She looked up. She seemed to have forgotten the question. Dave took a careful step toward her. They were on a teeter-totter. Any sudden movement could knock both of them off. He pulled her up gently by the shoulders. They were close to a point of no return, might already have passed it. Her eyes, he saw, were slightly crossed. It gave her a distracted look, as if she was listening to an inner voice.

She seemed ready for him to kiss her. He was ready too.

She tilted her face to meet him and closed her eyes. Her lips were large and soft and moved lazily against his. Her skin smelled warm and sweet. He put his arms around her and, as if in reaction, her tongue moved deeper inside his mouth.

Her T-shirt hung loose around her hips. Dave slid one hand up inside it, touching the impossibly smooth skin of her back. "Mmmm," she said. She seemed to have lost her nervousness. They'd moved into an area where she knew what was expected of her. Dave felt calmer too. His doubts had vanished in a surge of hormones. He kissed her throat and the line of her jaw. Her hands moved to the back of his neck and then into the short hair above his ears. She pulled him into another kiss, and by this time both of them were breathing hard. He tugged at the bottom of her T-shirt and she reached down, smiling, and pulled it over her head.

Underneath she wore a massive, flesh-colored bra. Dave reached around her arms and unhooked it by touch, a skill he was afraid he might have lost. She shrugged gracefully out of the straps. Dave held her bare breasts in his hands. For that one second he wasn't aware of anything but his own happiness. "You're really beautiful," he said. She acted like she hadn't heard him. He peeled off his own shirt so he could feel her naked skin against his chest and then he kissed her some more.

Finally he took her hand and led her toward the old lady's bedroom. She went in and sat on the bed. "Uh, one second," Dave said. "I'll be right there."

She lay back on the bedspread. "I'm not going anywhere."

Dave ran upstairs and found a strip of condoms in his sock drawer. When he got back downstairs Mickey had her back to the doorway, playing with the small gray cat. "Does she have a name?" she asked.

Dave sat on the bed behind her. "Not yet," he said. She had strong shoulders, and a dark mole below one shoulder blade. He kissed the nape of her neck.

She rolled onto her back. Her breasts flattened out, swelling at the sides. "She needs a name. You should name them all. She looks kind of like Liz Taylor. You know, a tad overweight, but booger-green eyes to die for."

"Okay," Dave said. "We'll call her Liz." He scooped the cat up and shut her in the hall. "Listen," he said. "There's a lot you don't know about me."

"You're not gay, right? No incurable diseases?"

"No," Dave said.

"Then we can worry about the rest later." She reached for his belt and tugged his pants down around his knees. Dave got out of them and put a condom on. He felt naked. In fact he *was* naked, except for the condom and his socks. He took the socks off.

He helped Mickey out of the rest of her clothes, kissing her at the same time. Her pubic hair was dark brown, with a reddish tint. It looked so smooth and symmetrical. He cupped his hand over it, feeling it crinkle between his fingers. The crevice between her legs was warm and slick. He kissed the inside of her thigh, smelling sweat and primal juices. Mickey grabbed him under the arms and pulled him on top of her.

He crawled over her on his elbows. She took his penis in her left hand and guided him inside. Dave thought he might faint. It was like God. He was in contact with the heart of the Mystery, the only one that mattered.

He didn't try for anything athletic or complicated, not this first time. Instead he took it slow, feeling the pleasure spread out through his chest and all the way down to his toes, where his feet were trying to cramp. He loved the taste of her mouth, a girl's taste, bubblegum and pep-

93

permint and fruit-flavored lipstick. He couldn't get enough.
He kissed the inside of her lower lip, felt along her back
teeth with his tongue.

Her breathing got very intent. Her eyes were unfocused,
staring off past his left shoulder. Then they closed and
she let out a long, wavering moan. Her arms wrapped around
his neck and held him tight. That was all Dave could handle and he went into his own final approach. It built up
for a long time and she opened her legs wide to take him
deep inside her. Finally he let it all go and hung on as they
slowly rolled to a stop.

It took him a while to get his breath. Mickey stretched
languorously under him and said, "That was nice. It was
like when you really want a pizza, and then you get one."

After a minute or so he kissed her on the shoulder and
got up. He went to the bathroom and knotted the condom, then buried it in the trash. He washed the medical-
smelling lubricant off his hands and stared at himself in
the mirror. Nothing seemed quite familiar. Which made the
girl in the next room even more of a stranger. What had
he done? He didn't even know her last name, let alone her
age.

It was not the time to ask, he knew that much. He went
back into the bedroom and lay down next to her, thinking of all the unanswered questions between them. The bed
smelled like sex. It worked its ancient chemical magic on
him and his doubts drifted away. He put his head between
her breasts and listened to her heart race. "That was really amazing," he said.

"It was sex, Dave," she said gently. "Not nuclear phys-
ics. Just about anybody can do it." She stroked his hair
absently.

"It's been a long time, is all," Dave said. "A long, long
time. I've kind of been out of circulation."

"Is this the part you worried about me not knowing?"

"Yeah. I didn't want to freak you out or anything. See, I just got out of the slam three days ago."

"The slam?"

"Prison."

"Oh, yeah."

"I know what it sounds like. But I'm not, I don't know, what you would think of as your typical ex-con."

"No, it's funny, see, because that's what skaters call it when they wipe out. A slam. Anyway, I already know about jail and stuff. I talked to your buddy Fred."

"What? Really?"

"Yeah. I found out he was Mrs. Johnson's lawyer and I called him up. Told him I wanted to buy the place. He kept asking if I worked for somebody named Nixon. He told me all about you. He said you could be anything you want, but you never wanted to be anything."

"God, he's even telling it to total strangers now. I'm not as bad as he makes me out. Not really. I just never wanted to be anything they already had a name for. I mean, some-where in there 'lawyer' stopped being what Fred *did* and it turned into what he *was*, you know? I don't fit in any of the precut holes."

"Is that why they put you in jail?"

"Sort of. I used to work in this used record store, part time, and they paid me in cash. So I never declared any of it. And the store got audited and I got caught and they told me I had to get a regular job so they could gar-nishee my wages for back taxes. And I basically told them to fuck off."

"Good for you."

"Yeah. I did six months in prison because I wouldn't let the government push me around. That's not being a hero, that's being stupid."

"I think it's pretty cool."

He turned so he could see her face. "Yeah?"

"Yeah."

He kissed the damp skin in the hollow of her throat. "So who are you? You're not even twenty-one, are you?"

"No. I'm nineteen. Does that, like, weird you out?"

"A little, maybe."

"I got a fake ID so I can drink and everything. All it takes is a birth certificate. I learned how back at Lakeside."

"What's Lakeside."

"It's a school for 'disturbed' kids."

Dave found the hint of danger excited him. "Really? You're a disturbed child?"

"It means my parents didn't know what to do with me. All you need is two shrinks to sign a paper and you're gone. It happens to kids all the time. It could happen to you. Grease the right people and then mom and dad don't have to deal with you anymore. They put you on Stelazine if you don't kiss ass, and the orderlies come around after hours for gang bangs. If you're not crazy when you go in you're sure as shit crazy when you come out."

"Jail is kind of like that. I mean, they don't make you into a criminal, exactly. They make you into a prisoner, which is worse."

"I used to get pretty weird. I mean, it was no picnic for my folks. I smashed things up as a kid. I still have a shitty temper. They told me—the doctors—it was because of how I was born. I was cyanotic, you know, where I almost strangled on my umbilical. Then I got all this bile in my blood. They had to change my blood, I had all these transfusions and everything. I mean, I was only like a few hours old and I was already fighting for my life. They said it really fucks you up. It makes you angry and depressed for the rest of your life, getting that kind of bad start."

"You don't seem that bad to me."

"It helps knowing about it. I mean, you can kind of see it coming. Besides, you're good for me." She rolled over on top of him and kissed him to prove it. The kiss lasted a while and Dave found his breath getting short again. He ran his hands down the small of her back and across her buttocks. She moaned and ground her pelvis into him.

Dave was ready to go again. He reached for the condoms and Mickey stopped his hand. "Check it out," she said. She took one out of the wrapper and popped it in her mouth like a piece of gum. Then she unrolled it onto him without using her hands.

"I'm impressed," Dave said. His voice wouldn't go above a whisper.

"Good," she said. She straddled him and rode him with something not far from desperation.

H E woke up feeling cold along his chest and the front of one leg. The windows were lighter patches against darkness. The curtains fluttered in the sea breeze. "Mickey?" he said. He reached out and found her sitting up in the darkness next to him.

"I guess I better go," she said.

"Why?"

"I can't stay here all night."

"Why not?"

"I don't know. It just doesn't seem like a good idea."

"I think it's a great idea."

"You don't have to be this way. Nice and everything. Just because we fucked a couple of times. I mean, I'm not really used to it."

"Maybe I like you."

"Yeah, well just go easy, okay?"

He seemed to have actually upset her, though he didn't know how. "I'll be careful," he said. "Are you at all hungry, by any chance?"

They had sausage and egg tacos in bed and talked until after one. She'd lost her virginity at thirteen, to a drummer in a big-name arena rock group. She'd gotten out of bed afterwards to go to the bathroom, and come back to find he'd put her clothes in the hall. Dave remembered the drummer's name, though Mickey had forgotten it. He had their first album on tape.

She'd slept with maybe a dozen guys who "counted." She assured Dave that he counted too. Being number thirteen didn't seem all that auspicious. Dave didn't think he'd ever slept with anyone who didn't count. Except, perhaps, Terrell. He found himself telling Mickey the whole story and was relieved that it didn't seem to upset her.

In the morning Dave woke up to her warmth and a ground-in, pervasive smell of sex. It was like waking up in heaven. His brain was still asleep at the same time that the entire surface of his body had turned into an erogenous zone. He slowly moved his chest against Mickey's shoulder blades and reached through her arm to touch the smooth skin of her stomach. Her hips began to turn and Dave's penis sprang to life again. She found it with her left hand and toyed with it for a while. It was sensitive from the workout the night before, which made everything that much more intense. Finally she put a condom on it and guided it into her from behind. The softness of her hips against his groin drove Dave wild. He cupped her breasts and chewed on her neck and ear and she cried out and bucked against him in a kind of frenzy. Apparently she hadn't entirely woken up either, because for the first time she seemed to really let go.

When it was all over she folded her arms over Dave's, holding them there. "That was nice," she said. "I came from all the way down in my toes." She dozed off again, still holding on.

S H E used his shower and borrowed one of his T-shirts. "There's water at the house," she said, "but it's always cold. It's going to be a bitch this winter."

Dave suddenly remembered that the beautiful concrete castle was doomed. He wanted to tell her but the words wouldn't come out. He hated to spoil the mood. It was delicious to sit on the bed and watch her dress, already wanting her again in an abstract, unhurried sort of way.

"You get off at four?" he asked.

"Yeah."

"You could maybe bring the T-shirt back then. We could go into Galveston, maybe see a movie. I don't know."

She looked at him for a second. He kept still, not wanting to seem to want it too badly. "I can give you the T-shirt back right now, if you're in a hurry."

"It's not the T-shirt."

"So what is it you're asking? I mean, all of a sudden you want me to like move in with you, or what?"

Her moods were a bit quick, he decided. "I just wanted to see you tonight."

She walked over and kissed him long and slow, tasting of Crest. Dave lifted the T-shirt and put his cheek against her bare stomach. "I don't know," she said. "Let me think about it, okay?"

"Okay," he said.

When she left he stood at the edge of the blinds to watch her walk away. If she looked back, he didn't want her to see him. She didn't look back.

D A V E ate three fried eggs, five pieces of bacon, two pieces of toast, and drank a quart of orange juice. He even offered the cats his leavings, which they ignored. He did the dishes and sprawled on the couch in nothing but his jeans and listened to *Sunshine Superman* all the way through. Then, in a fit of paranoia, he put fresh sheets on both beds, changed all the litter boxes, and set out fresh food and water for the cats.

When he was finished he went back to the office upstairs. He called up the program that ran the modem and dialed the number for the THRASHER board. To his amazement he got an answer. The screen blanked out and began to ask him questions.

It gave him an illicit thrill to work his way in. Nobody could see him, nobody would know that he wasn't some skate-crazed teenager. A survey asked him about his favorite skaters and favorite music. There were computer games like SK8BASH. Text files talked about everything from philosophy to how to build an atom bomb. He didn't understand half of what he saw. It didn't matter. He'd been granted instant electronic acceptance from the moment he logged on.

He finally turned the computer off with his pulse racing. He felt like some African explorer who'd stumbled onto a lost kingdom. Except this kingdom spanned the American continent and most of the world, its elect citizens chained together by fiber-optic cable. And instead of being a remnant of the past, it was an island of the future. How many other kingdoms were there, surrounding him invisibly even now?

He took a walk along the beach, his mind still in high gear. He hadn't meant to end up at Fonthill. He was genuinely surprised when he looked up and there it was. He could hear speed metal from the far side of the house. Behind the music was a sound like a knife against a grindstone.

He followed it to the drained swimming pool in the back yard. Suddenly a kid on a skateboard shot out of the deep end, straight up into the air. It was Bobby, the cast still on his arm. He grabbed the board and turned in mid-air and disappeared again into the pool. Dave heard a thud and a clatter and the hum of free-spinning wheels.

He ran up to the edge. Bobby was on his knees on the bottom of the pool. There was fresh blood on one elbow.

"You okay?" Dave asked.

The kid looked up for a long time before he decided to answer. "Yeah."

"How did you do that? It was unbelievable."

"It was shit. You're supposed to stay on the skate after."

"Well, it looked good to me."

Bobby shook his head and got slowly to his feet. He wore massive white plastic pads on his knees. They looked like they came off a space suit. He flipped the board over with one toe of a yellow high-topped sneaker and bent over to get his breath. His T-shirt had a lurid cartoon of a factory and a skateboarder on the back along with the words "Industrial Revolution." It was soaked with sweat and torn in a couple of places.

He straightened up and got on the board, pushing off with his right foot. He rolled back to the shallow end of the pool and ran partway up the low, curved wall as he

turned around. Then he pushed off hard for the deep
end. He leaned forward as he started to climb and then he
was in the air, grabbing the board and turning. As he
came down he set his feet too far back on the board and it
flipped out from under him. He twisted as he fell so that
he slid on the plastic kneepads. His chest heaved with the
effort.

Dave didn't say anything. After a while Bobby got up and
kicked the skateboard, hard. "Fucker," he said. He looked
at Dave. "Fucking cast fucks up my balance."

Dave nodded. He wanted to make him stop. It didn't matter so much whether the kid hurt himself, as long as Dave
didn't have to watch. "How do you learn something like
that?"

"Same way you learn anything. You work at it. You want
to take a shot?"

The kid's eyes were intent, a little contemptuous. Dave
found himself nodding. He put his hands on the edge of
the pool and boosted himself down.

"You ever do this before?" Bobby asked.

"No."

Bobby shrugged and tilted his head toward the skateboard. Dave carried it to the shallow end. It was heavier
than he expected. The sides were scuffed down to the wood.
The top was coated with a sticky black material for a better grip. He put his left foot on it, close to where the forward wheels were bolted on. It felt wrong. He changed
over to his right and pushed off with his left. He aimed it
across the narrow width of the pool, where it was level.
As soon as he quit pushing and tried to bring his left foot
up he lost all momentum. He tried to lean into it more.
One wheel hit a piece of gravel and the board stopped dead.
Dave came off the front and landed on his feet.

He didn't look back at Bobby. Sweat broke and ran under both his arms. The heavy metal on the jam box seemed terribly loud. He got on the board again and saw how the wheels turned when he shifted his weight, tilting the plane of the board. It was a kind of zen steering. He pushed himself around in a circle and then dug in hard for the deep end.

For two or three seconds on the downward slope he felt the speed really pick up. If he'd known what he was doing it would have been exhilarating. He got his left foot up on the board and tried to lean into it. Suddenly the end wall came at him, much too fast. The nose of the board went up and Dave fell off the back. He managed to land on his ass and the palms of his hands. It hurt, but he hadn't broken anything.

Bobby walked up. "Congratulations. Your first slam." He held out his hand. Dave reached for it and Bobby grabbed his wrist, pulling him onto his feet. "You did okay."

"I'd do better on someplace level."

"Come on," Bobby said. "I'll show you."

They climbed out of the pool. Dave walked carefully. He was going to be stiff the next day. Bobby showed him how to stand and balance himself. He was, apparently, goofy-footed because he put his right foot first. Bobby said it didn't matter. Dave pushed himself around the concrete patio. His left leg tired quickly. He couldn't imagine keeping at it for hours at a time. After a couple of circuits he jumped off and stepped on the tailpiece. "That was pretty great," he said. To his surprise he realized it was the truth.

There were metal lawn chairs set into the cement. Dave sat down in one of them, uncomfortable at not being able to tilt it back. What, he wondered, had given the guy who built this place such a horror of movable furniture?

Bobby said, "There's probably beer inside if you want it." His head and right foot moved irresistibly to the music.

"I'm okay."

"It's probably kind of warm anyway." Bobby fiddled with the Ace bandage that held his cast in place. "Mickey said you were forty or something."

"Yeah, thirty-nine."

"You're even older than my dad. My dad would never skate, though. He's a hippie."

"I used to be one of those. Sort of. I mean I used to go to all the marches and have long hair and stuff. I say used to. I still believe the same stuff I did then. Even if my friends don't."

"My dad's like losing all his hair so he grows it out in back. He has to do it so everybody'll know he didn't sell out. Even though he's a lawyer and has a Mercedes and a big house and all that shit. As if anybody cared."

"Yeah, this friend of mine's a lawyer."

"Is he fucked up too?"

"He didn't used to be. He seems to be kind of getting into it now, though. The whole lawyer trip." It was like a surrealist painting, sitting there in the immovable chairs around the drained swimming pool. "How long you been on your own?"

"Since the night I did this." He held up the cast. "I mean, I was in the hospital almost two weeks. I checked out early and hitched here. I was in deep shit, grounded, no skate, I figured what did I have to lose."

"How'd it happen?"

Bobby shrugged. "I was pissed off. They were like giving me shit for thrashing at school, and my fucking dad keeps trying to 'relate' to me, and my mother is on fucking Valium all the time, and my big brother is another fucking lawyer in progress. So I split. Just got on my stick and got out of there for good." He looked over at Dave. "Is your dad still alive?"

"Yeah."

"How can you stand it? I mean, that seems like the only good thing about getting older is that your parents finally die."

"I don't see him much. When I go home, like for Christmas or something, it's fine for a couple of days and then he starts trying to run my life again, like he always did."

"That sucks, man. You know what I hate? The whining. The world is going to shit, according to him. Every day it's something else. He's watching this baseball game, right? The manager shoves an umpire, the ump throws him out, the crowd boos, maybe throws a couple bottles. To my dad it's the end of the fucking world. It's anarchy, man, the crowd is like pissing on the American flag because they don't respect the umpire's authority. I mean, who cares? It's just a stupid fucking game. Sure things are shitty. They could drop the Big One any second and we could all fry. You ever been to Pasadena? You can't even breathe the air there, with all those refineries, I mean it's *brown*, you know? But you got to go on living. You can't sit around and cry because they cut down some trees and pave everything. Concrete is radical. Concrete is the future. You don't cry about it, man, you skate on it."

The tape ran out and the jam box clicked off. Bobby's foot kept moving, like he could still hear it in his head. "So anyway," he said. "I split and I try to get this girl I know to come with me. She's scared, though. She's only fourteen and everything. So I catch a ride over to Steve's—he was up there with his folks that week, you know, real food, hot water, that kind of shit. Only when I get over there he's out with some girl or something. Girls always hang around him. Like Mickey, you know. She's really in love with him."

"Yeah," Dave said. He felt the same as when he fell off

the skateboard, like everything had turned over on him. "Yeah, I could see that."

"Steve doesn't care. That's the trick, you know. Not caring. Girls can't get enough of that." Dave nearly made a sarcastic remark about taking lessons from a fifteen-year-old. Except the kid was probably right. "Steve always says, between skating and girls, skating is number one with him. That's how you get to really rip like he does. So anyway. I'm skating around and around and wondering what I'm going to do. There's cops all over the fucking place and I have to keep dodging them."

"They bust you for skating?"

"In Houston? Oh shit yeah, dude. You got to understand. Once you get up on that skateboard, like all of western civilization is out to get you. They got cars and bicycles and pedestrians and barricades and bulldozers, and they all got to use the same roads and sidewalks as you do. Only you don't have to sit in traffic jams or wait in line at the gas station or follow where the roads go. They hate that, man. They want to bust you down to where they are. But they got to catch you first. And I got skater's eyes. It's true. I can see shit they can't see. Medians and retaining walls and storm sewers and spillways. Except when I look at it, all I see is the lines, you know, the lines you can rip across it.

"I end up out by Town and Country Mall, where they're putting in that new turnpike and everything? It's got all these unfinished overpasses, it's really incredible out there. There's this one overpass where if you hit it just right it's like a ten-foot acid drop. Steve's made it like two or three times. It's just killer. So I'm kind of skating out there and I'm pretty stoked. Then I see these lights."

Bobby crouched on the edge of his chair. His forelock hung over his face and his eyes shone like polished agate. "It's a UFO. It has to be. It keeps circling and after a while I figure it out. It's there for me. It wants to pick me up, only it can't land. What it wants, see, it wants to grab me out of the air with like tractor beam, okay? So I come around and make a run off that overpass."

After a second or two Dave said, "Then what?"

"Cops must have scared it off. Suddenly the UFO is gone and there's just this cop car. And I slam big time. The next thing I know it's hospital city."

"I know somebody you ought to talk to."

"What, some shrink?" Bobby flopped back in the chair. "Forget about it. This place rules. I ain't going back."

"No, not like that. I know this guy Bryant C. Whitney that's got a whole church for UFOs."

"You mean that TV dude with the lame-o ties? Yeah, I seen that shit. He's just out for a buck."

"I don't know. He seems pretty into it."

"Where do you know him from?"

"He's . . . well, he wants to move in on the house where I live."

"Yeah. Like I said. People are so fucked up these days. Money is their religion. It really pisses me off. Their lives are so empty, that's what's wrong."

"Maybe they should learn to skate."

"Hey, dude, it's better than chasing bucks." Bobby stood up. "I got to get back at it before I get stiff. You want another shot at the pool?"

"Next time, maybe."

"Listen, there's going to be a contest this weekend, up in Houston. It's going to be pretty intense. Going to be pros there to judge and everything, Hawk, Caballero, Mountain. You want to see some skating."

"You going?"

"Yeah. Steve got me entered. If I can fucking skate by then." He waved his bad arm.

"I'll think about it. Take it easy, okay? Don't kill yourself."

Bobby shook his head. "People always tell me that."

D A V E passed Kitty's Purple Cow and then skidded to a stop in the middle of the rutted dirt road. The green Chevy with the black patches was back in the driveway.

He trudged over to the stairs. The sand seemed to suck his feet into the ground. His stomach had clenched tight and his arms dragged at his sides. Sitting at the bottom of the steps was Liz, the chubby gray kitten. "C'mere Liz," Dave said, feigning good will. She bolted sideways, stiff-legged, like a pony. A fat white male with calico patches stared at him from under Terrell's car. Burke sat outside the door, yowling to be let in. As Dave watched, Burke shoved against the door with his shoulder and it eased open. A scrawny yellow cat jumped out and climbed headfirst down the six-by-sixes that held up the porch. Dave felt tears start in his eyes. "I can't stand it," he whispered. He climbed the stairs. Burke darted in as Dave slammed the door behind him.

Terrell was on the phone in the kitchen. "No problem," he said. He winked at Dave and blew him a kiss. "Later, blood." He hung up the phone and said to Dave, "Did you miss me?"

"Terrell . . ."

"Don't even say it. It ain't what you think. I got me a small job of work to do, and then I am out of your hair forever. Going to Nicaragua. Those Sandinista motherfuckers have got some very together shit happening down there.

You'd never know it, from looking at the TV up here. I been talking to some of the brothers, and they got a place for me down there. Where I can get into some really heavy shit."

"That's great, Terrell."

"The only thing, I can't be going down there empty-handed, you dig? People be starving and shit down there. So I got to put together a little stake first."

"Stake?"

"I show you."

They went downstairs. Dave checked the highway for police cars. Terrell raised the trunk of the green Chevy and stepped back, snapping out his open left hand like a circus ringmaster. Dave saw three dark-green garbage bags. They looked like they might each have a case of longnecks inside them. He took a step closer. The air filled with a damp, spicy odor.

"Oh no," Dave said. "No. No way." He slammed the trunk and backed slowly away, like it might come after him. "Terrell, this is it, man. I can't go this far. This is too much dope. I can't do it."

"That there about seventy-five pound," Terrell said. "Should pull in maybe twelve grand. Less travel expenses, that should buy at least a colonel uniform. Won't that look cold? Gonna meet with my people tonight. Should have everything took care of first thing in the morning."

"You can't do this to me, Terrell."

"I got nobody else to turn to. I know it gets you all upset. It ain't for more than a day or two."

"Upset? Upset? I'm talking about *me* going back to *jail*. The cops have got to be looking for that car—"

"Not with the new paintjob."

"—and the license plates—"

"Stole 'em fresh this morning."

"—and when they find that dope in there—"

"Dave. Dave. Just chill, home. You too late. See? I told the people sold me this you was covering me on the money."

Dave opened his mouth. Nothing came out.

"I give 'em your account number, they call the bank, they hear all those zeros at the end of the number, they be happy. Now I know you wouldn't be calling no cops on me, on account of how we friends and all. Just so you understand. We together on this."

"How . . . how much . . . money . . ."

"Aww, no, man, you don't be paying for any of this shit. You my security. I have the cash by tomorrow."

Dave tried to think. It was no good. His mind was molten slag. "If I let you stay the night—just tonight—will you at least move the car? Not just across the street, but three or four blocks away? Someplace where it's not totally obvious from the highway? Will you do that?"

Terrell smiled. "I knew I could count on you."

D A V E took a can of tuna downstairs and tried to round up the missing cats. It was almost four o'clock. Time for Mickey to get off work. He tried not to look at his watch. Terrell came back up the dirt road on foot, a big smile on his face. He waved and climbed the stairs and a few seconds later the TV clicked on.

Liz finally came to check out the tuna and Dave put her inside. He chased down the scrawny yellow cat, getting phenomenal bursts of speed from sheer nervous energy. The one with the calico patches had bolted when Terrell started his car and was nowhere to be found. At seven past four he saw somebody that looked like Mickey walking toward him along the beach. He turned his back to her and pulled a couple of clumps of grass out of the garden in an attempt at nonchalance.

When Mickey said "Hi" he straightened slowly and turned around, slapping his hands together.

"Hi yourself."

She tilted her head. "Is that the TV?"

"Terrell's back. It was kind of a surprise."

"I bet." She put her left hand around his waist. It was a quiet, familiar gesture and it brought joy to Dave's heart.

"You want to go upstairs?" he asked.

"Sure. I got to give you back your shirt, don't I?"

MICKEY came in the bedroom behind him and shut the door. She reached up under the back of her T-shirt and unhooked her bra. Then she peeled the shirt and the bra off together. "Here," she said. "Catch."

She didn't seem to care that Terrell was in the next room. After a while neither did Dave. It was even more intense than before. Mickey seemed to feel it too. When Dave came it felt like everything he had. His ears rang afterward. He had tunnel vision and he couldn't have moved if he wanted to.

Mickey sighed. "That was nice. I came three times, once before you were even inside."

"Mmmm," Dave said. He drifted off for a while, and came back to the clamminess of the condom against his thigh. He got up and threw it away and stood in the doorway of the bathroom, watching Mickey. He couldn't get back to the way she'd looked to him at first. All he could see was how he felt about her. She was beautiful, but she wasn't entirely there.

"What are you staring at?"

"What's the story with you and Steve?"

"Steve's a turd. Why don't you come back to bed?"

He sat next to her, his hip against her thigh. "Bobby said you're in love with him."

"When were you talking to Bobby?"

"This afternoon."

"And he talked to you? I don't think he ever talked to anybody over thirty before."

"Just lucky, I guess."

"Yeah?" She pulled him over onto his stomach. "Where'd you get bruises on your ass since this morning? I think you went skating with him."

"Not for long. You're changing the subject."

"Maybe I *was* in love with him. So what? I fall in love easy. He never gave a shit. I already told you. As far as he's concerned I was just a fuck. That's all."

"He's an idiot."

"Isn't that pretty much what I said?"

The phone rang in the kitchen. Dave scrambled for his clothes. By the time he got his jeans on and a sheet thrown over Mickey, Terrell had answered it.

Dave opened the bedroom door.

"It's for you," Terrell said.

"Goddamn it, Terrell," Dave said in a strangled whisper.

"Thought it was going to be for me."

Dave ran to the phone. "Hello?"

"Who the hell was that answered the phone?"

"Uh, hi, Fred. That was, uh, that was . . . the plumber. I had to call a plumber. The toilet backed up."

"What's he doing answering the phone?"

"I was checking to see if he'd fixed it. The toilet, I mean."

"Dave, something's going on. You're not fucking up, are you? After me putting my ass on the line to get you this job and everything, you wouldn't fuck it up, now would you?"

"No way, man. No way. Nothing like that."

"And the cats? The cats are all right?"

"They're fine. Great! Never better."

"All twenty-three of them?"

"Every one."

"I better come out for a look. I don't like the sound of this. I'll be there around seven-thirty. And I'll have a little surprise for you."

"Really, you don't have to . . ."

"See you then."

Dave put the phone down. He stared at it for a second, started toward the living room, then turned back. He walked in a tight little circle and then out into the living room again. "I'm fucked," he said, looking at his feet. "Oh Jesus. Oh God. I'm fucked. It's all over. I can't fucking believe it. I'm going back to jail." He looked at Terrell. "And it's all your fault."

Mickey stood in the doorway, wearing nothing but Dave's T-shirt. "What's wrong?"

Dave pointed at Terrell, who sat watching the evening news and drinking Budweiser. "Him, for one thing. He's not some old friend of mine. He's an escaped convict from Bastrop. If they find him here . . . well, they just better not find him here. Then there's the cats. I don't even know how many Terrell let out. But I've got—" He checked the digital readout on the VCR. "—just over an hour to get them back. All twenty-three of them, safe and sound."

"Excuse me," Terrell said.

"Now what? Don't you have things fouled up enough?"

"Excuse me, but why do they have to be the same cats?"

"What?"

"Nobody but the old lady would know which of those cats was which. If she even did her ownself. So if you five cats short, get you five more cats. Nobody ever know the difference."

"Where am I supposed to get five cats?"

"The humane society?" Mickey suggested.

"It's kitty roundup time," Dave said. He grabbed Grease-ball, who immediately went limp. "Start putting them in the bedroom."

T H E Y each kept their own count. They looked under all the beds, in all the closets, inside all the drawers and cabinets.

"Four," Terrell said.

"Six," Mickey said.

"Shit," Dave said. "I got nine. That's . . ."

"Nineteen," Mickey said.

The kitchen door banged. Dave opened it and Burke stuck his head in. Dave grabbed him by the flea collar and yanked him inside. "Twenty," he said. "Three short."

It was twenty to seven on a Wednesday night. Dave grabbed the yellow pages. There was no animal shelter, no humane society listed. Nothing except an animal hospital on Brazosport. Dave fumbled the number twice, took a deep breath, and got it right.

"Clinic."

"Do you sell cats?"

"*Sell* them?" It was a woman's voice, and she seemed offended.

"I'm looking to adopt a cat. Three cats, actually."

"What sort of cats?"

"Any kind."

"Well, no, really, we don't usually handle that kind of thing. Sometimes we get notices on the bulletin board, but this is the wrong time of year for—"

"Who does?"

"Sorry?"

"Where do I go to adopt some cats?"

"You might try the adoption center in Galveston. It's part of the UT Medical Branch. Or you could try a pet store."

"I haven't got *time* to get to Galveston."

"What?"

Dave hung up, leaving his hand on the receiver. It was pale blue, a cheap generic wall phone. He took it off the hook again and threw it at the breakfast bar. It smashed one of the picture frames on the pass-through shelf and knocked a second one to the floor. The receiver swung back toward him and dangled there, mocking him with its dial tone. Dave dropped to his knees and started to pick up the broken glass. Immediately he cut his finger and blood dripped slowly onto the linoleum. He let go of the glass and rolled onto his side, hugging his knees against his chest.

Mickey knelt beside him. "I've had days like this," she said. "Easy, baby. Easy does it. It's okay."

"They might as well do it," he said. He wiped his eyes with the back of his hand. "It's the waiting I can't stand. It's going to happen and there's nothing I can do about it so they might as well fucking do it so I can stop worrying."

She took his head and pulled it between her breasts. The smell of her comforted him and made him crazy at the same time because he knew he was going to lose her. He balled up his hands in the back of her T-shirt.

Terrell's shadow fell over them. "You ain't going back to prison. You ain't the type."

"He's right," Mickey said. "Don't freak out. You got friends. We'll come up with something."

After a few seconds it passed. Everything was exactly the same as it had been, only now he could live with it. "I'm bleeding on you," he said to Mickey.

"It's okay," she said. "It's your shirt."

Terrell said, "Why don't you get you some cats off the street? They cats everywhere. Can't be too hard."

"In fact," Mickey said, "there's these alley cats where I used to work."

"Alley cats?" Dave said.

"You'll love them," Mickey said. "You'll see."

H E let Mickey drive. His panic had triggered a flood of brain chemicals, making the world weird, fantastical. They caught the tail end of a two-hundred-car train as it pulled out of Dow Chemical and Dave watched in resignation as the huge silver tanks of improbable chemicals rolled by: hydrochloric acid, toluene, chloroform, diethyl benzine. He was beyond impatience. On North Gulf they passed the Improved Order of Red Men Lodge, with a giant concrete tepee around the entrance. Earth-toned murals of Indians stared back at him from the south wall. It looked like something cooked up by his fevered brain.

Mickey turned in on Quintana Street, between a Shell station and the loading dock of Gerland's Food Fair. A dumpster sat against the tan brick wall of the grocery, surrounded by discarded grocery carts and a mountain of bound, flattened boxes. Mickey parked by the dumpster, which smelled of rotten lettuce and spilt milk.

Dave got out of the car. He felt like a retardation poster child. Mickey said, "Here, kitty kitty kitty."

Nothing happened. "Maybe we should have brought some tuna or something," Dave said.

"They'll show up. Here, kitty kitty."

"I'm sorry I fell apart like that," Dave said.

"It was okay. You were kind of cute."

She banged on the dumpster with a piece of broken crate. The back door of the store opened. A kid, maybe eighteen, with long black hair, stuck his head out. "Oh," he said. "It's you. How ya doing, Mickey?"

"Hey, Keith. You seen those cats around?"

"I don't know. They're around." He watched her with an obvious wistfulness. Dave could see history between the two of them that he didn't want to know about. "So," the kid said, "you doing okay?"

"Yeah, Keith." She sounded impatient. "We just need to borrow some cats."

"Oh. Okay. See you, I guess." He nodded politely at Dave, and Dave nodded back. He looked once more at Mickey then went back inside.

"I don't think this is going to get it," Dave said.

"Wait," Mickey said. She banged on the dumpster again and suddenly she had a scuffed orange tomcat against her legs. Mickey picked him up by his chest. "I figured he'd be here. We always called him Sid."

"Sid?"

"For Sid Vicious, you know?"

"Great," Dave said.

Mickey shut him in the car. There were two more cats in the narrow space between the dumpster and the back wall of the store, one black-and-white, the other solid white. They began to back away as Mickey moved toward them with soothing noises. "Easy, kitties. Just stay where you are."

Dave circled around the dumpster just as Mickey grabbed the black-and-white, going down on both knees. The white cat bolted. It saw Dave and swerved suddenly, leaping through the open door of the dumpster.

Dave looked inside. The garbage was a foot deep, mostly shades of green and white. The cat sat licking a piece of bloodstained butcher paper. Its fur had a yellow tinge, like the nicotine stains on a heavy smoker's fingers. "Here kitty," Dave said. It didn't bother to look up.

Dave leaned back, filled his lungs, and climbed inside. The cat jumped at the swish of his feet sinking into the garbage. "Nice cat," Dave said, squeezing the air through his tightened throat. His voice sounded hideously mechanical. The cat tensed and flattened itself, ready for another leap. Dave stayed between it and the door. "I'm not going to hurt you," he croaked.

He reached for the cat as his left foot came down on something slimy. His balance went. He reached out with both arms and fell face-first into a decayed cantaloupe. The cat planted all four feet in Dave's back as it shot out of the dumpster.

Dave got up slowly, trying to decide whether to throw up before or after he smashed the cat's skull. He trudged back to the dumpster door and saw Mickey smile at him, the black-and-white cat in her left hand and the white cat in her right. Dave climbed out. "Yuck," she said. "What did you do that for?"

Dave turned his back on her and got in the car, careful not to let Sid, the orange cat, get out. He perched on the edge of the seat and rolled the window down an inch.

Mickey drove home with Sid on her lap. Dave held the black-and-white against his chest with one hand and tried to keep it from clawing its way over his shoulder. With the other hand he held the white cat against the floor, not very gently. Mickey told him the black-and-white was named

Oreo and the white cat was called White Kitty. Dave nodded stiffly.

By the time they got to the house Dave's legs had begun to itch. The cats crawled with fleas and god knew what else. They were scrawny, scarred, with filthy matted fur. No one could possibly mistake them for house cats. All three of them seemed to be males—unneutered, of course.

It was seven-fifteen. Terrell met them at the top of the stairs. "I am out of here, home."

Dave nodded.

Terrell leaned toward Dave, sniffed, and made a face. "You better get you a shower. Anybody calls for me, take the number, tell them I get back to them tomorrow."

They got inside and shut the door. The alley cats sprang out of their hands like exploding toys. They sniffed the tile and the table legs and Dave's shoes, and then their back hair went up and their mouths opened. Four of the old lady's cats, which had been asleep in the living room, woke up hissing and spitting. They sounded like clogged faucets. Then all seven started to make siren noises. The pitch got higher and higher. Bloodshed was seconds away.

"Hey!" Dave yelled, and clapped his hands. They ignored him.

Mickey shrugged.

Dave got the leftover catnip out of the refrigerator and scattered it around the room. It divided the cats' attention, at least. Every couple of seconds they stopped hissing at each other to nose around in the leaves.

"I guess I better go," Mickey said.

"Did they scratch you?"

"I'll live."

"Let me see," Dave said, reaching for her shirt.

She slapped his hand away. "You smell like shit." He

could see how young she was in the way she stood, head
down, arms off-balance.

"Yeah. I guess I better get in the shower."

"I guess you better."

"Look, I didn't fall in the garbage on purpose."

"And it wasn't my fault either, okay?" She stomped over
to the door. "See ya."

He had sense enough not to ask her when. It was an awkward moment, that was all. It didn't have to mean anything. "Okay," he said.

D A V E tied his stinking clothes up in a garbage bag and
took a quick shower. It was already seven-thirty. He chased
the new cats down and washed them with damp paper
towels and got flea collars on them. As soon as Fred left he
would turn them loose again.

He heard footsteps on the stairs, then a second set, then
a third. His heart stopped. They were running, the three
of them, their feet slamming into the stairs in double time.
The door swung open and banged into the wall.

"Surprise!" Mad Dog said.

Fred came in behind him, watching for escaping cats.
Then came Anson, with a case of Bud on one shoulder.

"Mad Dog," Dave said. "Anson. Imagine my surprise."

Mad Dog was five seven, thin, with big bones. His hair
was short and thin too, and receding from his forehead.
He wore brand-new jeans with complicated topstitching and
a pearl-snap western shirt. He lifted Dave by his waist
and carried him all the way around the room, barking furiously. Anson, in old Levis and a pink T-shirt, carried the
beer into the kitchen, shouting, "All right! All right!" His

red hair was cut off below his ears and parted on the side. The last time Dave had seen him it had hung past his shoulders.

Fred slammed the door. "Beer!" he said. "Let there be beer!"

Anson pushed him aside. " 'Nother case in the car." He went out again.

Fred said, "Guy goes to see his kid's teacher. Teacher says, 'Your son tells me you play piano in a whorehouse. Is that really true?' Guy says, 'No, actually I'm a lawyer. But you can't tell *that* to a little kid.' "

Mad Dog howled. Anson trooped up the steps with a second case of beer. Fred grabbed a six-pack as it went by. He tore a can loose from the plastic and tossed it to Mad Dog. Mad Dog shook it up and sprayed himself as he popped the top.

"Dave?" Fred said.

Dave shook his head.

"Aw, loosen up, man. I won't tell Mrs. Cook on you."

"You want me to start rounding up the cats?" Dave asked.

"Rounding them up?"

"So you can count them." Sid, the orange alley cat, was pacing the living room. He had a look in his eye that Dave didn't like. Mad Dog's antics had chased the others under the furniture.

"Oh Dave, for Christ's sake, nobody cares about the fucking cats. I'm sorry if I was an asshole on the phone. Is the toilet fixed?"

"What?"

"You had the plumber here this afternoon, remember?"

"Oh yeah, right. Yeah, it's fine."

"Then I better go siphon the python."

Fred set his beer on the table and headed for the downstairs bathroom. Mad Dog strolled by, his own can held straight up over his mouth. He crushed the empty and tossed it in the general direction of the kitchen sink. Anson sprawled out on the couch. "Man," he said, "this is some crib. You must get more ass than a toilet seat. Okay if I move in? I'll just sleep on whatever women you don't need."

Mad Dog came out of the kitchen with a beer in each hand. "All right! Y'all ready to look at some cards?"

Anson brought up a battered grocery bag full of poker chips. Mad Dog showed Dave the latest pictures of his kids. Then he stacked chips while Anson showed him pictures of his new house. It was three bedrooms in far south Austin and he had the entire place to himself. There was even a photo of his CD player. "I can't help it," Anson said. "I'm in love. At least I know where the CD player is when I'm not home."

"Anson," Mad Dog said, "you'd marry a woodpile if you thought there was a snake in there fat enough to fuck."

"Be a cheap divorce," Fred said. "You can say that for it."

"To hell with women," Anson said. "I'm too set in my ways."

"Yeah," Fred said. "Fuck 'em."

"Yeah," Mad Dog said. "Let's."

Everybody took a chair around the dining room table. They got the sacred green vinyl tablecloth out of the grocery bag and unfolded it. Fred broke out two brand-new Bicycle decks still in cellophane, one red, one blue.

"We been playing dime-quarter-half lately," Anson said to Dave. "That all right?" When Dave had left the game, it was still penny ante.

Fred answered for him. "Hell yes it's all right. Dave is flush now. Soon to be, anyway. He can lose twenty-thirty bucks, no sweat."

Dave sat with his back to the corner. His heart was not

in it. The smile on his face could not have fooled anyone. Fred fanned both decks across the table, face up, and
they all nodded that everything was there. Dave peered
over Fred's shoulder toward the living room. He saw Sid
backing toward the sofa, his tail straight out behind him.
"Oh Christ," Dave whispered. He shoved his chair back
and sprinted for the cat, flipping him with the toe of his
moccasin before he actually sprayed. Dave wondered if anyone would notice if he quietly pitched the little bastard
out the bedroom window. Sid sprinted upstairs before Dave
could make up his mind.

He sat down again. Fred had dealt seven stud high-low
in his absence. Dave was high with the queen of dia-
monds. He was reaching to check his hole cards when the
phone rang. He turned the queen over instead and ran
for the phone.

"Hello?"

"Yeah. I called about these here solar panels y'all ordered?"

"You must have the wrong number."

"This the Marguerite Johnson residence?"

"Oh. Listen, Mrs. Johnson is . . . well, she's dead is what
she is."

"Sorry to hear that. Thing is, these here panels are paid
for. Installation and everything. What you want me to do
with them?"

"Could I maybe talk to you about this another time?"

"I reckon."

Dave wrote down the man's phone number and went back
to the game.

"Who was that?" Fred asked.

"It was for the old lady."

"Friend of hers?"

"I don't think so." That was Bastrop talking. Dave had
gotten in the habit of not volunteering excess informa-

tion. Here he was doing it again. It was like he was already back.

Mad Dog had a couple of spades showing. They were small enough that he could go both ways. Mad Dog loved to go both ways. He threw in two blue chips and said, "Up fifty. So what do you do here all day?"

"Not much. Still taking it easy. Getting back on my feet."

The phone rang again.

"Dave. Mary Nixon. Is Terrell there?"

"What?"

"Terrell. You know. Guy that lives with you? Big, husky, kind of dark-skinned fella?"

Dave turned his back to the poker game and hunched his shoulders. The kitchen light seemed hellishly bright, glinting off tile and linoleum and porcelain. "How . . . what . . ."

"I came by this afternoon, around four-thirty? I gather you were otherwise engaged." He would have been in bed with Mickey. He hadn't even heard her knock.

Mary Nixon sighed. "Terrell and I had a pleasant chat about the whole thing. I suppose I understand. You *were* in something of a hurry. I hope it works out with this . . . little girl of yours." Dave blushed, unable to tell her it was none of her business. "It's different for men, I understand, like a hydraulic pressure that just builds and builds. The longer I go without the more the whole idea becomes sort of . . . abstract. Still. I wish you'd considered how I might feel." She sighed again. "I'm sorry. I didn't call to get on your case. I really did have something to ask Terrell if he's there."

"Um, not right now."

"When will he be back?"

"Not tonight."

"Dave, sweetheart, are you all right? You sound a little stressed-out."

"Fred's here."

"My second husband used to say, 'A truly good person does nothing, yet leaves nothing undone.' "

"What's that supposed to mean?"

"It means tell Terrell I called. Do you still have my number, or did you throw it away?"

"I still have it."

"You're probably lying. That's all right. I'll try again tomorrow." The line went dead.

Dave sat down again at the table. "Mary Nixon," he said, before Fred could ask.

Fred folded. Mad Dog declared both ways. Anson beat him low and took the whole pot. Mad Dog howled and ran around the table three times. "You want to see my dick?" he yelled. "Is that what you want?" He climbed on his chair, unzipped his pants, and showed Anson his penis.

Anson didn't look up from shuffling the red deck. "Your deal, pup-pup," he said. "I hope you keep that thing clean."

Mad Dog sat down. "I only use it on Thursdays. Alternate Thursdays." He glared at Dave. "You think I'm kidding?"

"No," Dave said.

"It's his wife's day off," Anson said. "It's the only time he gets it anymore."

"I wish I *was* kidding," Mad Dog said.

"Down, boy," Fred said. "Sit. Stay. Dave, if that Nixon woman is bothering you, we'll slap a peace bond on her. She messes with you, she goes to jail."

"That's okay. Really. No problem."

"Suicide," Mad Dog said, dealing everyone a down card.

"How's that go?" Fred asked.

"Same as seven stud high-low."

The joke was as old as the round green tablecloth. They

went through the motions for the sake of comfort. Seven stud high-low was the only game they ever played. They had a hundred names for it. Whipsaw. Train Wreck. White Knuckles. Pit Bull. Cardiac.

"So, Dave," Anson said. "You getting any or what?"

"Yeah, Dave," Mad Dog said. "What's it like? What does it *feel* like? What does it *smell* like? My memory isn't what it used to be."

They'd caught him unprepared. He felt himself blush.

"Woop!" Mad Dog said. "Bingo! He's been dipping the wick! Look at him!"

"It's not like that," Dave said. "I met this girl in a, a grocery store. We went to a movie, that's all."

"What movie?" Fred asked.

"Movie my ass," Anson said.

"You lying motherfucker," Mad Dog said. "You put it to her! Was it great?"

The phone rang again. "Phone," Dave said.

He ran to the kitchen and caught it on the second ring. "Hello?"

"Dave? This here's Marc. Patsy's friend? How you doing?"

"I'm okay."

"Good, that's good. I was just wondering if maybe you'd heard anything from Patsy?"

"Heard anything? What do you mean?"

"Well, you know how it is. It was time for my bootheels to be wandering, as the song goes."

"You two broke up."

"Something like that, yeah. I got to feeling, you know, concerned about her. What with the suddenness of my departure and all. I remembered your number from when you gave it to Patsy the other day in the car."

Dave realized that Marc was about three-quarters in the bag. "Marc, did she kick you out?"

"Kick me out? Hell no. What would she do that for?"

"I don't know. You're the one called me, I figured you must have something on your mind."

"Well." He cleared his throat. "Like I was saying, what with the suddeness of my departure, Patsy don't exactly know my present whereabouts. And I thought maybe she might have called you to see if you'd heard from me?"

"I'm afraid not. Patsy threw me out too, and she didn't seem inclined to change her mind back then."

"Oh."

"Look, who knows. She might call. Just to pass the time of day or something. I could mention I heard from you."

"You'd do that for me?"

"Sure I would. Tell me where you are and I'll write it down."

"I'm over to Houston now. Staying with my brother-in-law. His name's Mark too, only Mark with a *K*. Doing okay. Doing okay. But there might be a message or something, you never know. Like I say, I did pull out kind of sudden."

"Go ahead and give me the number." Dave wrote it under the number of the man with the solar cells. "You going to be okay?"

"Oh yeah. You won't forget me, now. If you should happen to be talking to Patsy, I mean."

"I'll call her tomorrow."

"That's great. That's great."

"Goodnight, Marc." Dave hung up and started back to the table.

"Is it like this every night?" Fred asked.

"You probably won't believe me, but this is the first time it's . . ."

The phone rang again before Dave could get back in his chair.

"Terrell there?" The voice was high-pitched, male, with a heavy Latin accent.

"Uh, no." Dave felt the sweat start under his arms.

"Where the fuck is he?"

"I don't know."

"Listen, man, this is a lot of fucking money, okay? If he fucks me around, somebody going to get cut. You understand?"

"I understand."

"You tell that fat fuck that Enrique called. You got that?"

"I got it." He hung up and wrote "Enrique" on the pad. Then he unplugged the phone. He sat down at the table and looked at his cards. They were five cards into a game of seven stud high-low. Dave had two tens and some garbage.

"We kept you in," Anson said. "You're out a couple of bucks so far."

It took half an hour for Dave to lose twenty dollars. The best he did was four out of the first five cards toward a straight flush. The others folded and left him a dollar's worth of change. Dave could see the disappointment in their faces when he blew his last dollar.

Fred tried to sell him some more chips. "C'mon," he said. "I'll discount. Ninety cents on the dollar."

Dave shook his head.

"What," Mad Dog said, "you just going to watch?" Mad Dog was down at least twenty dollars himself. "It's only money. That's what I said to the wife when she wanted central air, which only cost four grand. Then I got the fucking electric bill."

"Maybe I'll buy in later," Dave said.

Fred shrugged and dealt three hands. "Snowball in Hell," he said.

"What's that?" Mad Dog asked.

"Same as seven stud high-low."

B Y midnight they were down to their last two six-packs. There were beer cans everywhere. If Dave had been drinking the smell probably wouldn't have bothered him. Finally Mad Dog knocked a beer over and soaked both decks.

"Shit," Mad Dog said. "Got any more cards?"

Dave shook his head.

Anson said, "Time to roll anyway. Mad Dog's got to drive us back to Austin tonight."

"I got room for you guys here," Dave said. "All three of you. Maybe you ought to stay."

"Fuck no!" Mad Dog said. "Tomorrow's the day!"

"What day?"

"It's his alternate Thursday," Anson said. "It's all he could talk about on the way up."

"Oh Jesus!" Mad Dog screamed. He had the tablecloth folded, ready to stuff in the grocery bag. "Dave, one of your fucking cats shit in the bag!"

"You didn't put the chips in yet, did you?" Fred asked.

Dave got a fresh bag. The chips were still okay. They packed up and walked downstairs. Fred's Porsche was in the driveway and Mad Dog had parked his Coupe de Ville behind it. Dave hugged Anson and Mad Dog goodbye. He could hear Mad Dog bark all the way to the highway.

Fred sat on the steps. "It's not the same anymore."

"No," Dave said.

"Why is that? Why do things have to change?"

"You guys are the same. I must have lost my sense of humor or something."

"No, we're not funny anymore. It's me too."

"What do you mean?"

"It's nothing I can talk about."

"The hell it isn't. We're friends, remember?"

"Yeah, okay. Let me get a fresh beer."

"You just got one."

Fred looked at the can in his hand. "Oh yeah. Okay. Shit."

Dave waited him out.

"I'm in trouble," Fred said.

"What kind?"

"Money trouble. What else is there?"

"There's love trouble. Just for instance."

"That's not trouble. I should have that kind of trouble."

"So what's the deal? You owe money to the Mob?"

"Nothing that dramatic. Finance companies."

"You're kidding."

"Hey, man, they'll loan money to anybody. The interest sucks, but they don't ask the wrong kind of questions."

"Like how you plan to pay it back?"

"Exactly."

"What did you do with the money?"

He took a long drink, then sat with his eyes unfocused, like he might throw up. "Real estate," he said.

"What, are you putting it up your nose?"

"You laugh. It's not funny. It's addictive. You see everybody you know get these checks in the mail for nothing, they don't even break a sweat to get them. People put these condos up on all sides of you and you think, Jesus, how much longer can this go on? They'll run out of land to grab. Somebody else'll make all the money. And first thing you know you don't sleep anymore and you keep counting your savings and you drop hints and ask leading questions. And finally somebody offers you a piece of the action. And it's more than you can afford but you can't let them know or you're out of the game. So you buy in and next thing you know there's delays. Cost overruns. They need more money to keep up your percentage. Meanwhile you're already supposed to be paying back your bank loan. And if they get even the faintest whiff of trouble, if they even start to think you might be the tiniest bit overextended, your name is shit and all the business goes somewhere else."

"Fonthill," Dave said. "It's you, isn't it? You're the one knocking it down."

Fred put up his hands. "Okay, call me an asshole."

"You're an asshole! How could you?"

"What do you care? The place is a monstrosity. You can't heat it or cool it. You can't even move the goddamn furniture. The winos and the punks have spray-painted it, pissed and crapped in it, filled it with garbage. It's no good to anybody."

"Bullshit. There's nothing broken in there. You could clean it up, sandblast the walls, it'd be as good as new. It's beautiful in there, man."

"Whoa. Wait a minute." He cupped both hands over his eyes like a two-dollar psychic. "The picture is becoming clear. Girl in a grocery, you said. Like maybe that bimbo with the black hair and the huge bazoobas, works down the street. You're putting it to her, aren't you?"

"Don't change the subject."

"I'm not. You got your vested interest, I got mine. Don't get self-righteous with me. Maybe I'm thinking with my wallet, but you're thinking with your dick. You don't want to see your girlfriend put on the street."

"It's more than that. There's a principle here."

"Shit. Give me a break." Fred stood up. His knees bent and he had to grab for the banister.

"You okay?"

"Yeah, man, I'm fabulous. What else? I got to get out of here."

"You don't want to be driving. Why don't you stay the night?"

"I'm fine." He stood up straight. "I wouldn't drive if I thought I'd get busted. I'm a lawyer. You think I want to end up in court?"

D A V E put the empty cans in a trash bag and carried them out. Then he put the leftover six-packs on the beach where somebody would find them. He still wasn't tired. He could feel the past all around him. He put on the first Buffalo Springfield album and sat on the porch. He remembered a Friday in tenth grade when Anson had borrowed five dollars from him. Dave had been flattered by the attention. Anson was generally regarded as crazy and therefore worthy of respect. The next Monday Dave learned that Anson had borrowed money from most of the class and spent it on a bus ticket for Mexico. Anson got expelled and never paid anybody back.

That same year Dave met Alice Edwards. She was dating Dorothy Chambers' brother Pete. Dave was dating Dorothy. All of them but Pete were in the Drama Club. Pete was a sort of genteel biker who sang Arlo Guthrie songs at parties. Dave kissed Alice a time or two backstage, when she and Pete were fighting. She was very short, with a breathtaking body. She made constant tiny movements with her head, like a wild animal, and had a way of looking up at him through her eyelashes. He didn't believe she would ever break up with Pete. Still he asked her out on a real date in February of his senior year and she said yes. A month or so later she said, as if to herself, "How can I be in love with two men at the same time?" Not long after that they made love on the floor of her mother's apartment. *The Tonight Show* was on TV and a quiet rain fell outside.

That summer his parents would go out for the night or the weekend and Alice would drive the thirty miles from Arlington. Dave would put *Buffalo Springfield* or *Rubber Soul* on his cheap foldout stereo. When one side finished he would get out of bed long enough to turn it over. Dave's ideas of love came from movies and books and this seemed indistinguishable. Kisses soft as sleep. Unendurable pain of a phone that doesn't answer. Warm, sweet smells of sex.

It went to hell, inevitably. They were only eighteen. It took a year. Dave away at college. Quarrels and dizzy forgiveness. Pete, lurking. Perfumed letters and long silences. A final letter, without perfume, the fall of his sophomore year. "This is the hardest letter I've ever had to write." Alice pregnant and in love, not with him or with Pete either. "For the first time," she said, "this is the real thing."

Dave hadn't seen her in eighteen years. He'd heard she was married, living in Austin, still with the father of her kid. There had been years he thought he would never get over her. Other times it seemed like no more than a powerful longing without direction, triggered by the smell of honeysuckle or the first cool wind of fall.

If Mickey had been there he could have taken his sudden passion and spent it on her, whether it belonged to her or not. Without her he kept coming back to things he didn't want to think about. Finally he changed clothes and ran a couple of miles along the beach, until the voices in his head went away.

H E came out of the bathroom naked, still damp from the shower. The bedroom was dark, the cats shut out. He was halfway to the bed when he heard voices.

His first thought was that Enrique had shown up to murder Terrell. He held perfectly still. Then a whiny voice said, "Barbara?"

"Shit," Dave said, and fumbled for his clothes.

He found the flashlight in the night table, zipped his jeans, and went out into the living room. The kitchen door was wide open. In the moonlight he could see Charles, the deaf man from Fred's office, standing by the kitchen table. His blind wife grunted from somewhere near Dave as she ran into the furniture. Two cats made it out through the door before Dave could find his voice.

"Freeze," he said, "this is the police." He turned the flashlight on and pinned the old man in its feeble glow. "Shut that door and come over here."

The man stood motionless. You idiot, Dave told himself, he's deaf. Another cat escaped.

"Charles?" the old woman said. Apparently she'd forgotten he was deaf too. Dave flipped on the overhead light and dodged past both of them to slam the door.

The old man stared at him wide-eyed. Dave pointed to the couch. "Sit," he said. "You too, Barbara." They both wore dark blue jogging suits with silver stripes on the legs and sleeves. When Charles sat down his shoulders hunched and his sad little stomach stuck out.

Dave suddenly realized he was barefoot in broken glass. The idiots had smashed a pane out of the door when it wasn't even locked. He stepped away gingerly and collapsed in a chair across from them. As if in sympathy, the glass cut on his hand began to hurt. "What in hell are you two doing here?"

Barbara turned her head toward Charles. Charles had been watching Dave's lips. Charles said, "Nothing!" in his thick-tongued voice.

"I don't want to call the cops," Dave said. "But I will if I have to."

"You said you *were* the cops," Barbara said in a slow whine.

"I lied."

"We want our map," she said.

Charles waved his hands. "No! Don't tell!"

"Fred already told me about it," Dave said. "There's no map here."

"There is so," Barbara whined.

"Have you ever seen it?"

"I *can't* see it! I'm *blind*!"

"Charles, did you ever see it?"

"See what?"

"The map, goddammit!"

"There's no call for that kind of language," Barbara said.

"I never saw it myself," Charles said. "But Marguerite said she had it and that's good enough for me."

"She forgot to put in the will that we was to have it," Barbara said. "And Fred wouldn't let us come look for it. What else was we to do?"

"Where did you know Mrs. Johnson from?" Dave asked.

"Galveston Historical Foundation. We go to all the meetings."

"She was real friendly with us," Charles said.

"She was the only one. Nobody else likes us at all."

"Really?" Dave said. "I'll tell you what. Why don't we all go home and go to bed? And in the morning I'll look around and see if I can't find the map. And if I do, I'll give it to you."

"You won't!" Charles said. "You'll keep it for yourself! The treasure's right here. It's right under this house."

"If you know where it is—" Dave said.

"They won't let us dig without the map to prove it," Barbara said. Suddenly her eyes narrowed. "*You* could let us dig."

"Forget it," Dave said. "If I find the map, we'll talk about it."

"We don't trust you," she said.

"Look," Dave said. His voice had gotten very quiet. "It's very simple. Either you trust me and go on home, or I'll call the police and have you thrown in jail for breaking and entering. When you look at it that way, it all seems very clear, doesn't it?"

Charles stood up. "Come on, Barbara. We don't have to sit still for this." He took her hand and half-dragged her out the door.

"And shut the goddamn door!" Dave shouted after them.

Barbara's arm appeared in the doorway. It grabbed the knob and pulled the door shut. The rest of the glass fell out of the broken window and shattered on the linoleum.

Dave was too tired to look for the missing cats. He only hoped Sid was one of them. He cleaned up the glass and taped a piece of cardboard over the hole and went to bed.

H E woke up at nine the next morning. He'd stayed up with a book on the history of Galveston after Charles and Barbara were gone, listening for noises in the night. The little sleep he'd gotten had left him with a headache and a

vague sense of alarm. He suddenly remembered his eleven
o'clock appointment with Mrs. Cook. His eyes popped open
and he dragged himself out of bed.

He put on his jeans and walked into the living room.
The cardboard was off the door. Terrell was asleep
on the couch and the TV was on too loud. Sid was
beating the living daylights out of Burke, and Liz yowled at
the door to be let in. Dave's ass throbbed from falling off
the skateboard and his hand stung where he'd cut it. Apparently he'd also cut his foot last night since he seemed
to be tracking blood on the carpet.

"Good morning, God," he said.

He wrapped a Kleenex around his foot and limped over
to turn off the TV. Terrell lifted his head groggily. "What
did you do, man?"

"I turned off the TV."

"Why?"

"You were asleep."

"I'm awake now."

Dave put the TV back on. Terrell immediately went back
to sleep. Dave yawned and went into the kitchen. Terrell
had finished off the orange juice and put the empty jug back
in the refrigerator. Dave made toast and instant coffee. He
looked at the messages by the phone and saw that he'd left
it unplugged. Restlessness, and some of the night's leftover
nostalgia, made him plug it in and dial Patsy's number in
Austin.

"Hi, it's Dave. I didn't wake you up, did I?"

"Are you kidding? I'm nearly late for work."

"I won't keep you. I heard you split up with Marc. I
thought I'd see if you were okay."

"Split up is a nice word for it. I threw his ass in the
street, is what happened. Did he call you?"

"Yeah. I got the idea he wanted me to put in a good word
for him. I think he was on the desperate side."

"That sounds like him. Where'd he slink off to?"

"Houston. His brother-in-law's place. You want the number?"

"Hell no."

"Oh well. At least I can say I tried."

"How are you holding up?"

"Can't complain," he lied.

"I can't believe Marc got you to do his dirty work for him. You always were a nice guy. A little too nice, maybe, sometimes."

"I'll bear that in mind." A man's voice yelled something in the background. That Patsy, Dave thought. She never wasted any time.

"Oh oh," she said. "I got to run. You take care now, and give me a holler if you're ever in town."

"I will," Dave said.

He tried Information for a local office of the Texas Historical Commission. The best the operator could find was the Galveston Historical Foundation, on the Strand. Dave thanked him and went back into the living room.

"Terrell."

Terrell shifted onto his back and opened one eye. "What now?"

"Somebody named Enrique called for you last night. He seemed pissed off."

"Fuck Enrique. Anything else?"

"I guess not."

"Good," Terrell said, and closed the eye.

Dave taped the cardboard back on the door. He put Band-Aids on his foot and hand. Then he put on his best shirt and a black knit tie. It was time to go to Galveston.

M R S . Cook met him in the lobby and took him back to her office. It was like he might try to escape.

"Now," she said. "It's time to settle down into a routine. We'll meet here once a month, on the third Thursday, at this hour. There will be no exceptions. Starting next month you'll bring your Monthly Report with you when you come." She handed Dave a sheet of paper from the manila folder that was lined up perfectly with the edges of her desk. It had spaces for him to document how much he earned, how much he spent, what he did with his free time. "We also need to work out your payment schedule."

"Payments?"

"Your court costs were a hundred eighty dollars. Your parole administration fee is forty dollars, as set by the judge in your case. I see here you had your own legal representation so you won't have to pay for a court-appointed lawyer."

"I always thought they were free."

She looked at Dave like he'd said a naughty word. "Fifty dollars per court appearance. Arraignment, pre-trial, trial, one or two resets—it usually comes to about two hundred and fifty dollars. Plus I see here you'll have some restitution payments as well, to the IRS. Let's set you down for two hundred a month for now, and then we can adjust that upward as you settle in."

"That's half my salary."

"Your room and board is covered, as I understand it. What did you plan to buy with the rest, more Budweiser?" Dave had to look away from her stare. "Now then. The next phase is what we call Case Management Planning. We hope

that you will take an active involvement in your own rehabilitation."

Dave had worked part time at a used record store and
been paid in cash, off the books. What was to rehabilitate?

"Did you have something to say to me?" Mrs. Cook asked.

"No ma'am."

"We have five categories, depending on the amount of
supervision we feel is required. Now ordinarily I would
have put you in the lightest category, since you're well-
educated and you were not convicted of a violent crime.
However. In light of that drinking episode last Monday, we're
going to place you in category two. This will require—"

"Ma'am?"

"Please do not interrupt."

"Ma'am, I wasn't drinking. I swear to you—"

"I would also prefer that you did not swear in this office. Now. Category two requires occasional visits by the
case officer to the home or workplace. Well, here the home
and workplace are the same, aren't they?" She smiled as
if Dave was supposed to find this amusing.

It occurred to him that his twelve years of primary and
secondary education had really been about this moment.
They had trained him to sit here and feel twisted up inside
with guilt because this woman, who was every teacher and
every principal and every dean he'd ever known, had passed
judgment on him. Because, he thought, without that brain-
washing, anybody in their right mind would simply get up
and walk away.

"Do you remember the conditions of your parole? That
I gave you on Saturday?"

"Yes ma'am."

"What are they?"

"You want me to, what, recite them for you?"

"That is the idea, yes."

"Uh, I'm not supposed to hang around in bars, or be around drugs, or associate with criminals."

"And you will report . . ."

"Uh, any tickets or other violations to you personally."

"Within . . . ?"

"Forty-eight hours."

"Very good." She handed him another sheet of paper. "I've written those conditions out for you. I'd like you to be able to recite them for me next month. Word for word, if you please."

He didn't know if he could endure much more of this. His thumb left a sweaty ridge in the paper as he took it from her hand.

"I'm sure this seems juvenile to you. However I believe very strongly in our parole system. You have seen prison from the inside. You know that criminals are not rehabilitated there. Parole is the only hope our society has to bring the wayward sheep back into the flock. Prison is the last resort for those who cannot change. I would truly hate to abandon you. But understand me. If you do not follow the rules I have given you, I have no choice but to assume the worst. You *will* go back to jail. If I ever find you in a condition similar as to what I saw Monday, you *will* go back to jail. If you give me any further reason not to trust you, you will be outfitted with a Black Box."

"Black Box?" Dave whispered.

"It is attached to your leg. Oh, you can't get it off. Don't even think about trying. Then another part attaches to your telephone. Now I don't understand any of this newfangled computer business, but what seems to happen is the computer here calls your phone every so often, and the box on your phone tells it if that box on your leg is there. Doesn't even ring. If you're not there, it prints the time and date on a report. That way we always know you're where you're supposed to be."

"I'm sure," Dave said, and stopped to clear his throat.
"I'm sure that won't be necessary."

"I hope so too. Remember, the length of your probation
is at my discretion. It can last a few months, or it can go
on as long as ten years."

"Ten *years*?"

"In extreme cases. Now. Your file does not show a religious preference."

"No, ma'am." Ten years. It was inconceivable. He would
be fifty years old, a broken shell of a man.

"Why is that?"

"I guess I don't have one."

"A religion, or a preference?"

"No preference," Dave said. He told himself he was a
coward. He should tell her religion was bunk. Sure, he
thought. He could tell her that for ten long years.

"I feel duty bound to suggest to you that if you were to
accept Jesus Christ as your personal savior, you would
find your rehabilitation would progress more smoothly. My
husband and I, for example, attend the First Baptist
Church here in Galveston. I'm sure the Reverend Lansdale
would be proud to have you in his flock."

"I'll take that to heart, Mrs. Cook."

"Oh, I can see that you're not convinced. You see, the
issue here is compassion. You don't see how you committed a crime of cruelty. You avoided paying your rightful
taxes. Where would that tax money have gone?"

Dave was unable to stop himself. "Into weapons to kill
other people."

"Some of it. I deplore those weapons as much as you
do. Unlike you, however, I belong to a number of groups
who seek to abolish those weapons by peaceful and legal
means. And what of the rest of the money? The money
that would go to aid the sick and the poor and the help-

less? Can you deny that you withheld that money from
society?"

"No ma'am."

"Is there something in your throat, David?"

"No ma'am."

"Society has the power to heal as well as punish. We are
here today to begin to bring you back into society, to heal
you. If you understand that much, we will have made some
real progress today."

"Yes ma'am."

"Very good. Now relax and tell me everything you've done
since the moment you left prison."

FORTY-FIVE minutes later Dave staggered out into
the October sunshine. Somehow he had managed to discuss
his last hundred and twenty hours without mentioning
Terrell, Mickey, Bryant C. Whitney, or Mary Nixon. He
said he hadn't associated with anybody but Fred. Mostly,
he told her, he had watched TV. She had approved,
grudgingly, though she felt his time would be better spent
reading.

He put more quarters in the meter and walked the four
blocks to the Strand. At the end of the nineteenth century this had been the city's financial district, the "Wall Street
of the Southwest." Galveston had been the biggest city in
Texas as late as 1885, often compared to Manhattan for
the beauty of its natural harbor.

The only problem was hurricanes. One came through in
1900 that destroyed a third of the city and killed six thousand people. It was the worst natural disaster in the history
of the United States. When the bloated dead finally stopped

washing onto the beaches, Galveston tried to save itself. It built a concrete seawall and raised the height of the island by as much as eleven feet, jacking up the buildings and filling under them with sand and mud dredged from the bay. It was too late. The port traffic moved to the new city of Houston and the banks moved to Dallas. Galveston was on its own.

Lately they'd given the Strand a facelift, going for a sort of French Quarter ambience. The Victorian facades and wrought iron balconies had been freshly painted in reds and whites and greens. The lower floors were crowded with T-shirt shops and overpriced restaurants.

The Historical Foundation was in the same block as the Hendley Market, which now sold antique clothes and souvenirs. The offices were up a broad flight of wooden stairs. On the walls were pictures of the first causeway being dedicated, and a map of the bay dated 1721. One photo showed the wreckage from the 1900 storm. It was impossible to tell where the wreckage of one house left off and the next began. Lumber was strewn evenly across the landscape. There was even an engraving of Jean Lafitte, the pirate and hero of the Battle of New Orleans. He was shown in profile, with hawk nose, long sideburns, and dark eyes.

The man at the information desk was not much older than Dave. He had thin hair and bifocals. Dave said, "I need to see about getting a house declared a historical site or something."

"Is it here in Galveston?" The man had an Eastern accent. Philadelphia, maybe.

"No. It's a poured concrete house in Surfside, actually."

"Ah, Fonthill. I didn't know it was in danger." The man tsked. "Not anything, really, we can do for you. You want to get it declared an RTHL, and the nearest place for that is Houston."

"RTHL?"

"Recorded Texas Historic Landmark."

"What does that get you?"

"I couldn't tell you offhand what the specific protections are. They'd know in Houston or Austin, though. So. They're after Fonthill. That's a shame. It was actually written up in *Fine Homebuilding*, you know. Winter 1981 issue, if I'm not mistaken. Henry Chapman Mercer was the man that built it. Used to make ceramic tile. You know how he put the roof on that place? Put boards across his scaffolds, then filled the rest of the inside with old boxes and hay and dirt and anything else he could find. It's true. Laid the tile out on top of the dirt, face down, and just poured the concrete over it. Built the whole place with ten workmen and a horse named Lucy."

"There has to be a way to keep them from knocking it down. It's not right."

"I agree with you. But I'm afraid we're in a minority." The man sighed. "You get used to disappointment in this business."

D A V E drove down to the seawall and parked. The sea was running high. The surfers were lined up out past where the waves started to break. As Dave watched, a big wave humped up and three of them paddled furiously to catch it. One of them missed and the other two got up on their boards. The boards were shorter than what Dave remembered from the movies. The two kids pivoted their boards hard, moving up and down within the wave, playing chicken with each other. They seemed to act out of territoriality rather than any sense of fun. One of them bailed out and the other rode on until the wave stalled out. Then he slipped into the water and paddled back out to sea.

Dave was too depressed to see any joy in it. For every ride they had to struggle back against the swell. Ten years, he thought. Ten years on parole. Ten years of not being able to live his own life. How could anybody stand it?

He drove back to Surfside and parked under the house. He could hear the TV set already. He got out of the car and walked away. He found himself on the highway, half-way to the Surfside Grocery, when his brain kicked in again. Don't do this, he thought. You're pushing. Here you're not having a good day, and you still want to push things.

He ended up at the grocery just the same. Mickey stood at the register, ringing up some cigarettes for a battered old shrimper. Dave paged through *Time* magazine until the old man was gone. The Living section, at the back, pronounced skateboards no longer a fad but "a national turn-on."

"Look at you," Mickey said.

He realized he was still in his tie. He tugged at it nervously. "Just tell me one thing," he said. "Please? Tell me you'll come see me when you get off work. It would really make me happy if you did that."

She leaned over the counter on her forearms. The neck had been ripped out of her T-shirt and Dave could see the tops of her breasts. "C'mere," she said.

Dave walked over to the counter. She leaned out and kissed him in a way that nearly made him faint.

"Does that answer your question?" she said.

Dave nodded and started unsteadily for the door.

"What did you say to Bobby yesterday?" she asked.

"Nothing. Honest."

"No, he likes you. He said to ask if you wanted to go to the contest with us tomorrow."

"You're going?"

"Yeah. Steve's probably going to win. I should be there. You know."

"Are you sure you want me there?"

"Sure. Why not?"

"What's Steve going to say?"

"Fuck him. Who cares what he says?"

Dave shrugged. It was what he wanted to hear. "Is Bobby going to skate?"

"He says so."

Dave knew if he left town, even to go as far as Houston, he had to report it to Mrs. Cook. Ask her permission, actually. And most likely she would say no. Dave went claustrophobic. He couldn't seem to get enough air into his lungs.

"Dave? Are you okay?"

I can't live this way, Dave thought. If they send me back, they send me back. As long as I'm out I have to live like a human being. "Yeah," he said. "Let's do it. Why not?"

"It's overnight. I mean, tomorrow's just the qualifier. The contest's Saturday."

"Where would we stay?"

"Santa Cruz is buying Steve a hotel room. We can all crash there."

"Hell," Dave said. "I've got money now. I'll get us our own room."

"Whatever."

A middle-aged woman in a pants suit came in to pay for gas. She looked at Dave suspiciously. Dave had the sudden, horrible conviction that she worked for Mrs. Cook. "Good," he said. "Good. Fine. We'll do it." He opened the door again. "I'll see you later."

Mickey nodded, distracted. "See ya."

W H E N he got home there was a brand-new navy-and-tan Lincoln parked behind Mrs. Johnson's K-Car. It blocked the entire driveway. There were ivory-colored statues of Mary and Joseph on the dashboard. They seemed to exclude the possibility of Mrs. Cook. Dave climbed the stairs cautiously.

The door opened before he got to the top. A short, heavy-set Chicano with razor-styled hair stepped out. He had one of Terrell's bales of dope, still in its green garbage bag, under his left arm. When he saw Dave he raised his right hand shoulder high, palm out. "Hey, hombre, man, what you know?"

The voice was familiar. Dave lifted his own right hand, not sure what was expected of him. The Chicano shook it, Movement style. "You must be Dave. Enrique. How ya doing?" He glanced at his Rolex and touched the hair over his right ear with two fingers. "Got to run. Later, hermano."

Dave backed against the wall to let him by. Enrique waved as he rounded the bottom of the stairs. Dave went inside. Terrell, from the couch, said, "Hey, man, we almost out of beer. You didn't bring some, did you?"

Dave shook his head. He took off his tie and hung it on a dining room chair. He didn't want to watch TV with Terrell. He was too jittery to sleep. It would be another two hours before Mickey got off work.

He went upstairs, to the old lady's office. He'd promised Barbara and Charles he'd look for the treasure map. He opened all the blinds and pulled a box down from the top of the metal shelves. It was filled with dolls. They looked to be as old as Mrs. Johnson. Their dresses had yellowed with age and their crudely shaped heads had chipped and lost their hair. They all looked angry. They were probably worth a lot of money to a collector. Dave couldn't see that they'd be much fun to play with.

He tried another box. This one was full of old papers and a scrapbook. The book was covered in green cloth that had worn away along the edges. In places the cardboard underneath had frayed into separate sheets. The manila pages were crammed with photographs, some so old they were no more than smears of greenish brown.

Dave was mystified by the initials "CIA" under pictures too old to have anything to do with covert government agencies. Then he found a newspaper article that referred to the College of Industrial Arts in Denton, Texas. On the next page was the first clear, full-length shot of Marguerite Johnson. She had broad lips and a heavy jaw and strong, dark eyes. Her stocky body was probably admired at the time. In another picture, at the bottom of the same page, she was shown with the CIA women's tennis team. The caption read: "The Time We Got Licked." It was a gag photo of the twelve women, all in dark skirts to their ankles, done up in bandages and canes and slings. Dave supposed they wore those skirts even on the courts. Clippings showed Marguerite as president of the Texas Intercollegiate Press Association and talked about her campaign for women's rights.

Dave flipped ahead. There were fewer photos every year until 1941. Then came six pages where photos labeled "Gordon" and "HIM!" had been ripped out.

There wasn't much after that. A few scallop-edged photos of a brick house in Corpus Christi, a picture of someone's baby, two pictures of a black-and-white cat named "Buster." Stuck in the back was a wedding invitation, a two-page magazine spread on "Children of CIA," and a copy of the Houston *Chronicle*'s *Tempo* section from 1976.

The invitation was to the wedding of State Senator Gordon Powell Childers, to the daughter of a Houston man with an LLD after his name, in June of 1946.

The *Tempo* article was titled "An Early Feminist Remembers." Apparently Marguerite had been thrown in jail at least six times, had written nearly a hundred published articles, had even been approached to run for the Corpus Christi city council in the fifties. This last she had refused due to a "horror of politicians." Typical, Dave thought, that an anarchist should fall for a politician. She probably hadn't taken him seriously enough to defend herself until it was too late.

Anyway, she said, she would never have been elected because of her child. It turned out she'd had a son out of wedlock and made little attempt to hide it. She'd fought to give it her own last name, and had put "Unknown" for the father's name on the birth certificate. The kid had died of influenza at eighteen months.

Dave flipped back to the unlabeled baby picture. He pried it out of the black paper corners that held it to the page and turned it over. On the back, in pencil, was the name Lucas Gordon Johnson and the caption: "1st birthday, 7/13/47." If he'd lived, he would only have been a couple of years older than Dave.

He picked up the *Tempo* section again. The baby's death had taken the heart out of Marguerite. She stopped most of her marches and protests, though she kept on writing. She was opposed, as far as Dave could tell, to government of any kind. She talked a lot about the "voluntary society." She and Terrell would have gotten along.

He put the album back in the box and sat down at the computer. He called up the menu for the modem, started

to call the THRASHER bulletin board, then stopped to look
at the list of other boards the old lady already had on
file. One of them was called CIRCLE-A and Dave thought of
the symbol on the hood of Terrell's car. He punched it
up for the hell of it.

A black-and-white cat jumped up on Dave's lap. "You
must be Buster," Dave said. "I saw some pictures of your
great grandpa." The cat gave him a sidelong glance and
climbed onto the desk, knocking papers onto the floor.

Dave picked them up and went back to the computer.
He had to give his name and phone number as well as
his computer model. The screen blanked out, displayed a
big A in a circle made up of little A's, then gave way to a
menu. Immediately Dave sensed that something serious was
going on. The menu was divided into Software, Services,
How-To, and Messages. He selected Services and got another menu that included Barter, Legal Aid, Protection,
Taxes, and another dozen categories.

"What are you doing?"

Dave jumped. He'd lost track of where he was. He turned
in the chair and saw Mickey in the doorway. "I didn't
hear you come in."

She looked over his shoulder. "You on Circle-A?"

"Yeah," Dave said. "What is it?"

"Anarchists."

"You're kidding."

"No. They got a list of people who'll take barter instead
of money. Chickens or books or whatever. They got it broken down by area for all of East Texas. Then there's people who'll show you how to handle your books and stay
out of jail and all that."

"Is this legal?"

"Hey, man, it's information. No law against that."

The significance of it started to hit him. "How many . . .

my God, how many people are there that live like this? Underground?"

Mickey smiled. "More than you think. You see somebody on the street every day, you wave, you say hi, you don't know if they're who they say they are. They could have fake ID, fake MasterCard, fake everything. You'd never know."

Dave spun around in the chair. He'd read somewhere that ideas were like viruses. They used people to reproduce themselves and they did it by making fundamental changes in the host. He felt feverish himself, as if the infection had just set in.

"C'mon," Mickey said. "Shut that thing off and come downstairs. I'll show you what I've been thinking about all day."

A R O U N D dusk Mickey got up and put her clothes on. Dave rolled over to watch.

"I got to go home for a while," she said.

"Are you coming back?"

She shrugged.

"I was just wondering," Dave said.

"Can I use one of your videotapes?"

"Sure," Dave said. He pulled on his jeans and followed her into the living room. Terrell was on the couch, watching a beauty pageant in Spanish. "You can use the tape that's in there." At that point Dave didn't care if he ever saw Bryant C. Whitney again.

She rewound the tape and started it off on NBC. Her fingers moved across the controls with easy familiarity. When she was done she touched one finger to Dave's mouth and headed for the door.

"You let me know if that works out for you," Terrell said to her.

"I will," she said.

"If what works out?" Dave said.

"Nothing," Mickey said.

"Don't do this," Dave said.

"Terrell did me a little favor. Don't worry about it." She went out the door. Dave looked at Terrell and Terrell shrugged.

Dave went out the door after her. She was halfway down the stairs. "What favor?"

"Jesus Christ, keep your voice down," she said.

"I'll shut up if you tell me what's going on."

She stopped at the bottom of the stairs and Dave caught up with her there. "Terrell got me something for Bobby."

"Bobby smokes grass?"

"It's not grass, okay?"

"What is it?"

"It's smack. It's smack, okay? And it's not any of your business."

"Oh fuck." Dave sat down on the bottom step.

"They gave him Demerol for two solid weeks in the hospital, as much as he wanted. Now he can't sleep. He's in a lot of pain."

"I don't want to see him using that shit. It's bad news. Not to mention it's dangerous for me to be around it if anybody finds out."

"More bullshit rules," she said. "If Bobby was still with his folks they'd give him any kind of painkiller he wanted. What's the difference if he gets it from me or from his parents?"

"He could get hooked."

"He's already *hooked*. Don't you get it? They *hooked* him in the hospital. He needs something to get him through this. I hate this bullshit. Everybody's so fucking paranoid about drugs. Like alcohol's *not*. Or cigarettes. Or TV or anything else. They don't kill on contact. I did some skag when I was fifteen, and it was not that big a deal. I don't need attitude from you. If you're going to turn into my father we might as well pack it in."

"It's not like I'm telling you what to wear or what to eat. We're not just talking about a couple of joints or a few mushrooms, here."

"Why don't we not talk about it at all?" Her face had changed. She was smiling in a way Dave didn't like to look at, like she was grinding her teeth. She took about ten steps then turned back. "Just stay out of it. Just stay the *fuck* out of it."

"Mickey . . ."

She grabbed a walnut-sized rock and threw it at him as hard as she could. Dave ducked and it whizzed by his ear, hitting the side of the house with a loud whack. "Stay the fuck *out* of it," she said, and turned and walked away.

H E went to the kitchen to get a 7-Up. He turned around from the refrigerator with the can in his hand and saw Terrell by the phone.

"What was all that about?" Terrell said.

"Smack," Dave said. "I don't like it."

"I don't like it either."

"You sell it."

"If I don't sell it, that don't make it go away. People got to stop wanting it. Most junkies, they live long enough, they quit on they own. They get tired of it. You don't hear that in no presidential campaigns. It's the truth, all the same."

"I don't know what to think anymore," Dave said. "When I was a kid drugs were fun. Recreation. Now I see people fucking themselves up all the time."

"They do, that's they own business."

"Yeah, I know. It just seems different somehow."

"The world ain't the same. I read somewhere, what you *want* a drug to do change what it does. Everybody took acid in the sixties to see God, so they saw God. Now they take it to get stupid, that's what happens."

"Well, that's fine. All I know is, the stuff you got around here is going to get me sent to jail." He opened the 7-Up and had a drink. "I saw my parole officer today. She's going to make surprise visits here and check up on me. There's not supposed to be any beer or anything here. Not to mention, like, bales of dope, escaped convicts, firearms, that kind of thing. I just wanted to tell you that. So you'd know."

"I be gone by tomorrow."

Dave sat at the kitchen table. "To Nicaragua?"

"Better." Terrell brought a book from the living room. It was called *How To Start Your Own Country*. It was published by somebody called Loompanics and it had a cheap blue paper cover. Dave could barely read the title through the rippled water pattern printed on it. "Place called Operation Atlantis. Going to start a new country in the Caribbean. Got a ship and a bunch of folks and everything."

"Where? I mean, are they going to buy an island, or what?"

"I can't tell you that. It's secret. All that sovereignty shit. The US or Russia find out what you up to, they try to shut you down. Especially someplace like this, proprietary community, no laws."

"No laws?"

"Right. Everybody sign a contract say they won't engage in coercive action. Anything else is okay."

"No rules. Like the skaters say."

"Exactly. This the wave of the future. Government can't protect you no more. Can't do nothing about terrorists. Can't do nothing about tax havens. Can't do nothing about pirates."

"Pirates?"

"Video pirates, data pirates. Print up they own stuff, don't pay royalties. Big business, man. You spend you whole life chasing pussy? Don't you pay attention to the world? You got to get the message. Don't look to no government. They only out to cover they own ass. Don't look to no cops, they don't know who you are. All you got is your friends, your partners, whatever kind of networks you got. Otherwise you on your own."

"Unless you're in jail," Dave said, thinking of Mrs. Cook again.

"Everybody in some kind of jail. Now, speaking of friends, I went and got some more beer. You can have one if you want."

"I just told you—"

"Yeah, yeah. Parole officer say you can't. Don't mind if I have me one, though."

Terrell opened the refrigerator. There was a knock on the door. Dave looked at Terrell. He heard the knob turn and the hinges squeal. He closed his eyes.

"Hi," said Mary Nixon's voice. "Anybody home?"

"Come in," Dave said. She was inside, with the door closed, before he finished the sentence. At least, he thought, she hadn't let any more cats out.

She wore a fuzzy pink sweater and a tight pair of jeans. She had pearls around her neck and red high-heeled pumps on her feet. She had on a lot less makeup than before. The lines around her eyes made her look more human. Dave couldn't stop thinking about Mickey, about the rock she threw at his head. Maybe things were over between them. Relationships were hopeless; his sex life might be over for good.

"You look nice," Dave said suddenly.

"Why thank you, darling. I'm glad you noticed. Hi, Terrell. Did you get the goods?"

"Right here," Terrell said. He went back to his usual station on the sofa. He pushed beer cans and supermarket tabloids aside to make room on the tabletop. Two of Mrs. Johnson's framed pictures fell on the floor. Terrell set a gallon ziplock bag of dope in the clear spot and held up a pack of E-Z Widers. "Want to smoke a little?"

"Great." She sat next to him on the couch, leaning forward expectantly.

"Oh," Dave said. "Business."

Dave took the chair by the TV. "Terrell, have you got a gun?"

"What you want a gun for?"

"I was thinking, if you had one? You could get it and maybe hold it on me when you did stuff like this. So it wouldn't look so bad for me."

Terrell quickly ran the finished joint in and out of his pursed lips to seal it up. "That Dave," he said to Mary. "What a kidder."

"This is all because of the house, isn't it?" Dave said to Mary.

"All of what?"

"This cozying up to Terrell and everything. You're going to get me busted so I lose my job and the old lady's will gets broken."

"I beg your pardon?"

"You mean to say that you never pretended to be related

to Mrs. Johnson? That you're not after the house? And the money?"

"I don't see what that has to do with you and me."

"Everything," Dave said.

"My second husband would say, 'Forget the entanglement of love; forget not to practice charity.' "

"What's that supposed to mean?"

"It means can't we start over? Try and be friends?' "

"How can we? You're just like Terrell or Barbara and Charles Whatever-their-names-are or Bryant C. Whitney or any of the others. You're using me." Dave stood up. "You don't care about me at all."

Terrell fell back on the couch, giggling. Mary Nixon took the joint out of his hands and gave Dave a serious look. "I'm sorry you feel that way."

Dave stomped out of the house and slammed the door.

H E went to Kitty's Purple Cow for a shrimp sandwich. The marijuana fumes had left him starved. He lingered over his food, talked to a couple of old men at the bar about the weather. The shrimpers were waiting for the full moon to bring them a decent catch. Dave didn't ask about Mrs. Johnson or TEDs. After an hour and three 7-Ups he knew he'd started to look suspicious. He said goodnight and went outside.

Halfway home he saw Mary Nixon come down the stairs. She was leaning against the side of her car by the time he got there. "Are you okay?" she asked.

Dave shrugged.

"Problems with your girlfriend?"

She seemed to mean well. "Maybe," he said.

" 'To shine is better than to reflect.' "

"Another fortune cookie."

"It means be yourself. Not what you think other people want you to be."

"I'll keep that in mind."

Terrell had gone to bed. There was enough moonlight to see by. Dave cleaned up the beer cans and set the picture frames back on the table. Then he said to hell with it and put them all in a drawer in the bureau.

He sat for a long time without thinking. The VCR whirred quietly in the background. First one cat, then a second and a third got on the couch with him. When he looked again there were a dozen of them, all around. He switched on the floor lamp and picked up the *Weekly World News*. Elvis had been sighted in a Burger King in Kalamazoo, and in a supermarket checkout line in Indiana. THE KING'S DEATH WAS STAGED, said the headline, SO HE COULD LIVE OUT HIS LIFE IN PEACE. Though Elvis was now balding and wore a beard to hide his identity, he couldn't seem to stop wearing white jump suits. It's always the little things, Dave thought, that trip us up.

He didn't hear the kitchen door open. He saw something move out of the corner of his eye, and before he had time to be afraid he saw it was Mickey. She sat in the chair by the TV without saying anything. Dave didn't want to talk either, at first, in case she was a hallucination. Finally he said, "Hi."

"Hi. Is it okay if I look at the tape now?"

"Sure," Dave said. He saw she was not going to mention the heroin, or the rock. He thought that was just as well. He put his arm up on the back of the couch. Mickey stopped the tape and rewound it. She turned the TV on with no sound and came to sit next to him.

He thought of things to say and didn't say them. The

tape finished rewinding. Mickey started it with the remote, then switched to FAST FORWARD. "What was it you wanted to see?" Dave asked.

"Just . . ." She gestured vaguely with the remote. "It's the only way I can stand to watch TV. Otherwise I'm sitting there thinking, you know, get *on* with it."

She sped through two hours of sitcoms and comedy/drama. She only stopped the tape for commercials, and then she clicked the PAUSE button through a series of single frames. Her favorites seemed to be the car commercials, all hot reds and matte black, with stark sexual imagery and high-dollar special effects. Her left knee bounced with pent-up energy as she stared at them. During the shows, as the characters raced frantically through their oddly high-ceilinged homes, the motion seemed to calm her.

The tape ran out. Dave got up to turn the TV off and Mickey said, "Wait." It was the ten o'clock news from Houston. Dave turned up the sound. The screen showed skateboarders in drainage ditches, cutting in front of each other, making each other slam. It reminded Dave of the surfers he'd seen that afternoon. They showed a close-up of a skinned, bleeding elbow and another of a kid with a scar over one eye. The announcer spoke in bright, authoritative tones. He came down hard on words like "alarm" and "accident" and "danger." Angry neighbors complained to the camera about noise. A gang of cops lined kids up against a squad car.

When they cut back to the blonde anchor she promised they would wrap up their week-long series tomorrow with coverage of the National Skateboard Association qualifier from right there in Houston. As they cut away for a commercial they showed a kid skating on a ramp in the shape of a wide, open-ended U, down one side and across the bottom, his momentum carrying him up the curved transition, past the lip of the other wall. He flipped over in mid-air and started down again. Suddenly the screen filled with a glistening hamburger.

"Kill it," Mickey said. Dave shut off the TV. He was still standing in front of it when Mickey got up and put her arms around him from behind. "Let's go to bed," she said. "It's been a long day."

D A V E lay in the darkness and thought about life. He had learned early on that he would never truly understand anything. The best he could hope for was a working misunderstanding. Through careful refinement, a working misunderstanding might actually lead to successful predictions. This, as he understood it, was called science.

Tonight had brought him closer to a working misunderstanding of Mickey. The next time she blew up or threw things, maybe he wouldn't take it so hard.

Or maybe not.

"Dave?"

"What?"

"Are you really coming to Houston tomorrow?"

"I guess so." He turned to look at her. "Is that okay? Is that what you want?"

"It's fine."

Mickey shifted around on the bed. She seemed to shake it harder than she needed to. Dave wondered if he should try to make love to her one more time, tired as he was. Anything might happen in Houston, with her and Steve together.

In fact he was emotionally exhausted. He felt sleep coming up fast on his blind side.

Glass broke in the living room.

He came out of bed groping for his jeans. He got into them and threw open the bedroom door. He could see a rectangle of lesser darkness by the kitchen, and the red glow of a flashlight with a hand over it. The silhouette was tall and thin, apparently male. The man whistled softly, as if calling the cats. A couple of them padded by him and ran down the stairs. Muted light flickered over shards of glass on the linoleum. Why, Dave wondered, couldn't he have torn off the cardboard over the window that was already broken?

Dave was about to shout something when the flashlight went flying though the air and Terrell's voice said, "Surprise, motherfucker, surprise!"

They crashed into the dining room table. Dave switched on the overhead light and found Terrell sitting on a man in black clothes and a ski mask. Terrell peeled back the mask to reveal Bryant C. Whitney. "Where's my glasses?" Whitney said. "I can't see anything without my glasses."

"What the fuck are you doing here?" Terrell said.

"What are *you* doing here?" Whitney said. His groping fingers connected with his glasses and put them on. "And who's *that*?"

He pointed to Dave's left. Dave turned and saw Mickey in the bedroom doorway, wearing nothing but a T-shirt.

"There's something fishy going on," Whitney said, looking at Dave for the first time. "Who are all these people? What are you up to here?"

"These are my friends," Dave said, crossing the room to shut the door. He got a broom out of the kitchen and started to sweep up the broken glass. "And you're in no position to talk. You're the one broke in here."

"You know this guy?" Terrell said.

"More or less."

"Then you don't want me to kill him?"

"Excuse me?" Whitney said. "Kill me?"

"I don't know," Dave told Terrell. "I don't want to rule anything out just yet."

"Listen," Whitney said, "I was just, uh, I was just . . ."

"You were going to let all the cats out," Dave said. "Then you were going to get me fired and Fred fired and try to jockey yourself in as executor."

"I'm a desperate man," Whitney said. "They've got a buyer for the church. I'll be out on the street in two weeks."

"Aren't you that preacher with the UFOs?" Mickey asked. "I knew I'd heard that voice somewhere. I saw you on TV."

Dave dumped the broken glass in the trash. "That's him all right. I am so goddamned sick of this. I am being hounded night and day by every greedy, moneygrubbing bastard on the Gulf Coast."

"Let me kill him, then," Terrell said.

Mickey came over to hold Dave's left arm. "Easy, Dave."

"I didn't want to hurt your cats," Whitney said. "I never used to care about money at all. But how can you live without it?"

Against his will Dave began to feel sorry for him.

"We can make a deal," Whitney said. "I don't say anything about seeing all you people here and you let me go. That's fair, isn't it? What do you say? I mean, it's not just me. I'm part of a network. If any member of AASK is abducted by a UFO, we have to try to persuade the Visitors to pick up as many fellow members as possible. If you break that chain, you risk everything."

"Is he crazy?" Terrell said.

"Yes," Dave said.

"All across America," Whitney said. "Hundreds, maybe thousands of people, driven to build their own flying saucers in their basements and garages and back yards. Wanting nothing more than to rise up, escape, transcend." Whitney's eyelids fluttered alarmingly. "Can't you trust me? For their sake?"

"We cut out your tongue," Terrell said, "we don't have to worry if you talk. Hey. You listening to me?" He looked at Dave. "Motherfucker fainted. You believe that?"

"Let's put him outside," Dave said.

"What if he decide to call the police?"

"I think you made an impression on him, Terrell. I don't think he's going to tell anybody."

Terrell took Whitney's arms. Dave and Mickey each took a leg. Dave heard Whitney's head bounce at least twice as they carried him down the stairs.

"You ever really kill anybody, Terrell?" Mickey asked.

"Only in prison," Terrell said. "Sometimes people be fucking with you, you got to do it."

"He didn't like it," Dave said. "He's more sensitive than you might think."

"Didn't mind it that much. I believe in world peace and all that shit, but by the time some motherfucker got it in his head to be fucking with you, it's too late. The time to work all that shit out is before somebody actually get in your face." They came over the rise and staggered onto packed sand. "Shit, this far enough. Put the motherfucker down."

Dave dropped Whitney's leg and turned to face the breeze that blew in with the tide. Whitecaps flashed in the night. Otherwise it was impossible to tell the sky from the ocean. The air was cool and thick. Dave shivered slightly. "We better get back inside."

Mickey smiled. "How about a swim instead?"

"You mean right now?"

Terrell shook his head. "I'm going to the house. You two

sort this out amongst your own selves." His feet crunched in the sand as he walked away.

"I don't have a suit," Dave said.

"Who cares?" Mickey peeled off her T-shirt and threw it in the sand. She patted his front pockets and took a condom out of the left one. "Ah," she said. "My perfect boy scout." She kissed him and ran naked into the water.

Dave looked at Bryant C. Whitney, who seemed on the verge of coming around. Then he stepped out of his jeans and threw them behind a dune. He ran for the ocean, his penis slapping against his leg.

The water was warmer than the surrounding air. Mickey waited for him in shoulder-high water. As Dave struggled out to her, his brain surged and pounded like the ocean, nagging him about the trip to Houston, about Whitney, about Mrs. Cook, about leaving Terrell alone with the cats.

The sea lifted Dave off his feet and tried to throw him sideways. A wave broke over his face and he wiped the salt away. "You're crazy," he shouted. He wanted to be back in bed, warm and dry and asleep.

Mickey swam over to him and put her arms around his neck. Her eyes were bright and intent. She kissed him, her mouth firm and wet and tasting of salt. She wrapped her legs around his waist and her sea-slick breasts rubbed against his chest. The water flashed green around them. Excitement hit him like a jolt of electricity. He felt Mickey's hands put the condom on him underwater. The empty package floated to the surface a few feet away. If he found it on the beach later, maybe he would pick it up then. He felt the strength of the tides and the sensual reek of marine life all around him. Mickey's face went serious. She kissed him hard. A second later she rose up and guided him into her, one liquid sensation giving way to another. Her legs tightened around his waist. A wave covered him and he didn't feel it. The ocean began to sound like a choir, holding one long note. He didn't think he'd be able to come standing up. The water made the two of them nearly weightless and he hardly knew where he was. He was looking into Mickey's face when it happened. Her hair hung in black ropes and there were beads of salt water on her eyelashes. He couldn't remember anything more beautiful. Then he was the ocean. He was miles deep and thousands of miles wide. Vast, eternal, rhythmic. Everything made sense. He saw where he had to go and what he had to do and who he had to become.

When they staggered back onto the beach Bryant C. Whitney was gone. They picked up their clothes and walked naked back to the house and slept the sleep of the dead.

D A V E woke up around eight. Mickey slept next to him with total concentration, face down on her pillow, one leg thrown over his. Her breath rasped faintly in the back of her throat. Dave gently worked himself free and put on his clothes.

Except for the cats he had the place to himself. It was warm and sunny and Dave opened all the windows. The gulls were on their morning patrol, knocking over garbage cans, chasing small animals, fighting bitterly over the tiniest scraps. The cats sat in the window and let out short strangled cries, as if they already had a bird by the neck. Dave put out fresh food for them and changed their litter and gave Morpheus his ointment. Then he made himself some orange juice and sat on the couch. Mickey and Terrell slept on.

Dave closed his eyes and thought about the night before,

in the surf with Mickey. He remembered everything he'd felt afterwards and it still seemed true. It wasn't something he could put in words, exactly. It was more like seeing the direction the light came from and knowing that was where he had to go.

He got up and dialed Marc's number in Houston. After the second ring Dave realized it was only nine o'clock. By then it was too late to hang up. A groggy voice answered on the fifth ring.

"Is this Marc?"

"Yeah."

"This is Dave. In Surfside?"

"Who?"

"Is this Marc with a *C*?"

"No it ain't. Just a minute."

He heard Mark shuffle away. Loud voices filtered through the phone. A few seconds later a voice said, "Yo."

"This is Dave. In Surfside?"

"Yeah, Dave. I reckon ol' Patsy gave you a shout, did she?"

"Well, no. Not exactly. This is to do with a conversation we had that day you and Patsy picked me up in Bastrop. You were talking about a line of work you used to be in?"

"I never did much in the way of work, actually."

"This was more like a craft you used to practice."

"Dave, you seem to be having God's own time getting to the point this morning." Marc yawned.

"I'm trying to keep both of us out of trouble in case this phone is tapped."

"Why? Did you want me to burn someplace down for you?"

"Listen, Marc, maybe I better talk to you in person. I might be in Houston this weekend, maybe we can get together. Like, say, Saturday morning?"

"Don't see why not. Could you make it a little later in the day, maybe?"

"I'll call you," Dave said.

He hung up and the phone rang in his hand.

"Is Michelle there?" asked a woman's voice.

"You must have the wrong number."

"Is this Dave? Just tell Michelle it's her mother."

"Hold on."

Dave went into the bedroom. "You know somebody named Michelle?"

Mickey got up and put on a T-shirt. "It's my mom, right?"

She went to the kitchen and picked up the phone. Dave sat on the edge of the bed. "Michelle?" he said softly. He could hear her laughter. Finally she came back and rubbed his hair.

"Mom said you sounded cute."

"Well," Dave said. "I'm glad somebody gets along with their parents."

"She's sweet. I just can't stay with her for more than a few days. She worries about me too much." She got into her jeans.

"Your real name's Michelle?" Dave asked.

Mickey made a face. "I hate it. That fucking Beatles song, you know? But what can I do? She's my mom."

T H E Y drove to Fonthill to pick up Bobby. Dave walked around the front of the house while Mickey went inside. He could see where an old stone house had been built into the design, encased in concrete arches and pillars. Mercer had raised the roof and poured new windows and doors.

Mickey called his name.

"Coming," he said. He laid both hands against the cool cement. There was a ridge in the concrete where two edges of the form had met. Dave closed his eyes, trying to let the stillness of the house flow into him. Then he headed back to the car.

Bobby had on turquoise high-topped All-Stars, red sweat-pants, and a red-and-black T-shirt that said Vision Street Wear. The shirt looked like it had seen a couple of years of hard use. It didn't fit as loosely as fashion demanded. He had his skateboard and a Gerland's sack with pads and a helmet showing through the plastic. Mickey got in the back seat so Bobby could ride up front.

Dave was edgy, no doubt about it. All resolutions aside, now that he was here, committed, it was hard not to imagine the phone ringing back at the house. Mrs. Cook on one end, Terrell on the other. Search warrants and All Points Bulletins.

"288's the best way," Mickey said, arms folded on the back of the seat. "You have to go back toward Freeport to pick it up."

Dave glanced over at Bobby. The kid looked like he'd been into the smack. His eyelids drooped and he didn't show any interest in the world outside. Dave turned the car around and drove back past the old lady's house. He promised himself he wouldn't look, and then he looked anyway. No cop cars. No sign of trouble. He turned right at the Surfside Grocery, went up over the Inland Waterway, and kept going straight instead of turning left for Freeport.

Bobby flipped through a shoebox of Dave's cassettes. It was mostly sixties stuff that he hadn't heard in a while. "Hey, all right," Bobby said. "The Doors." He put the *Strange Days* side into the player.

"I saw them," Dave said. "Back in '68." He checked the rearview mirror. Mickey stared out the window, unimpressed. Bobby didn't seem interested either. The concert had been in June, the summer after Dave's freshman year at college. He went with Alice. Jim Morrison wore black leather pants that looked like he'd stuffed a sausage down the front. Alice threatened to rush the stage. Dave was working construction all day and only saw her on the weekends. She and her mother had moved to Dallas. It didn't seem to make things easier. They were back to making love on her mother's floor, playing records on the stereo, stripping the music off of them and replacing it with raw emotion. It was still on the records, and Dave could play it back whenever he wanted.

Sometimes it came back when he wasn't prepared for it. Right then, for instance. It made him feel like he hadn't learned anything since high school, that he was still making the same emotional mistakes.

Like the way he let Mickey keep him on an emotional roller coaster. Most of the time he didn't mind. Except that afterwards he found himself on the phone to Patsy or staring at Mary Nixon or thinking about Alice. All these women were like the places he'd lived, and there were countless other women that were like the places he'd never seen. They all had claims to pieces of him. The urge to travel fought with the urge to settle down and dig in.

Physicists were still looking for the fundamental structure of the universe. Dave had read up on it. One week it was supposed to be quarks, the next gauge fields, the next super strings. Dave thought Fred was closer to the truth when he talked about paradox. The universe was built up, piece by piece, from contradictions. When the physicists talked about "broken symmetries" that was clearly what they meant.

The salt marsh wastes gradually filled in. There were gas stations, then convenience stores and fast food. They were in civilization. They merged with Brazosport Boulevard and turned north toward Houston. Bobby hit the EJECT button in the middle of "Horse Latitudes." The smack had worn off and he looked more lively.

"Can I play one of mine?" he said.

"Sure."

He took a tape out of his bag and put it on. It was power chords, screaming solos, a rough-voiced lead singer, young, having problems with parents and teachers and sex. "Who is this?" Dave asked.

"The Suicidals. Suicidal Tendencies."

"They're okay."

"My dad can't stand them. He can't even stand the idea of me listening to them. He thinks I'm going to kill myself."

I hope Mickey is noticing, Dave thought. All these chances to make a remark about the heroin and I'm not saying a word.

"That's such bullshit," Bobby said. "People don't kill themselves over songs. My friend Mike snuffed it. He did it because he busted up with his girlfriend. My dad can't understand what the music says. Don't fear the reaper, that's what it says. You can't live if you go around afraid all the time. You end up like him. Fat and old and hanging on to your Mercedes like it means something."

"Sure," Dave said. "Look at me. If my parole officer knew I was doing this, she'd put me back in jail."

"You're on parole?"

"Yeah."

"That's pretty cool."

"Not like you might think."

"Are you scared?"

Dave hesitated a second, then nodded. "Yeah. What about you? You nervous about the contest?"

"Some."

"You ever done it before?"

"A contest? No. I skated this ramp plenty of times. It's super fast. The top layer's metal, see."

"What is it usually?"

"Masonite. So it's really hard, really slick."

"How do you have a contest for skateboards, anyway? I mean, I thought you guys didn't believe in rules and like that."

"There aren't any rules, hardly. There's judges. They get pros to judge. And you only got so many chances to skate. It's not like ice skating where you have to do certain tricks. The judges don't really care about flash. They want to see you in control, see you skate hard and tough. The thing is not to slam."

"Does Steve skate today?"

"No, man, Steve's been in forever. He qualified, like, this summer. There's thirty spots for tomorrow. Twenty are for kids that qualified in other regionals, like Steve. Locals get to thrash it out for the other ten. Steve, man, Steve's sponsored and everything. Santa Cruz sends him to contests all over. They want him to turn pro."

"What's that involve?"

"It's a salary and everything. He'd get his own model deck and do all this promotion and shit. He's going to do it, too. End of the year."

Mickey said, "Really?" It was the first thing she'd said since she got in the car.

"That's what he said last night."

"He didn't tell me," Mickey said.

"You haven't been around. He says after he turns pro he's moving out to California."

"You really think he'll go?"

"Sure, man. He's going to be a pro. He can do whatever he wants."

Dave checked the mirror. Mickey was staring out the window again. "Hey," Bobby said. "There's a McDonald's. Can we eat?"

"Not there," Dave said. McDonald's reminded him of prison: the regimentation, the uniforms, the plastic smell. He pulled into a Red Top and got a couple of bags of food to go. Mickey didn't want anything but a chocolate shake and then she didn't drink it.

T H E Y drove in toward the center of Houston. Dave could see clusters of mammoth buildings to the north, obscured by smog and pine trees. Mirror-glass towers in subdued shades of green and brown came up on both sides of the road, which had swollen to three concrete lanes in either direction. Traffic was thick and never slowed down. Houstonites seemed comfortable driving bumper to bumper at seventy. Dave, sweating, found his way onto US 59 North. If he kept on it long enough it would take him through the Big Thicket, Lufkin, and Nacogdoches. A billboard overlooking the intersection claimed to have 98,100 viewers daily. To Dave it seemed an indictment of Western civilization rather than something to brag about.

Once they got outside Loop 610 the road deteriorated to blacktop. They passed salvage yards and used car lots and peeling white fences decorated with hubcaps. Bobby leaned forward. "It's around here somewhere. Maybe you should go ahead and get off."

They crawled along the access road for a mile or so. Men in white undershirts watched them from the porches of decaying businesses. Some were black, some burned nearly black by the sun. Bobby recognized Aldine Mail Road and

Dave made a U-turn back under the freeway. They passed
a strip center with a parking lot full of pickup trucks and
turned right at a cheap motel.

The skatepark had a yellow portable sign in front. It made
Dave feel at home. The neighborhood around it was full
of trailers, and houses that were either being knocked down
or moved. There were a few scrub oaks and a lot of weed-
choked lawns. It was less festive than Dave had imagined.
They parked on the grass in front of a green metal shed.
A sign on green astrobrite posterboard said, "Go beyond
this point at your own risk." Another sign said, "Closed
Friday for preliminaries. Open Saturday 12 noon for contest."

Beyond a hurricane fence Dave saw four ramps, varying
in height from four to ten feet, all painted deep blue. He
recognized them from the TV news report. Bobby seemed
wound up, in a hurry to get started. They followed a walkway made of two-by-fours around the metal shed to a
glassed-in pro shop. The man inside directed Bobby to
the judges' stand to register.

"Listen," Dave said, taking Bobby aside. "Are you covered for the entrance fee and everything?"

"It's cool," Bobby said. "Don't worry about it."

Close to a hundred kids had already showed up. Some
of them had helmets and pads and some were clearly only
there to watch. Despite the difference in their ages and the
length of their hair, they had similar postures and the lines
of their clothes were the same. Bleachers were set up next
to the biggest ramp. The youngest kids and a few parents
sat there, shoulder to shoulder. The older kids leaned against
the fence or the exposed framework of the other ramps.

Wooden stairs ran up the back of each of the ramps. Ten
skaters waited on the arm of each U to drop in. Some of
them stood with both pairs of wheels hung out over the
edge, the board held in place with one foot on the tail-

piece. A skater in flowered jams came up over the lip and tried to spin around in mid-air. He came loose from his board and slid on kneepads down the curve of the ramp. His skateboard flew off at an angle and slammed into the chain-link fence. As soon as he got out of the way two more skaters leaned forward and shot down from opposite sides. Some invisible etiquette prevailed and one of them held up at the top of the opposite wall.

The judges' stand was a long wooden table and some folding chairs. The table held a big Peavey amp, speakers with horns, and a cassette deck. A long-haired kid in his twenties, wearing a Thrasher T-shirt, jams, and a knit Rasta cap, sat behind the table with a microphone. Harsh, urgent music blared out of the speakers. Dave recognized Metallica. The noise of the urethane wheels against the metal ramp was loud enough to be heard over the music. Every few seconds the kid in the Rasta cap would interrupt with comments like, "All right, a really ripping frontside grind."

The next skater was Steve. Dave recognized him even with the short, bicycle style helmet and his hair tied back in a pony tail. He wore red sweatpants and a black T-shirt with a grinning skull. Everyone else had been smooth, graceful, had made it seem effortless to float into the air, to keep the skateboard glued to their feet. Steve raged. Even the sound of his wheels was louder. He attacked the lip with the bottom of his board, skidded the length of it and dived back into the trough. When he turned his body he turned tight, hard, and fast, arms pumping, hands clenched into fists.

Dave saw Mickey five feet away, watching. "He's good," Dave said.

Mickey shook her head and looked away with a faintly contemptuous smile. Like Dave was an idiot to even bring it up.

"I thought he didn't have to skate today," Dave said.

"He didn't *have* to. He's taking warm-ups. Getting the feel of the ramp."

"Did Bobby get registered okay?"

"Yeah, he got in. His heat isn't till five."

Dave checked his watch. It was ten after one. "I've got to run an errand. Will you be okay here for a while?"

He got the ironic smile again. It was like, Dave realized, she was embarrassed to be seen with him. He said, "You can tell Bobby I'll be back by five. I promise."

"Whatever."

D A V E had been to Houston a couple of times in high school for football games with rival St. John's. He'd spent a weekend there during college because of a Houston girl named Kristi. It was the same as Dallas except for the pine trees and the seaport. Concrete and mirror glass ruled. The downtown area had atrophied while giant malls like Galleria had turned into arcologies. People could live and work and shop there and never go outside. They'd tried to revive downtown with a frenzy of oddly shaped architecture, then discovered there was no one left to rent it to.

Dave took 59 South to the university area. With a map he managed to find the Texas Historical Society on Bissonnet. It was in a two-story granite building surrounded by bookstores and fern bars. The secretary sent him back to see a woman named Sue. She was six feet tall, with strong legs and intermittent gray in her hair.

"We're out of applications for the RTHL at the moment. We could mail you one. But from what you told me, I don't think it's going to give you what you need. All it says is you can't change the protected structure without sixty days' notice."

"I don't want to sound antagonistic," Dave said, "but what good is that?"

"If the developers are after it, it would give us time to try to find another buyer. Or make an offer ourselves, if we had any money."

"And if they don't give notice?"

"Then we can take our historical marker back."

Dave handed her the printed sheet she'd given him. "Thanks. I guess."

"I'm sorry. I know how you feel. Helpless, right? Money talks. History walks."

V I T A L Statistics was on the first floor of the Harris County Administration Building downtown. Dave headed north on San Jacinto from Polk Street. It was like driving backward in time. The tinted glass and turrets and triangles of the First City Tower gave way to metal projections and parallel lines out of the fifties. Then came the brick and granite offices out of the twenties and thirties, gray with soot, plywood in some of the windows. Dave swung around in front of the civil courts and found, to his surprise, a place to park.

He took the set of plastic windows out of his wallet and put it in the glove compartment. It had all his identification in it. He still didn't know if he had the nerve to go on. He put the newly flat wallet in his pocket and got out of the car. Then he nearly locked the car with the keys inside. A wino eyed him from a bench and decided he wasn't worth getting up for.

The County Administration Building looked like a parking garage, its concrete walls streaked from dirty rain. Inside, the paint had the yellowed look of entrenched bureaucracy. The clerks sat behind windows and had clear plastic signs over their heads. It was impersonal enough to ease his nerves.

It struck him that he was not particularly afraid of being arrested. His most blatant fear was of being seen through, of getting another lecture like Mrs. Cook's.

He got in a long line and waited. Boredom became a calming influence. Finally he got to see the man in front of him go through the procedure. No complicated story necessary, only a card to fill out. Still when he stepped up to the window his hands trembled.

He held the metal-topped ledge in front of him and said, "I need a duplicate birth certificate?"

The woman, a thin blonde with hooded eyes, handed him a card. He completed the lines for "Full Name" and "Date of Birth" and "Place of Birth" and "Mother's Maiden Name." Under "Father" he wrote "Unknown." The woman took the card and $7.50 and told him to stand in a second line until his name was called.

It was another ten minutes. He pictured supervisors being brought in, then the police. When the voice said "Lucas Johnson" it took a full two seconds for the name to register. He went to the window and a man handed him a fresh-minted photostat of Lucas Johnson's birth certificate.

His relief was instant and overwhelming. He wanted to click his heels. He was cunning and powerful and free. Anything seemed possible.

TRAFFIC was already bad. The car in front of Dave, as he crawled down Highway 59, had a rear window full of signs on suction cups. "Playboy on Board." "Stud in Car." "Bulldog Fan on Board." The guy behind the wheel was too bulky for his Toyota Supra. He looked like a football player gone to seed. He had a terrycloth headband on, as if driving demanded all his athletic skill. He darted back and forth across the lanes without doing himself any good. Dave kept his distance and listened to KLOL and dangled his left arm out the window.

Even with the congestion he made it back before five. He found a spot where he could lean against the eight-foot ramp and still see everything. The crowd had thinned. There was a certain frenzy to the skating and Dave figured the heat was almost over. He didn't see Mickey or Steve around and it made him uncomfortable. Okay, he admitted, jealous. It made him jealous. Mickey hadn't done much to make him feel otherwise.

The four judges were down front on the other side of the ramp, inside the chicken wire that held the spectators back. They all had white Vision Street Wear T-shirts, still with creases in them, that a company rep had given them. They had clipboards and pencils which they didn't seem to use. They mostly talked and kidded with each other. The DJ with the Rasta cap got on the microphone and said, "Okay, people, we need to clear the ramp for the last heat." It took a while. Everybody wanted a few last licks. Finally the ramp was clear and the next group was all lined up across the top. There was room enough there for a couple of folding chairs and for a photographer, who'd been shooting his flash in the skaters' faces all day.

Bobby was the last one up. His left arm looked out of
proportion. Then Dave saw he'd taken the cast off and
wrapped his forearm in Ace bandages. It scared Dave that
the kid could have so little regard for his own body.

The DJ read off the kids' names and starting positions.
Half the kids seemed nervous and unsure what they were
supposed to do. The others were wired, laughing and trac-
ing out their runs in the air with their hands. Bobby was
different. It was like he didn't see anybody else up there.
He slowly pushed his board out past the edge, one foot
on the tailpiece. The DJ kept reading. Dreamily, without
seeming to intend it, Bobby stepped out onto the board
and dropped in.

He rode with no apparent effort. There was no moment
when Dave could see him throw his weight or suddenly
lean forward to make his board climb the wall. Suddenly
he was clear of the far side of the ramp and falling back
again, backwards this time. On the near side he straddled
the coping with his board and rocked for a second, then
shot back over the edge. He went five feet into the air on
the far side, high enough to grab the board and kick one
leg straight out into space.

"Could we clear the ramp, please?" the DJ said. Nobody
paid attention. All day long he'd announced rules—no vid-
eotaping, no parking in neighbors' driveways, no climbing
the fences—and everybody had ignored him. Now they
whistled and cheered for Bobby. Bobby did a one-armed
handstand on the edge of the vertical drop, his left hand
holding the board onto his feet. The crowd yelled. The DJ
went back to the list of names. Bobby made another ten
or twelve passes and finally missed a trick, riding it out on
his knees.

"Okay, Bobby," the DJ said. His voice echoed back flat
and metallic from the steel ramps and sheds. "We see you.

How about giving somebody else a turn?" The crowd yelled
some more. Bobby held his skateboard over his head as
he walked off the ramp.

As he climbed the steps in back of the ramp his eyes met
Dave's. Dave knew better than to wave. Bobby gave him
a short, serious nod, and Dave nodded back.

Bobby hogged the action for the entire heat. He took off
on other skaters and never gave ground. After a while he
would only make two or three passes and then sit and pant on
the ledge at the top. Then he would nose his board out
and go again. He bailed out twice, not counting the slam
at the end.

That was the bad one. Dave saw the bandaged arm fly
out and hit the wall before Bobby could get himself aligned
to land on his kneepads. He got up slowly and shook his
head. Dave wanted to go out to him, like some kind of
overprotective parent. Instead he made himself look away.

Bobby only took one more run after that, a short one,
nothing fancy. Enough to show he was still in there. He
waited until the DJ called the end of the heat to do it, like
he was making a point.

Dave let himself move with the crowd toward the back
of the ramp. Bobby was the last one down. He still had
his helmet and all the pads on. He saw Dave and pushed
his way through to him.

"What'd you think?"

"You looked good," Dave said. "Doesn't that piss the
judges off, that business of skating early and cutting people off and like that?"

"Snaking," Bobby said. "I guess we'll find out. They knew
who I was, anyway. They want you to skate hard, they
can't come down on you for being aggro. Could you maybe
help me with these pads?"

He stuck his right thumb under the side of one kneepad.

He didn't move the left arm at all. "How bad is it?" Dave said, pulling on the other side of the pad.

"How bad is what?"

"Your arm," Dave said. "I saw you hit it."

"It's okay. It's fine."

They got the other kneepad and the right elbow pad off. Dave reached for the left.

"Leave it for now," Bobby said. "You seen Steve?"

"Not lately. Mickey's off somewhere too."

"Did they see my run?"

Dave considered lying for a second. "I don't know. Maybe."

"Yeah."

"You hungry?"

"Yeah. I got to see if I qualified first." He looked past Dave's shoulder and his face relaxed. "How ya doing, Mickey?"

"You looked awesome, dude. You really ripped it."

"Yeah?"

"Yeah."

The DJ said, "Can I have all riders to the judges' stand. All riders to the judges' stand, please."

Bobby moved to the head of the crowd. Dave hung back with Mickey. He thought maybe she would say something about where she'd been. She offered Dave a piece of Super Bubble and he shook his head. The DJ, off mike now, read the names of the ten qualifiers. Bobby made tenth.

Bobby pushed his way back to them, his left arm behind his skateboard. He looked like some ancient injustice had been set right. It was less than a smile, and his eyes were slightly damp. Mickey kissed him on the mouth and said, "Congratulations."

"Yeah," Dave said. "Right on, man."

"Thanks," Bobby said. "I'd like to clean up. And maybe eat?"

T H E pros were staying at the Holiday Inn, a mile and a half toward town on the access road. Supposedly it was the best around.

It looked all right to Dave, clean and new, two stories of rooms covering a block or so, orange brick walls and turquoise trim. Mickey waited in the car with Bobby while he went in.

It only took ten seconds. Dave came out again and said, "Full up. He said we could try the Motel Hong Kong, or the Sunshine."

"Yuck," Mickey said. They'd passed both on the way. "No thanks. Steve's got a room here with two double beds in it. We could take one and put Bobby on a rollaway."

Dave wondered how Mickey knew the contents of the room. "What's Steve going to say about it?"

"I'll go ask," she said, getting out. The gentle sway of her walk gave Dave an involuntary pang.

"What about you?" Dave asked Bobby. "You want to stay with Steve?"

"Sure," Bobby said. "Why not?"

Mickey came back two minutes later with the key. The rooms were laid out in an L behind the office. There was a pool in the center with white metal furniture and umbrellas that were once the same color turquoise as the trim. Dave drove around back and parked by the room. Beyond the motel's back fence were cheap houses—shacks, really. A bunch of Chicano kids played basketball around a hoop nailed to a tree. Dave opened the trunk and brought up his duffel bag and Bobby's grocery sack. Mickey had everything she needed in a big black purse.

Both beds were made, Dave noticed. The walls were white, with light fixtures and mass-produced landscapes over the beds. Steve sat on the bed nearest the door, bare to the waist, hair wet from the shower, watching TV. He nodded to Dave and said, "Maid's bringing the rollaway."

Bobby went straight into the bathroom and started the shower. Mickey sprawled across the second bed, face down. Dave sat awkwardly on the edge, not quite touching her. Nobody said anything. Dave didn't feel like it was his place to start.

Wheel of Fortune was on TV. It was a very popular show in Bastrop FCI. The players clapped for themselves and cheered self-consciously as the wheel went around. After the wheel they took turns at Hangman, like Dave used to play in grade school, and then the winner got to go shopping right there on stage. Dave knew Terrell would have the same show on back home in Surfside. It was the American Dream, shrunk down to fit a 19-inch screen.

Bobby came out wrapped in a towel. Dave couldn't help but notice his left arm. The muscle had atrophied from the cast, and a fresh bruise was coming up yellow and purple behind the wrist. The kid's eyes were squeezed almost shut and his teeth dug into his lower lip. He got his grocery sack and went back into the bathroom.

The game show ended and Steve changed over to MTV. Madonna was on in a video full of scenes from one of her movies. Steve snorted in disgust but left it on.

There was a knock at the door. Dave jumped to his feet, heart pounding. Steve gave him an irritated look and Mickey said, "Jesus, Dave."

"Sorry," he said. "Nerves." Since he was up he went to the door. A woman in a white polyester uniform had one hand on a rollaway bed.

"Need any help with this?" she said. Dave shook his head,

gave her a dollar, and set it up on the far side of the room. Bobby came out of the bathroom in clean jams, T-shirt, and a flannel shirt with the sleeves rolled up.

"Hey, Steve," Bobby said. "You want to get something to eat?"

"Nah. Santa Cruz reps supposed to take me out later. You got your own key and shit, right?"

"Yeah," Bobby said.

"Then that's cool." He hadn't looked up. It was like they were already gone.

T H E Y ended up at a Western Sizzlin' Steakhouse. None of them knew the area and Bobby wanted red meat to prime himself for the next day. Dave didn't think Bobby had been into the smack yet. He was twitchy and had plenty of appetite. After dinner he got in the back seat and said, "You want to drive around for a while?"

Dave looked at Mickey, who shrugged. "Sure," he said. "How's your arm? You okay?" Bobby had held a fork in it, awkwardly, long enough to cut his steak, and after that had left it in his lap. When they stood up he'd carried it in his right hand like a carton of eggs.

"It's okay," Bobby said. "No problem, okay?"

They took 610 to the Pasadena Freeway. It was Friday night, date night. The couples sat shoved together in the front seats of pickup trucks, or had arms over the back of each other's seats in little Japanese sportscars. They all drove too fast. Dave got off on Red Bluff Road and followed Bobby's directions into the heart of Pasadena. They passed an island city of refineries that dwarfed the chemical plant in Surfside. Flames shot out of the tops of the towers and a thick brown cloud hovered overhead. The air smelled like a distillation of rotten leaves and cigarettes and hardboiled eggs. It felt oily going down into the lungs.

"Welcome to Pasadena," Bobby said.

Gilley's, the gigantic C & W bar with the mechanical bull, had made the area famous. The oil crisis and the end of the urban cowboy fad had killed Gilley's, and it hadn't done the rest of Pasadena much good either.

Bobby steered them into a middle-class neighborhood a lot like the one Dave had grown up in: brick houses, station wagons among the pickups, precisely edged lawns. "That one there," Bobby said.

Dave pulled up across the street. The house was nothing special, a mud-brown stucco with wrought-iron burglar bars over the windows and big wrought-iron hinges on the door. Through gauzy curtains Dave could see the glow of a TV set and a man's legs on a recliner.

"Boy, that really makes me feel weird," Mickey said.

"Me too," Dave said.

"It's like they're a real family and we're a joke family. Mom and Pop and Junior here in the back seat." From that angle, Dave had to admit, what he had with Mickey looked pretty hopeless.

"It only looks like a real family," Bobby said. "From the inside it really sucks."

"You don't miss it at all?" Mickey asked him. "I mean, sometimes I just have to go home for a few days, till Mom gets used to me and starts, you know, complaining about my hair and all."

"I would never go back," Bobby said. "And if I did they would never let me out again."

Dave wasn't convinced by Bobby's tone. Maybe it was more to do with him than Bobby. "That there," Dave said, "is what everybody wants me to be. Straight job, mortgage, wife, kids, the whole package. What kills me is I sit here and look at it and I still feel, I don't know. Like I'm missing out on something."

"They program you to feel that way," Bobby said. "With TV and school and movies."

Dave let the car roll forward. "It's not like I really want to live like that. I guess I miss believing in it. That someday I would wake up and be an adult and everything would make sense and I would know what I was supposed to do."

"You ever talk to them?" Mickey asked Bobby. "Since you split?"

"I called one of those hotline deals, had them tell my folks I was okay and everything. So they wouldn't, like, drag the bayous and put my face on milk cartons and shit. They'll be okay. They got my brother. He'll grow up to be a good little lawyer, just like Dad." The house shrank to nothing behind them. "This is getting to be a drag. Either of you dudes into video games?"

They found a "Family Recreation Center" off 610. Dave provided the quarters and let Mickey and Bobby show off. Mickey's favorite was a driving simulator called Out Run. It had a young couple in a convertible and a real wheel and gas pedal. When the car went off the road and rolled, it scared Dave out of his wits. Mickey couldn't get enough of it.

Bobby didn't do so well. There wasn't much he could play with only one arm. Dave could see the frustration and pain building up. He called it off after an hour and drove them back to the motel.

They got in around ten. The room smelled like Cashmere Bouquet and fresh ironing. Steve was still not back. Mickey turned the TV on with no sound and sat up on a stack of pillows. Bobby went into the bathroom with his grocery bag. Dave sat and stared at the TV, not seeing it. He knew Bobby was shooting up. He didn't know how to stop it. He kept checking his watch. After ten minutes he couldn't stand it anymore and knocked on the bathroom door. "You okay?" His nerves were all twisted up again. "Bobby?"

"Yeah, yeah, I'm fine. Can't a guy take a shit?"

Bobby came out a couple of minutes later moving slow. He must have given himself a pretty good jolt. He lay on the rollaway and watched TV with unfocused eyes. Dave stripped down to his underpants, hesitated a second, then took them off too. He got under the covers and fell asleep thinking about the birth certificate out in the glove compartment of the car.

W H E N he woke up the room was dark and silent. He was sprawled out on his back. The taste of the air conditioning told him where he was. That and the lack of cats. He almost missed them. He started to turn over, then felt a familiar warmth in his groin. Mickey was under the covers, stroking his penis. He felt her roll a condom onto it and suddenly he was wide awake.

The other bed creaked as Steve shifted his weight and sighed. Dave froze. Mickey's mouth moved up his chest and over to his ear. "Relax," she whispered. She sank her teeth gently into his earlobe and moved on top of him. It was too late to argue. She said "Oh" very softly as she fitted herself onto him. He could see her now, the vaguest of outlines, black on black. The bed whimpered gently under them. Dave, embarrassed, excited, confused, grabbed her buttocks with both hands and leaned up into her, a futile attempt to quiet the bedsprings. Mickey raked her fingernails across his nipples and after that the noise hardly bothered him at all.

Afterwards, after he'd been to the bathroom and settled down again with Mickey pressed against him, before he fell back into sleep, he thought he saw Steve's face in the darkness of the bed across from him, eyes open, calm, watching.

W H E N he woke up again it was light. The digital read-out on the TV said seven-thirty. Steve's bed was empty. Dave put on his jeans and went outside to look at the morning. He heard a car start on the street behind the motel and then saw Steve in the parking lot, warming up. He was in shorts, socks, and tennis shoes, touching his toes. Dave nodded to him, unsure of where they stood.

Steve nodded back. "Want to run some?"

"I haven't got anything to wear."

"Those sneakers you had on last night'll work. I'll loan you some shorts. Come on."

They ran south along the 59 access road, past an orange-and-white Whataburger and a giant supermarket called the Fiesta Mart. Steve kept the pace down to where Dave could handle it. He was the closest to cheerful Dave had ever seen him. "This isn't how I pictured you," Dave said.

"I don't recommend this for everybody," Steve said. "Somebody like Bobby, he's probably got to keep fucking himself up for a few more years. That's cool. You need that too. I'm not sorry I did all that when I was a kid. It's just, after a while the engine starts to miss. You get tired of feeling poisoned all the time."

"Clean living?"

"A joint or a beer every now and then won't hurt you. Even that doesn't get me off like it used to."

"You know Bobby's shooting smack."

"Yeah. I don't like it. I could tell him to quit. He'd take off."

"I guess," Dave said. They ran on for a while. Dave had never run with anyone before. It was pleasant. Despite the air that tasted like auto exhaust and the brittle, patchy grass littered with cans and cups and fast-food napkins. The land was flat, the interruptions man-made: on and off ramps, embankments, overpasses.

They ran by more auto wrecking yards with chain-link fences, and turned back at the Wing Motel, a pink brick building with interlocking hexagons on its sign. "This'll be plenty," Steve said. "I just want to take the edge off. Don't want to get worn out."

"I saw you skate yesterday. I don't know much about it. You looked like the best up there."

"Yeah? Thanks. The trick is not to slam. I get too aggro sometimes, go after it too hard."

"Bobby said you're turning pro."

"Yeah. Been waiting a long time for it. Guess I'm ready as I'm gonna be. If I win today, then I could sign with Santa Cruz after the Nationals."

"I kind of envy that," Dave said. "Ambition, I mean. Everybody I know seems to want something. Money, usually. All my friends turned into lawyers or insurance adjusters or programmers. Even the ones that didn't care about money had something they wanted to do. Teach. Paint. Something. So what's left for the rest of us?"

"I guess I never thought about it."

They came up on the Fiesta Mart again. "Ever been in there?" Steve asked. "They got the goddamnedest vegetables. Fresh stuff you've only seen in cans. Canned stuff you've never seen before. Whole aisles for these little jars of Burmese food."

"Vegetables," Dave said.

"Yeah. I'm into them."

"I've been thinking about a garden. You know, for something to do."

"Gardens are good. I been meaning to fix up that old greenhouse out back. Fresh is always better than you can buy in stores. Even in Fiesta Mart. Also you can get outside the system that way. Barter instead of money. The whole scene."

They ran around the back of the motel. Dave noticed signs of recent landscaping. There were small green yucca plants and hedges only a couple of feet high. Steve slowed to a walk and then started stretching in front of the stairs. "You can have the first shower," Steve said. "I got to warm down for a while."

"Thanks," Dave said.

He took a long shower and got dressed in the bathroom. Mickey and Bobby were still asleep when he came out. He wrote a note for Mickey and put it by the phone. It said he'd be back by eleven. Steve was already stripping down for his shower. It felt strange to leave him there naked with Mickey. He told himself he really had no choice.

He called Marc from a pay phone in the lobby. "Is this Marc with a *C*?"

"Yeah."

"Did I wake you up again?"

Marc yawned. "That's okay, I had to get up to answer the phone."

"I'm sorry."

"Let's just don't let it turn into a habit. What's on your mind?"

"I'm in town, out around 59 north of 610. Can I meet you someplace?"

Marc gave him directions to a Jack-In-The-Box off 610 West. "I'll meet you there in half an hour."

"Half an hour," Dave said. "Great."

Dave found the place and sat inside for forty minutes, staring at his hands. He was too nervous to eat. Marc finally arrived, still with exactly two days' growth of beard and the same crumpled hat. He waved and got in line at one of the registers. Dave joined him and paid for his food.

"So," Marc said, carrying his sack to the table. "You want me to torch someplace for you?" He opened his sack and took out tacos, onion rings, a fried pie, and a large coffee. He poured hot sauce on the tacos. Dave looked away.

"It's like this," Dave said. He waited in vain for the right words. "Yes," he said at last. "Yes, I want you to torch someplace for me."

"You want an onion ring?"

"No thanks."

"Where is it?"

"Surfside. The place I'm living in."

"Insurance?"

Dave shook his head.

"I don't get it," Marc said, biting deep into a taco. "Not to be nosy, but what's the problem?"

"The problem is everybody wants a piece of it. No, scratch that. There's a long line of people, and they all want the whole thing. Either the phone's ringing or somebody's breaking in or I'm being drugged or seduced—"

"Them last two don't sound bad. Drugged or seduced either one."

"It was bad enough. I'm going out of my mind. I can't take any more. And the more I find out about the old lady

that used to live there, the old lady whose money they all
want, the more I think she'd want it this way too."

"What about them cats you're supposed to be watching?
I thought this job was the only thing stood between
you and the hoosegow."

"Well," Dave said. "I don't have that part entirely figured out yet."

Marc finished the last of the tacos and wiped his mouth.
"For a old friend of Patsy's I suppose I could do it for a
thousand. Plus expenses."

"What kind of expenses?"

"Okay, make it a thousand even."

Dave nodded. "How much notice do you need?"

"I got all the pieces laying around, here and there. However long it takes to get to Surfside, I guess."

"That's great. Do you need, like, an advance or anything?"

"I could use five bucks."

Dave passed him a ten and left his hand out. Marc looked
at the pie in his right hand, set it down, wiped his fingers
with a napkin, and shook. Dave stood up. "Thanks. I really appreciate this."

Marc shrugged. "Hey. What are friends for?"

T H E maids were cleaning the room when Dave got back.
Everyone else was gone. His note was where he'd left it.
It had been scribbled on, as if Mickey had tried to get a
pen to start writing. Or maybe she was pissed off. There
was no message.

He went on to the contest. The lot was full and he had
to park on the street. He could hear Guns 'N Roses blast-
ing over the sound system as he got out of the car. This

time it cost him six dollars to get in. The man in the booth stamped his hand with a picture of a camera and gave him a National Skateboard Association sticker. A couple of hundred kids were already there, mostly male, a lot of them fifteen and older. They were decked out in their finest: neon yellow shoes with tiny printed skulls, sweatpants with a row of Thrasher logos, loose berets that looked like flattened chef's hats. One kid had a Trojans T-shirt that said, "To Serve and Protect."

Steve and Mickey stood talking to the DJ on the flatbed truck. Mickey looked nervous. She had her head at an odd angle and kept pulling at her hair with her left hand. Bobby sat next to the stairs behind the ten-foot ramp. He looked seriously fucked up.

Dave walked over. "What's happening?"

"Where'd you go this morning?" Bobby asked.

"I had something I had to do."

"We didn't know if you'd be back for the contest or what."

"Of course I was coming back. I left a note."

"Yeah, okay. Forget it."

"How's the wrist?"

Bobby shrugged and looked away.

"Are you going to be able to skate?"

"Sure. Why not?"

His attitude pissed Dave off. "Because you're fucked up on smack, that's why not."

"I can handle it. I know what I'm doing."

"Right," Dave said, and walked away. That's good, he told himself. You can act like a fifteen-year-old too. Congratulations.

There was no place left to sit, nothing to lean against. Dave stood at the back of the crowd with his arms folded. They were only kids. He could see over them. The DJ went through a complicated explanation of how the first round worked. What it came down to was only the best run counted. The top five went straight into the finals, and the next ten went into a second elimination.

It didn't matter if Dave understood or not. The kids didn't need his approval. It was a pocket universe where they could accomplish something real, something of their own. They couldn't do that in the adult world, the world in which Dave was supposed to be rehabilitating himself.

Dave could feel the nervous energy in the shifting of the crowd, in the brittle voices of the kids waiting to skate. A stiff breeze pulled at Dave's shirt. Clouds dimmed the sun then blew on past a second later.

Finally it started. Dave listened in on the kids in front of him and picked up some of the language. The axles were called trucks. Skating backwards, tail first, was a fakie. Rocketing vertically off the ramp was catching air.

Steve was in the first heat. He skated like he had on Friday, only harder and faster. His airs cleared the ramp by at least six feet. When he ground his trucks along the coping he drove the other skaters all the way back from the edge. He skated so hard he couldn't stay on his board. He had to bail out of both his practice runs and on his first scored run he went off the floor of the ramp and rode his board for twenty feet in the dirt. At the end of his second scored run, his last chance to qualify, he spun completely off the wall, turning over at the same time. "All right!" said a kid next to Dave. "McTwist!" Steve didn't make it. He hit the wall face-first and rolled down the curve of the ramp as the DJ called time. He was so wired that he grabbed his board and ran up the face of the ramp and pulled himself onto the top.

The judges gave him 79s, good enough to put him in the eliminations. Bobby didn't skate till the third heat. Dave felt his stomach relax and went to the concession stand for peanuts and a 7-Up. He assumed Mickey was in the crowd somewhere. He hadn't seen her. He didn't want to make a point of looking. She could find him if she wanted.

He walked out to the street. The highway was a long block away, the cars most likely headed for the malls. He wondered how it would look to one of Bryant C. Whitney's UFOs as it hovered over Galleria. Like some kind of religious ritual, probably. The carefully chosen clothes, the excitement, the crush of people. Jobs existed so people would have money to shop with. Cities, cars, TV, the stock market, the IRS—all necessary and inevitable offshoots of the basic shopping experience.

He looked back in time to see a twelve-year-old kid hang suspended in the air above the ramp. Time stopped. Dave forgot to breathe. The guitar on the PA held a single long, screaming note. The wind puckered the kid's shirt and pushed at his hair. For as long as he could stay up there, all laws were suspended, no rules applied.

And then everything lurched into motion again and the kid disappeared. Dave sat on the hood of the K-Car and finished his peanuts. It was the kind of thing that made somebody think. The maximum somebody could sink into skateboarding was a few hundred dollars, counting pads and helmet and Vision Street Wear. For a fraction of that a kid could skate in old clothes. Either way there was no gas tank to fill up, no dock fees to pay, not even air to put in the tires. No ski lifts to ride, no boat that had to be hired, no partners to work out a schedule with. When Bobby or Steve got on their boards and pushed off, they were on their own.

Dave tried to imagine an entire world like that. It didn't seem half bad.

BOBBY'S heat started at two-thirty. There was trouble from the start. He was slow to get off on his first practice run. His balance was lousy. He tried to ride up onto the lip and didn't make it all the way. He came off the back of the board. The song on the PA ended while Bobby was still in the air. There was the ominous hiss of the speakers and then a heavy thud as he hit the floor of the ramp.

He was slow to get up. The DJ reminded him he had thirty seconds left. He got on his board and tried to pump back and forth and work up the speed to get to the lip again. He wobbled and fell off and slid down the wall on his knees.

Dave pushed his way up to the chicken wire and stood there, fingers through the wire, squeezing it. He couldn't tell if Bobby had landed on the bad arm again. In the shape he was in, Bobby might not have known either.

Bobby picked up his board and went around to the stairs and climbed back up. When they called his name for his second practice run, one of the other skaters nudged him. Bobby waved him away and the next kid went on.

He was up and ready in time for his first scored run, board shoved out over the edge. Dave could see his hands shake. The board got away from him as he dropped in. He slid down the transition on the seat of his pants. The crowd laughed. At first the laughter made Dave furious, then it made him ashamed.

The riderless skateboard rolled back and forth under its own momentum. It took Bobby too long to chase it down. The crowd started to hoot. When he finally caught it he lifted it over his head and threw it into the dirt. It bounced and landed against the chicken wire, wheels up and spinning. The painted face on the bottom leered at Dave with spiral eyes. Bobby headed for the parking lot, jerking at the strap on his helmet.

Dave leaned over the fence and picked up the skateboard. Nobody stopped him. He was an adult in a land of children. He carried the board out to the car and put it in the trunk.

Bobby sat under a tree, looking off into the distance. He still had his pads on. When Dave walked up Bobby said, "I don't want to talk to you."

"Okay," Dave said. He sat down a few feet away. After a couple of minutes he heard Bobby start to cry. Dave lowered his head until it rested on his knees. That way Bobby would know he wasn't watching.

Eventually Bobby said, "Why don't you leave me the fuck alone?"

"Good question," Dave said. "I don't know."

"Maybe you just like losers. Me, Mickey. You."

"Yeah, maybe." It sounded like Bobby was through crying so Dave lifted his head back up.

"What a bunch of shit," Bobby said. A few seconds later he said, "I mean, who cares? Streets and pools are real skating. This is a lot of bullshit. I shouldn't even be here."

Dave said, "Seems to me like you don't know what you can really do until it counts for something." He didn't look at Bobby, just talked quietly like he was talking to himself. "Yesterday you skated a lot harder than you did in that pool."

"Yeah, well. The real pressure was on today and I fucked up."

"*You* didn't fuck up. You *were* fucked up. If it wasn't for the skag, you would have placed."

"The what?"

"Skag. You know. Heroin."

"My dad always says, 'If the dog hadn't stopped to whiz he would have caught the rabbit.' "

After a minute or so Dave said, "What does it mean, when you get sponsored?"

"What's that got to do with anything?"

"I just wondered what it is Steve gets from Santa Cruz."

"They pay his way to contests, they give him decks and T-shirts and all like that."

"Okay, well, here's the deal. You get off the smack, and I pay your way to contests. As soon as somebody offers you a real sponsorship you go with them. If you shoot up again, you're on your own."

"I don't get it. What's in it for you?"

"I don't like feeling helpless. I don't like to watch something happen that pisses me off and not do anything about it."

"Where are you supposed to get the money?"

"That's my problem." Dave got up. "You think about it. You decide you want to do it, you tell me."

D A V E went back into the park to watch Steve win.

It was never in question. He kept skating the way he had been and he stopped coming off the board. He made it look like he'd slammed just to keep everybody else in the contest. He finished at the top of the second elimination, pulling off the McTwist he'd missed earlier, practically grinding the coping right off the lip of the ramp, rocketing six and seven foot airs, balancing it all with moments of perfect stillness that made the next run seem even harder and faster.

The top ten skaters were all headed for Phoenix. They had a final jam to settle their positions. They lined up and skated in order, no time limit, going until they slammed or wore themselves out.

A swollen sun lay behind the pine trees, turning the air fifteen kinds of blue and pink. The stereo was cranked until the bass and drums blurred into a single pulsing wave of noise. The lead guitar sailed over it and climbed into the sky with the skaters and the sunset. There were stretches when Dave, just watching, forgot who and where he was. The music and the power of the hurtling bodies filled his entire consciousness. He couldn't have asked for more than that.

Finally it was over. The DJ read the names of the final-ists, starting with the alternates. Steve stood by the judges' stand, smiling easily, talking with one of the other riders, not seeming to pay attention. Dave thought Mickey would materialize somewhere near Steve in the crowd. He couldn't see her. He didn't know if she was riding back with him and Bobby or not. It was one more thing he had no con-trol over.

Then he felt a hand on his arm. She leaned her head on his shoulder and said, "You ready to split?"

Dave held up one finger. The DJ called Steve's name for first place. The crowd cheered hard and long. Dave made his way through them and held out his hand. Steve shook it, smiling. "I'm heading out," Dave said. "It was intense."

"Yeah," Steve said. "Thanks. I'm going to get fucked up with the reps and see what happens."

Bobby was asleep in the back of the car. Mickey made it to the Houston city limits and then went to sleep herself, her head in Dave's lap. Dave put on KLOL and kept the volume down, listening to Aerosmith and Van Halen and Bon Jovi. He stayed calm until Angleton, twenty miles from home. From then on, every time he passed a phone booth he stared at it and wondered if he should call ahead, find out what he was about to walk into.

The old lady's house was dark as he drove past. He told himself everything would be all right. Mickey woke up as they pulled into Fonthill's gravel driveway and said, "Are we there?"

"Depends. You want to stay here or come home with me?"

"With you, I guess. The shower's better."

"Thanks."

She kissed him distractedly. "Don't get all bent out of shape. I'm going to run in and get some clothes."

She woke Bobby up. He crawled out of the car and stumbled into the house without even a thank you. The ungrateful little shit, Dave thought, gathering up his skateboard, pads, and grocery sack. It amazed him how easily the attitude came to him. Dave's own parents had probably had occasion to feel the same way. He left the stuff on a concrete bench in the big front room.

Outside it was genuinely cold. He stood in the wind and shivered. It would be nice to stay there, not go back to Terrell and the phone and the real world. The sky was clear and Orion was straight overhead. With a little push he should be able to swim off into space.

Mickey came back outside. She trailed her fingers lightly around his waist and got into the car. Dave got in and started the engine. He rolled his window down as he hit the highway and let the cold air bring tears to his eyes.

Terrell's car sat in the driveway. Dave tiptoed up the stairs and tried the door. Unlocked, of course. Not that it mattered, with the two squares of cardboard where glass should have been. The litter obviously hadn't been changed since Friday morning. Mickey made a face and wandered off to bed. Dave checked the pad by the phone for messages.

There weren't any. He cleaned the house, happy in the mindlessness of it, fed the cats, and gave Morpheus his medicine. Liz kept butting against his legs and squalling. Dave picked her up and held her against his chest. "Come on," he said. "You're not going to tell me you actually missed me." Liz closed her eyes, purred, and then tried to bite his hand. It was past one when he crawled into bed next to Mickey, exhausted.

S U N D A Y came up cloudy and cold. Dave wasn't sure what kind of heat the old lady had or how to start it up. It seemed foolish to bother when he was warm where he was. He kept dozing off and it was ten-thirty before the smell of coffee from the kitchen finally got him up.

He put a flannel shirt on over his T-shirt and jeans, and put on thick socks and high-topped sneakers. He went into the living room to find the kitchen door wide open. Oreo and one of the black cats strolled outside while he watched. "I give up," he said. He walked into the middle of the room. "You hear me, Terrell, wherever you are?" He was not quite shouting. "I give up."

He found a thermostat on the wall behind the couch. He set it for 72 and switched it to heat. There was a click and a comforting hum.

From the doorway Terrell said, "I hear you. What you on about this time?"

"Nothing," Dave said. "Forget it. Anybody call for me this weekend?"

"No, man. Nobody called. Shit, it cold."

Dave turned to look. Terrell had a bulging green trash bag in either hand. "Now wait," Dave said. "I thought we had an understanding."

"Forget understanding. I like you, Dave, but you don't understand shit. Try and understand this. In two hours I am out of here forever."

"Heading for Atlantis."

"Naw, those motherfuckers don't know a good thing when they see it. Where the money come from, they want to know. Gonna start my *own* country. Think I'll call it . . . Terrell-Land. What you think?"

"It's you, Terrell. What can I say?"

"Gonna be vonu for me, son."

"Vonu? Where's that?"

"It ain't a where, it a what. Vonu means 'invulnerability to coercion.' You dig? What you got when they can't fuck with you. Can't make you pay taxes, can't make you fight wars, can't even find your ass."

"Terrell, where do you come up with all this shit?"

"Books, man, books. You should read more your own self. Give you something to think about besides you dick."

"You keep saying you're leaving and you never do."

"You be ready to watch my dust, man. My bags all packed."

"Then why are you bringing all this stuff *in* instead of *out*?"

"We won't be long. Everybody be here by eleven o'clock, be gone by eleven-thirty."

"Everybody?"

"Don't you get all panicky on me, Dave. This got to be done."

Dave had moved instinctively to shut the door. He suddenly noticed two gallon-size plastic bags of white powder on the kitchen table. "Holy shit," he said. He shut the door and sat down. "Is all that heroin?"

"Hey, it wasn't for your girlfriend I wouldn't fuck with it either. But I got to buy in bulk, you understand?"

"Terrell, who's coming here?"

"Enrique, a couple other heavy players. Don't let it weigh upon your mind. You take your vacuum sweeper around this afternoon, clean up real good. Don't forget to throw the dirt bag away when you done. You be fine."

It was a beautiful image. Dave held it in his mind. "Listen," he said. "Maybe Mickey and me will go down to her place until it's all over."

Terrell had been untying the garbage bag. He turned around slowly and let Dave see that his smile was gone. "I can't let you do that. You understand? We almost through this shit, and nobody leaves until it all over. Don't make me get ugly about it."

He came for the heroin. Dave had to step out of his way. Terrell took the bags back into the living room and started moving furniture. It looked like he was getting ready for a tea party. The bags and bales of drugs were laid out on the coffee table like trays of cookies and watercress sandwiches.

Terrell went upstairs. Dave watched him, wondering how far he would get if he ran. It was no good. He couldn't leave Mickey there alone. Terrell came back down with a worn leather suitcase. It was exactly like one he'd seen in the old lady's study. Dave looked at the suitcase, then at Terrell.

"Yeah, okay, I borrowed the suitcase. You want me to pay for it? I buy it off you. How much you want? Hundred dollars?"

Dave held up both hands. "Easy, man. Take it. With my blessings, and the old lady's too."

Terrell set it by the door. "See? All ready for departure." He got a beer and sprawled out on the couch. Heavy footsteps pounded up the stairs and a fist knocked on the glass. Dave heard the thin glass crack. He ran to the door and opened it.

"Hey, bro," Enrique said. "What you know good?"

"Not a lot," Dave said. He showed his teeth nervously. Enrique's tan polyester jacket was stretched so tightly over his gun that Dave could see the checks in the walnut grip.

"Hey, is the Oilers game on yet?"

"I don't know," Dave said.

"It's in New York and they got a early starting time. Okay if I turn on the TV?"

"Go ahead. It's over there."

"Get the man a beer," Terrell said. Dave stared at him. "Shit," Terrell said. "You could at least ask him does he want one."

"You want a beer?" Dave asked Enrique.

"Sure," Enrique said.

Dave brought him a beer. He'd settled on the couch next to Terrell and was clicking through the stations with the remote control. He paid no attention at all to the drug buffet laid out in front of him.

There was another knock. The TV was on too loud. Dave hadn't even heard anyone on the stairs. "Terrell?" Dave said. "You want to get that? I mean, I don't know who's invited to this thing . . ."

"If they ain't cops," Terrell said, "let 'em in."

An enormously tall, muscular-looking black woman stood at the door. Dave figured her to be in her forties. Her hair rolled back from her forehead in a single stiff black wave. She wore a wine-colored pants suit and blouse that tied in a bow at her throat. She had rhinestone glasses and an expensive leather briefcase. "You must be Dave," she said. "I'm really thrilled to meet you. Terrell has told me so much about you."

"Great."

"You got the Oilers on?"

"I don't really know."

He heard the shower start up. Mickey. He should warn her. There was another knock before he could take a single step toward the bedroom. This time it was a short white man with bad acne scars and a tucked-and-rolled leather jacket. Like the others he had a briefcase and a gun. He was very happy to finally meet Dave too.

"You want a beer?" Dave asked, pointing him to the living room.

He shook his head. Terrell said, "You can bring me another."

Dave went into the kitchen. He couldn't seem to get his breath. He opened the refrigerator and stood there for a second, unable to remember what he'd come for. His hand shook so badly the jam jars rattled on their shelves. How could anybody live with this kind of fear every day?

Budweiser, he thought. His hand closed on the can, took it out of the refrigerator, pulled open the tab. He started back for the living room. The voices were louder than the TV now. The air had started to fill with cigarette smoke. All the lights were on and the room was too bright. When the knock came, he reached over without thinking and opened the door.

For everyone else the noise must have gone on like before. For Dave there was a pocket of silence. All he could hear was the blood moving inside his own head. The beer can slipped out of his numb fingers.

He stared into the cat-eye glasses of his parole officer, Mrs. Cook.

D A V E turned and looked into the living room.

Terrell had a beer in each hand. Two pistols lay on the

table. The man with the scarred face had a small dab of white powder on the end of a huge switchblade. Enrique had just lit a joint and the black woman was in the middle of rolling another.

Dave turned back. He watched Mrs. Cook's eyes. He saw them look from the guns to the knife to the bags of white powder to the joints and back to Dave.

The bedroom door opened. Mickey, naked except for a towel held loosely in front of her, said, "Dave, what in the fuck is going . . ."

She saw Mrs. Cook. Mrs. Cook looked at her.

"Oh shit," Mickey said. She backed into the bedroom and closed the door.

A man appeared behind Mrs. Cook in the doorway. He was her age, mid-forties, with a large head and black hair combed straight back. He had jowls that made him look like a basset hound.

"My husband," Mrs. Cook said. "Mr. Cook."

Dave lurched over to pick up the beer can, which was still gurgling beer onto the carpet, endangering Mrs. Cook's open-toed shoes. He managed to get beer all over his hand. He wiped the hand on his jeans, started to offer it to Mr. Cook, then thought better of it. He put the beer on the kitchen table and said, "I can imagine how this looks."

Mrs. Cook turned to her husband. She smiled sadly and shook her head.

"Come inside," Dave said. "Sit here in the kitchen, I'll explain everything."

"I don't believe that would be appropriate." She took her husband's arm and turned him around. "Come along, dear."

Dave took a step toward her, meaning to follow her out. "For God's sake, take me with you, then. They—"

A shadow moved in his peripheral vision. He saw what

was coming and grabbed Mrs. Cook from behind, around the waist. He only meant to pull her out of Terrell's way. He felt her suck in a lungful of air to scream and he slapped his other hand over her mouth.

By that time Terrell had already grabbed her husband by the coat collar, dragged him inside, and kicked the door closed. The cracked pane of glass fell onto the porch and shattered. Mr. Cook hung limply from Terrell's hand, completely passive. Mrs. Cook fought furiously, trying to kick Dave in the shins.

Terrell waved the index finger of his free hand in her face. "Bitch," he said, "*relax.*"

She quit struggling. Dave stepped away from her, ready to grab her again if he had to.

"Who these people are?"

"Nobody," Dave said. "You should—"

"I am this man's parole officer," Mrs. Cook said.

"This is nothing to do with me," Dave told her. "I didn't want any of this. You have to believe me."

"She don't have to believe shit," Terrell said. "I guess I put them upstairs where they be out of the way."

Mrs. Cook looked at Dave. "This is kidnapping, you know. A capital crime. Better you let us go now and take your medicine."

"You come quiet, you understand?" Terrell said. "You see those guns in there. Those folks get upset, they likely to start shooting. Don't none of us want that."

Terrell led Mrs. Cook by one arm and her husband by the other. The dealers looked up from the TV and nodded to them. Mrs. Cook nodded back and smiled horribly. She had gone quiet, her eyes flicking from side to side, taking in details for future testimony.

Dave went into the kitchen. He reached for the phone, pulled his hand away, walked across the kitchen and back.

He chewed on his fingers. It was the end of the line. Unless he killed both Cooks or kept them prisoners for the rest of their lives, they would go to the police. There was no way out.

In the space of a few seconds a million thoughts went through his head.

He would probably never see his parents again. All his business with his father would have to stay unfinished. There was no point in kidding himself that they would ever have settled things. Dave supposed it was always that way. They would have gone on in strained silence until the old man eventually died. At least, Dave thought, he was making the decision for himself. In time they might learn to forgive each other.

Alice. Until five minutes ago he might have called her, talked to her, to her family. Made some kind of peace with his feelings for her. Found out what those feelings were, what they meant. Now she was lost too. Again.

There was so much undone. Shelves of books upstairs to be read. History to learn. Skills to develop. His life lay in pieces around him. The shape it might fit into was impossible to foresee. The end, one ending, had come in the middle of the story.

He called Houston. "Is Marc there? Marc with a *C*?"

"He ain't here." Dave felt like a tire that had sprung a leak. "This is Mark. Can I take a message?"

"This is Dave, in Surfside. Do you know where he is?"

"He's over to the He's Not Here to watch that Oiler game."

"Where?"

"It's this bar down the street."

Mark didn't have the number. Dave got it from Information and dialed it. He waited through seven rings. A sharp, hot pain moved up from his stomach and into his chest.

On the eighth ring a woman picked up the phone. "He's not here," she said.

"What? Oh, I get it. Listen, I got an emergency here. I need to talk to a guy named Marc. With a *C*. He's got two days' worth of beard and a beat-up straw hat. Tell him it's Dave. Say it's an emergency."

The phone clunked onto the bar and the woman shouted something. He could hear the TV in the background and the crowd going wild over something happening on the field. Dave wrapped the phone cord around his wrist and watched the veins bulge out in his hand. He started to hit his head gently against the kitchen wall. A bit harder each time. Soon it made a distinct sound.

"Sorry hon," the woman said. "Don't seem to be . . . wait a sec."

"Dave? This is Marc."

"Oh Jesus. I thought I was going to have a heart attack. Listen, I need you. Like immediately. Now. It's time."

"Jesus, Dave, there's a football game on."

"Life and death, Marc. I'm serious."

"Yeah, okay, buddy. I can listen to it in the pickup."

"Hurry," Dave said.

Mickey came out of the bedroom, tucking one of Dave's old T-shirts into her jeans. He felt a pang at the sight of her.

"What's going on?" she asked. "Who was that old woman?"

"My parole officer. I'm fucked. Don't ask any questions. Don't come back here. Don't worry about me. I'll see you tonight at your place. If not tonight then in the next couple of days."

"Dave? What are you doing?"

"No questions. I mean it. I don't want you to get dragged into this. Go to work. If anybody asks, you never heard of me."

"You have to promise me you're going to be okay."

"I can't promise that. I promise I'll try."

Dave couldn't stand to look at her anymore. She was so goddamn beautiful. He closed his eyes. He felt her lips touch his. When he opened his eyes again she had closed the door behind her.

Dave ran upstairs to see what Terrell had done to the Cooks. He found them both sitting on the upstairs bed. Terrell was searching for something in his dirty clothes. Dave hoped it wasn't a gun.

He ran downstairs. The three dealers seemed increasingly restless as they watched the football game. Enrique said, "Where's Terrell? Is anything wrong?"

"No, hey, everything's fine. Listen, why don't we go ahead and settle up? If everybody's got what they ordered?"

"Sure, man." They opened their briefcases and put envelopes of money on the table.

"You want to count it?" asked the white guy.

"No," Dave said. "No, I'm sure it's all fine. Pleasure doing business with you. I hate to rush you, but . . ."

"You sure everything's okay?" Enrique asked, squinting.

"Positive," Dave said. "Never better."

O N C E they were gone Dave started grabbing cats and throwing them outside. True to form, they now fought to get back in. He found thirteen of them right off. He would look for the others as he went.

He scooped up the envelopes of money and took them over to Terrell's suitcase. As he was about to put them in he saw Terrell watching him from the balcony. Dave opened one of the envelopes and took out two five-hundred-dollars bills. "Okay?" he said.

"Okay," Terrell said. "Save some of that for the phone bill, which may be on the nasty side when it come in."

"What happened to your credit card?"

"You be better off you don't know."

Dave put the rest of the money in the suitcase. "If there's anything else you want," Dave said, "better get it now."

"Might take the TV," Terrell said.

"I'll put it in your car."

Dave carried the TV downstairs and put it on Terrell's front seat. He watched the highway for a while. No cars went by. Everybody was inside watching football. A pearl-gray Cadillac sat across the street, next to the Cedar Sands. It had to belong to the Cooks. Dave walked over to check it out. They'd left it unlocked. He got behind the wheel and stared at the featureless dash, which would light up in digital glory when once the ignition was on. The gray velvet upholstery suffocated him. Dave popped the hood and got out. He took off the distributor cap and tossed it in the sand by the wall of the motel.

Before he went upstairs he got the birth certificate out of Mrs. Johnson's K-Car. He took it into the kitchen and sealed it in a ziplock bag so he wouldn't sweat through it. Then he stuffed it down the front of his pants.

"Okay," he said.

He picked up the phone and dialed Fred's number in Galveston. "It's Dave," he said.

"Hi, Dave. Good to hear from you. I've always said a lawyer should never be ashamed of his convictions."

"We need to talk."

"No doubt. But there's an Oilers game on. What could be more important than that?"

"In an hour from now, more or less, Mrs. Johnson's house is going to burn to the ground."

"You now have my attention."

"Here's the deal. With no house and no cats left to support, you can use her money to buy Fonthill and turn it over to the Texas Historical Society. You can even do it in the name of your company so you can get a tax break and some photo opportunities and maybe a medal. Then if you still want to build condos, you can build them here. It's a better location, you got the beach view, you won't have to knock anything down to make room."

"One second." Dave heard a chair drag across tile and a beer can pop open. "What happens to the cats? You're not killing them, are you?"

"I'm kicking them loose. Any of them want to can move up to Fonthill with me."

"Ah. So you're moving to Fonthill, then."

"Right. I'm going to be the caretaker."

"Who's going to pay you?"

"The estate can probably afford to pay me some. In cash, unreported. And pay to fix up the old greenhouse and so forth. Then I'll barter crops wherever I can. I know it's going to be tough for a while. The cops will be looking for me. But I'll lie low. Maybe I'll grow a beard. And I'll have Mickey and Bryant C. Whitney to help out."

"Whitney. The UFO nut, we're talking here. He's living there too?"

"I haven't asked him yet. I know he'll go for it. He needs a new church and there's plenty of room."

"Okay, now let me see if I've got this. You're going to take care of the old lady's cats, same as before, only now you're going to do it at Fonthill, with Bryant C. Whitney, instead of the old lady's house. Why? Because the old lady's house is about to burn down. Maybe the UFOs are going to burn it down with their heat rays. Maybe it's going to spontaneously combust. That's a detail. Otherwise, do I have the gist?"

Dave let out a long sigh. "That's it."

"Dave? Next time you get in the catnip and decide to make a crank call? Don't do it in the middle of the goddamn Oiler game." He slammed the phone down.

Dave dialed again. "I'm not kidding, Fred. The place burns in an hour. There's a guy on the way here I hired to do the job. If you don't help me I'm going back to prison. I don't know what the consequences will be for you."

"You're serious."

"I'm not trying to blackmail you or take advantage of you or anything like that. I'm saying you're already in it. I regret that, but there it is. I've been thinking about this since the day I got out of Bastrop. It's what I want to do with my life."

"Burn down houses?"

"Just live. Make my own decisions. Know where my food comes from. Be responsible. Take care of myself and my friends. It's a full-time occupation. And I need you, man."

After a long silence Fred said, "Yeah, okay. I'll see you in a couple minutes."

The phone rang as soon as Dave put it back on the hook. He watched it ring twice, then three times. Nothing good could possibly be on the other end. Still he couldn't stand not to know. He picked it up.

"Dave? It's Mary Nixon. Is everything all right?"

"Funny you should ask."

"I mean, Terrell said he was supposed to finish up his business this morning, and I thought I'd call and see if it went okay."

"No, not hardly. My parole officer showed up. Terrell's got her upstairs, her and her husband both. She'll make a dash for the cops the second we let her go. So I'm history. I am out of here. Gone."

"You need a ride?"

"I don't understand. Why do you want to get mixed up in this? I can't do anything about the old lady's fortune anymore. I don't know if I can save my own ass."

"You can be awfully obtuse sometimes."

"What exactly do you want from me?"

"I want to know if you need a ride. You don't have to try to get me into bed, you don't have to give me a million dollars, you don't even have to treat me like a normal human being. All you have to do is tell me if you want a ride or not."

"In that case," Dave said, "yes."

HE found Terrell sprawled across the upstairs bed reading *Playgirl*. "Where's the Cooks?"

"Who?"

"The people you were supposed to watch."

"I handcuffed them to the toilet."

"How bad are they hurt?"

"I didn't hurt them none. And I got the key right here." Terrell tossed it to him and Dave put it in his shirt pocket next to the money. They walked down to Terrell's car. Dave carried a couple of cats that he'd found upstairs. He set them down and they bounded across the street to join a half a dozen others, worrying a giant fish head in the motel dumpster. Another three or four wandered around the carport, sniffing the cold air, clearly unsure of what to do with themselves. Clouds blew past overhead. The sun would flash white for a second, then disappear. The sudden shadows made everything seem to jump.

Terrell put the suitcase in his trunk. Dave said, "Send me a postcard when you get where you're going, okay?"

"Where do I send it?"

"Good point. Just get on a computer somewhere and leave me a message. It'll get to me."

Terrell hugged him, rocking him back and forth. "Going to miss you, blood."

"Things won't be the same around here," Dave said. "That's for sure."

Terrell got in and turned the key. The car started on the third try. It rumbled and shook and spewed black clouds out of dual tailpipes. Terrell gunned it a couple of times, backed it out into the dirt road, and sent it lurching toward the highway. A huge black arm came out the driver's window and waved goodbye. Dave waved back. He kept expecting to see the car wallow to a stop, see the taillights come on, see it back up toward the house again. It didn't happen. Terrell sailed through the stop sign and onto the highway and roared off toward Freeport and parts unknown.

Dave stood and watched the dust settle onto the road. A mob of seagulls came to fight with the cats over the fish head. The wind blew and the cold worked through Dave's flannel shirt. It was time to go upstairs.

T H E house felt deserted without Terrell or Mickey or the cats. The life seemed to have gone out of it. Dave made a careful sweep through all the rooms, under the beds and inside the closets. He found two more cats and put them out. To make sure, he dumped fresh food into the trough in the kitchen. There were no takers.

He went up to Mrs. Johnson's study. Having Mary Nixon to drive him would make some things easier. He unplugged the computer and took it downstairs, then filled up a box with books and papers, including the faded green photo album. From the window he saw Fred's Porsche pull up next to the motel, with Mary Nixon's Buick right behind.

Dave started down with the box. As he passed the bathroom, Mrs. Cook said quietly, "If nothing else, you might think about your immortal soul."

Dave stopped. Mrs. Cook sat on the edge of the tub, leaning forward awkwardly. Her husband had his back against the vanity and their hands met behind the toilet. "I'll let you go as soon as I can," Dave said. "I'm sorry I can't make you more comfortable."

He set the box next to the computer on the kitchen table. There were cats on the porch and Dave chased them away, screaming. It felt so good it was hard to stop. Fred hesitated with one hand still on the door of his Porsche. He didn't seem to want to come any closer.

Mary Nixon ran up the stairs and hugged him. She wore jeans and a white sweatshirt and no makeup. She looked wonderful. Dave patted her awkwardly on the back. He found himself suddenly aroused, either in spite of the danger or because of it. "If you still want to help," he said, "there's some stuff you could take."

"Of course."

They put the computer and the box of books in the trunk of her Buick. Fred watched with his arms folded.

Dave walked up to him and said, "No lawyer jokes?"

"I can't believe this."

"It's happening."

"Now?" He looked nervously at the house.

"No, not yet. But let's stay out here just the same."

"Why?"

"Because Mrs. Cook is in there."

"Oh no."

"Chained to a toilet with her husband."

"You're not seriously thinking of . . ."

"Nobody's going to be inside when it burns. Not Mrs. Cook, not her husband, none of the cats. Nobody gets hurt. I promise."

"Are you sure we can't find an easier way around this?"

"Mrs. Cook walked in on a major drug deal this morning. It was put together by my former cellmate from Bastrop, who escaped from prison last week. You talked to him on the phone the other day."

"The guy you said was the plumber."

"That's right."

"This is serious."

From the highway came the sound of an engine running full out. A pickup roared toward them, wheels barely skimming the road. It was old enough to have odd curves and bulges, and the lavender paint job had been brushed on by hand. It fishtailed to a stop and Marc hopped out of the cab. He didn't bother to turn the motor off.

"It's halftime," he announced. "Let's blow this little buddy and see if I can't make it back to the He's Not Here for the two minute warning."

Dave took him upstairs. Marc walked around the living room and kitchen, tapping the outside walls. He took his hat off and scratched his head. "Wood house like this, it'll go up like flashpaper. Hell, it's all you can do to *keep* it from going up." He hesitated and looked toward the upstairs bathroom. "Is there somebody here?"

"They'll be long gone, don't worry."

"That's good," Marc said. "I can't feature you as the cold-blooded type."

They went outside. Marc put on a pair of Playtex Living Gloves and attached a cardboard box to the ceiling of the carport. That put it under the middle of the living room floor. He used plastic package tape to hold it in place. There was a window cut in the side of the box and Dave could see metal behind it.

"The beauty is," Marc said, "ain't nothing in that box you wouldn't find in a house anyway. Except your thermite, of course. I like to use acid to eat through your detonator wire instead of your mechanical timer. Not as accurate, but it don't leave no evidence, either. And no nasty ticking noise."

He handed Dave the wireless remote control from a Panasonic VCR. "When you're ready, get within thirty or forty feet of the hole in that box, point this doohickey at it, and push PLAY. You'll have about five minutes."

"That's all there is to it?"

"That's it."

Dave pulled Terrell's five-hundred-dollar bills out of his shirt pocket. "Here you go. I really appreciate it." Marc looked at the money for a second and shifted his feet. "Go ahead," Dave said. "Take it. It's not really mine anyway."

"Thanks," Marc said. "I still owe you ten."

"Keep it," Dave said. "Expenses."

"Adios, then," Marc said. "Let me know how it all comes out." He hopped in the pickup and spewed sand and gravel as he spun it around toward Houston.

"This is it," Dave said. "You guys go on. I got to get the Cooks the hell out of there."

"Dave," Fred said. "You don't want to do this."

Mary Nixon kissed his cheek. "There's a joint called the Shove It Inn a couple of blocks up the road. I'll be waiting in the parking lot." She ran out to her car.

Dave started up the steps. "Wait," Fred said. Sweat ran down his face. "We could hide you out. I'll send you to

Mexico for a year. All expenses paid. How hard could it be?"

"You don't want to be here when the Cooks come down," Dave said.

T H E Cooks were exactly where they'd been. Dave had to force himself to slow down. He was in a terrible hurry for it all to be over. He sat on the edge of the tub next to Mrs. Cook.

"This is probably a waste of time," he said. "But I want you to understand. This has gone too far. We're not talking about parole anymore, we're talking about going back to prison. You know what prison does to people. You know I don't belong there."

"Are you going to kill us?" her husband said. "I don't want to die."

"No," Dave said. "This isn't your fault or mine. It's a problem with the rules. They won't stretch to fit me."

"If you surrender," Mrs. Cook said, "you will have a fair trial. Running away will only make it harder on you."

"I had a trial," Dave said. "It wasn't fair. It wasn't about people. It was about laws and evidence. It was set up so nobody had to be responsible for what happened to me."

"Sooner or later," Mrs. Cook said, "you'll have to answer."

"I'm leaving," Dave said. "Leaving the country." It was true, he realized. Not physically, but psychologically. He got out the key and leaned over to unlock the handcuffs. Out of the corner of his eye he saw Mr. Cook's fist arc toward him. He pulled back and took the feeble blow on his shoulder. It knocked the key into the toilet.

Dave suppressed the urge to hit him. "Now look what you did," he said.

"Henry," Mrs. Cook said, "leave him alone."

Dave rolled up his sleeve and fished out the key. "I'm not going to hurt you. I'm letting you go. You can call the cops and everything. There's pay phones down at the 7-Eleven." He got the cuffs off and tossed them in the wastebasket. "Go on," he said. "Get out of here."

Mrs. Cook stood up and rubbed her right wrist. Her husband hurried to the door, then looked back. Mrs. Cook stared at Dave for another second or two, as if there was something she didn't understand. Then she shook her head and led her husband to the stairs.

Dave watched from the landing until they were gone, then went down to shut the back door. The last thing he needed was to have one of the cats sneak in. He wandered nervously through the living room one last time. He could feel Marguerite Johnson's presence all around him. "Sorry," he said to her. "I didn't know what else to do."

He went out onto the porch and shut the door. Broken glass crunched under his feet. Burke stopped halfway up the steps to stare at him. "Scram," Dave said. He clapped his hands. "Get the hell away from here." The cat turned and sauntered back down.

Mr. Cook had the hood of the Cadillac open. He said something to his wife, slammed the hood, and gave Dave a poisonous look. Then the two of them started for the highway on foot.

Dave positioned himself in the middle of the dirt road and took the remote control out of his back pocket. The Cooks had their backs turned, walking away. Don't think about it, he told himself. He pushed PLAY and saw a red light wink on inside the box.

There, he thought. It's done.

He looked at his watch. It was 12:37. He wiped the remote with his shirttail and pitched it into the motel dumpster. He stood there for a second, trying to decide if he should go or wait for the fire to start.

Go, he thought. Don't take chances. If it doesn't work there's nothing you can do.

He started toward the beach. Go, he thought. Run. Instead he took one last look over his shoulder.

Burke was climbing the stairs to the house.

Dave spun around. He cupped his hands over his mouth and shouted, "Hey! Get away from there!"

The cat hesitated on the landing, staring like Dave had lost his mind.

Dave grabbed a rock and threw it at the porch. It smacked loudly into the underside of the stairs and Burke, startled, jumped through the broken window into the house.

D A V E stared at his watch, waiting for his blood pressure to come down enough that he could see. 12:38. And a half. Surely nothing would happen before 12:40 at the absolute earliest. He didn't stop to think any more about it. He ran up the stairs.

Crunching noises came from the kitchen. It astounded Dave that creatures supposed to be as delicate as cats could make so much noise when they ate. He ran into the kitchen and made a grab for Burke's flea collar. Burke saw him coming and took a shortcut through the breakfast bar into the living room.

Dave bounced off a cabinet and turned himself around. He got into the living room in time to see Burke climbing the stairs. "Nice kitty," Dave said bitterly. "What's the matter with you? Are you stupid? Do you *want* to die?"

The cat ran straight across the walkway and into Mrs. Johnson's office, as if he had something in mind. Cornered, Dave thought. Please. He raced up the stairs and into the storeroom and shut the door. He could hear the small clatter of the cat's tags.

He looked at his watch, knowing he shouldn't. 12:41. "Shit!" he yelled. As if in answer a cardboard box crashed to the floor on the far side of the room. The cat landed on a piece of paper and couldn't get a grip with his claws. Dave snatched him around the middle and shook him a couple of times to settle him down.

Then he saw the paper the cat had landed on. It was old, yellowed around the edges, torn and waterstained. The paper itself was thick and wrinkled, probably parchment. There was writing and a diagram. Dave recognized the butterfly shape of Galveston Bay and the two thin arms of Bolivar Peninsula and Galveston Island.

It was Jean Lafitte's treasure map.

For two seconds he stood there paralyzed, knowing all he had to do was pick it up and put it in his pocket.

There was a muffled whump under the house. Dave went cold to the center of his bones. To hell with the map. He wrenched the door open and ran for the stairs, trying to stuff the squalling cat in his shirt.

The center of the living room was a fountain of fire. Air rushed up through the hole in the floor and pushed a cylinder of flame to the ceiling, where it mushroomed out toward the walls. There was already enough smoke to make it hard to breathe. Burke heard the noise of the fire and tried to claw his way to freedom through Dave's stomach, kicking out with his powerful back legs. Dave pinned the cat harder under his arm and stumbled down the steps into the living room.

He couldn't see the kitchen door. Smoke poured off everything in the house. One second the couch was smoking, the next it was covered in flames, the next it collapsed in ashes. It wasn't like any kind of heat Dave had ever experienced. It was active, murderous, unquenchable. He'd had no idea. How could he have turned something like it loose on the world? Clearly there was nothing that could ever stop it. His only consolation was that he would be dead and would not have to watch it sweep across the face of the entire planet.

The coffee table shattered with a crack like a rifle shot. A sudden blast of heat took off Dave's eyelashes and split his lips. He could feel the floor under him sway and moan with the violence of the fire. He'd lost his sense of direction. He looked behind him to find the porthole, to orient himself again. There was too much smoke. The walls behind him were burning now. The air was too hot to breathe. He didn't have but a couple of seconds left, he figured. It seemed ridiculous to get this far and lose the cat too. If he could get to a window he could at least fling the little bastard clear.

At that second the kitchen door came loose from the wall and Dave got a glimpse of the sky. He put his head down and ran for it. Suddenly he was on the porch and hurtling down the steps. The battleship-gray paint under his feet blistered and smoked, the wood itself shrieked in pain. The stairs collapsed when he was only a step from the ground. He landed on his feet, dimly aware of something hitting him in the back.

He was in the road. The front of him was cooler now, but his back was still hot. He realized he was on fire. He threw himself at the ground, both arms still wrapped around the cat, and rolled into a sand dune.

For a second he lay on his back, watching. The fire

erupted through the roof, scattering ash and flaming scraps of paper. It was like the fire saw it had no place else to go. It flung out its seeds and screamed in rage and hunger. Dave got onto his knees, then his feet. He could still see the blistered, smoking paint from the porch. That was how his skin felt. He came over the top of the dune at a dead run, headed for the beach. He got both hands around Burke's middle and held him out at arm's length. He plowed straight into the water and as soon as it got above his knees he threw the cat out to sea and dove into the next wave.

H E swam underwater as far as he could. It seemed like miles. When his head came up the air was bitterly cold. Nothing had ever felt quite as good. He crouched in four feet of water, showing only his head, and turned back to face the beach. That was when he saw Mrs. Cook.

She stared out to sea from the top of a dune. Clouds of thick black smoke rose behind her. She seemed to look right at him. She nodded and for a second she almost seemed to smile. Then she turned and walked away.

A siren sounded in the distance. Dave had no idea what had just happened. He only knew the sirens were coming for him. He was amazed to find he still cared. He flailed his way back to dry land and ran north along the beach. From nowhere Burke appeared, dashing back and forth between his legs, yowling the entire time. Dave was too weak to kick him out of the way.

Mary Nixon and Fred were parked side by side in front of the Shove It Inn. It was a lifetime since Dave had come there to hear the band, and yet it had only been a week ago, his first night out of prison.

"Jesus!" Fred said.

"I'm okay," Dave said.

Mary Nixon found a beach towel in her trunk and wrapped him in it. "I'll take him home," she said.

"I can't go home with you," Dave said, through chattering teeth. "I have to go to Fonthill. Please?"

"I know that, dear," Mary said.

Fred said, "Are you sure? Don't you think he ought to go to the hospital?"

"In the circumstances," Dave said, "no."

Fred stuck out his hand. Dave held on until he forgot it was there. "Be careful," Fred said. "I'll be by to check on you."

Dave nodded and got in the car, careful to sit on the towel. Burke hopped in after him and got in his lap and began to clean himself furiously.

AT Fonthill Dave discovered he was too weak to walk. Bobby helped Mary Nixon get him upstairs. They put him in Mickey's room, on her battered mattress and sleeping bag. Dave passed out for a while. When he faded back in, Mary had sponged him off and was putting ointment and bandages on the worst of his burns.

"It's not that bad," she said. "Remember, 'Joys are often the shadows cast by sorrows.'"

"Thank you."

"Take these." She gave him a handful of aspirin. Dave swallowed them and watched her leave.

Mickey got home a few minutes later. "Oh my god," she said when she saw him. "I heard the cops and fire engines and everything from the store. I went up there and there wasn't anything left of the house. I was scared to death."

"I'm fine," Dave said. Talking hurt his lips. They felt like they were coated in stiff plastic. "I forgot to ask you if it was okay to stay here."

"Don't be dumb." There was no place she could touch him that didn't hurt. She lay down next to him and he slept for fourteen hours.

I N the morning he sent Bobby to the grocery store for apple juice and a copy of the Brazosport *Facts*. The fire took up the entire front page. The headline read, LOCAL MAN BURNED, FEARED DROWNED. Among the witnesses was a Mrs. Sylvia Cook, Federal Parole Officer, who claimed to be the last one to see David Stokes alive. "He went back into a burning building to save a cat," she said. "Whatever his flaws, you have to admire his compassion." Mrs. Cook said she saw the man fall into the ocean, his clothes smoldering, and did not see him come up. Police divers continued to search for the body.

Dave read the article three times. She must not have seen him. If she had, she would have told the police. That was the only logical conclusion.

Logic, Dave thought, wasn't everything.

"What's wrong?" Mickey said, waking up.

"I'm fine," Dave said.

"You're crying. Is there something in the paper?"

"Good news," Dave said. "That's all. Good news." It was a free country. He could believe what he wanted.

She started to take the paper from him and then reached up to stroke his head. "Did you always have this much gray hair?"

"That's a hell of a thing to ask."

"I'm serious," she said.

He went carefully into the bathroom. Without windows or electricity, he had to use a flashlight to see himself in the mirror. He did look grayer, especially around the temples.

Mickey came up behind him. "You can dye it," she said. "There's that Grecian Formula stuff."

"No," Dave said. "I kind of like it." No one would fail to recognize him, and yet he seemed different. It was more than the hair, more than the seared-off eyelashes and swollen lips. He looked calmer, wiser, more in control. "What about you? Think you could get used to it?"

Mickey looked at him. Her face was so full of regret that he didn't want to know the reason.

"Forget it," he said. "Forget I asked."

T H E Y sang "Happy Birthday" and Dave blew out the candles. They'd put all forty onto the cake. Mary Nixon had bought it from a fancy bakery and had managed to get Dave's favorite, white with chocolate icing. Dave believed it wasn't often enough in life that things could be black and white.

Everyone clapped and cheered. Outside, the first winter rains were coming down. Inside it was warm and dry. Mrs. Johnson's solar cells were on the roof, and had taken on enough of a charge before the rain to power a few electric heaters and floor lamps. Fred had brought deaf Charles and blind Barbara, like Dave had asked. Steve and Bobby and Mickey were there, and Mary Nixon had come in from Freeport. Bryant C. Whitney had moved in the day before and tonight he'd dressed up in a plastic tie with a live goldfish inside.

And Burke was underfoot. He never got more than a few feet away from Dave anymore. Liz was there, and Buster and Greaseball and Morpheus, and a half-dozen others, including Sid from Gerland's. More straggled in every day. Dave had built a cat door in the kitchen and brought in sand from the beach for their litter boxes.

Mickey handed him a gift-wrapped package. She seemed nervous. The box was a foot wide and two feet long. Dave opened it up. Inside was a brand-new skateboard. On the bottom was the name Steve Winslow in flame letters that came out of a dragon's mouth. There was a castle in the background that looked like Fonthill.

"I did the graphics myself," Steve said. "That's the first one. They'll be in stores early next year."

"Happy birthday," Mickey said. "And it's, like, also . . ." She had to swallow to get the rest of it out. ". . . a going away present."

"Yeah, okay," Dave said. "I'll be out of here by tomorrow."

"Not you," Mickey said. She looked at Steve. "Us."

"Oh."

"I tried to tell you. It was, like, really hard. Steve's got this job with Santa Cruz and everything. At least he will in January. And he's going out there to get settled in. And he asked if I, you know. Wanted to come with him."

"Right."

"Oh, Dave. Are you going to be okay?"

"I guess it's a little sudden," Dave said. "When is this supposed to happen?"

Mickey looked at Steve again. "Well, we thought we might leave tonight. After the party and everything."

Dave nodded. The silence stretched until it sounded like it could go on forever. Finally Mary Nixon clapped her hands and said, "Dave, cut the cake. Fred, get everybody some beer. And is there music without quite so much screaming in it?"

Dave got on the skateboard and circled the room, to cheers and whistles. After a couple of circuits he sat down next to Bobby on the stairs. The party went on without them.

"You okay?" he asked Bobby.

"I feel like shit, you want to know the truth."

"Still not sleeping?"

"A little last night."

"Drink a couple of beers," Dave said. "Maybe it'll help." Bobby got a beer and came back.

"Steve and Mickey are going to California," Dave said. He got it out quickly to keep the words from tearing him up.

"I know."

"I guess everybody knew but me, huh?"

"Nobody wanted to have to tell you."

Dave nodded. There was a clarity to the pain that was its own reward. It took him closer to the truth. That was more important than how much it hurt. He could see that now.

"I think she's crazy not to stay here," Bobby said. "She was happy with you. She'll go to California, they'll fight, she'll end up out on the streets or something. But you can't stop her."

"No," Dave said. "I guess you can't." Mary Nixon brought him a piece of cake and a 7-Up. She touched his cheek and walked away again.

Dave ate his cake. "Did you see Steve's deck?" he said.

"It's pretty cool," Bobby said.

"You want to try it?"

Bobby put his beer down and got on the skateboard.

"You have to give it back when you're done," Dave said. Bobby nodded and slalomed into a darkened hallway.

Dave went over to the table where Barbara and Charles sat by themselves. He took a piece of paper out of his pocket and handed it to Charles.

"I didn't have a chance to save it," he told them, "but I found an old map before the house burned down. I think I got it pretty near right. If not, let me know and I'll try again."

Barbara made squealing noises in the back of her throat. Charles looked at the folded paper and then at Dave's mouth. Dave smiled and nodded. Charles grabbed Barbara's arm and took her into a corner. They worked the paper open with trembling hands.

Fred took a beer out of the ice chest and said, "Why is it New York has so many crack addicts and Texas has so many lawyers?"

"Is this a joke?" Dave asked.

"It's because New York got to pick first." He drank some of the beer. "Did you really find the map?"

"It was *a* map, anyway. And I let it burn. I didn't really see what it said at all. But I wondered if maybe they didn't need the chase more than they needed the gold."

Fred shook his head. "I don't hardly know what to make of you anymore."

Dave climbed up to the balcony to watch the party from a distance. Mickey stayed close to Steve without ever seeming to look at him or touch him. She'd turned into a stranger. Dave found himself wondering what she would be like in bed, as if it had never happened between them.

He heard a toilet flush and water run into a sink. They even had hot water now. Bryant C. Whitney came out of the bathroom and sat next to Dave. "Great party," he said.

"It was a real surprise."

"Not as much as when you asked me to move in. I can't tell you what that means to me. I thought the church was finished."

"You didn't go to the cops about Terrell. That impressed me a lot. Anyway, it's a big house. I guess there's room enough for us all."

"That's all I ask. A roof over my head until They come for me."

"They?" Dave asked.

Whitney looked up to the ceiling.

"Right," Dave said.

"I'll be back in a minute," Whitney said. "I need to change."

"Change?" Dave said. Whitney smiled and walked away.

Bobby skated back in and got another beer. Fred talked to Mary Nixon and kept checking his watch. Dave closed his eyes and tried to put Mickey out of his head. He thought about the next day, working on the greenhouse, building a bed from the scrap lumber Fred had brought.

"Dave!" Fred shouted. "Get your ass down here!"

Dave made his way downstairs.

"I got to get these people back," Fred said. "Since you don't exist anymore, it's hard to use you for an excuse."

"Sure I exist," Dave said. He got out his wallet and showed Fred his new driver's license, with Lucas Johnson's name and Fonthill's address. Mickey had used makeup to cover the effects of the fire and he looked almost like himself.

Fred took it away and stared at it. "Hell, according to this, today isn't even your birthday! Stop the goddamn party!"

Outside, the rain had tapered off to a light mist. Charles led Barbara out to Fred's car. As she got in she said, "If anybody asks, I'll say I never saw you!" Charles pushed her gently into the front seat. Fred turned the car around and drove off toward Galveston.

Mickey kissed Dave softly on the mouth. She had a paper bag with her things in it. She got into Steve's car and waved and then they were gone too.

There were two layers of clouds, one low and moving fast, the other high up and motionless. The moon was only a crescent and the few stars that showed through were fiercely bright. Whitney came out and stood next to Bobby. He'd put on a silver lamé jump suit.

"A good night for UFOs," he said. "I believe I'll take a walk."

"Okay," Dave said. "Be careful."

Bobby said, "I'm going up and see if I can crash for a while."

"Okay," Dave said. "Listen . . ."

"Yeah?"

"It gets easier."

"Sure," Bobby said.

Mary Nixon said, "Sweet dreams."

Dave found himself alone with her.

"I'm sorry about you and Mickey," she said.

Dave shrugged. "I'll be okay. I guess it was a pretty screwy relationship."

"A lot of them are."

Somewhat to his surprise, Dave found he was holding her hand.

"This is nice," she said. "My last husband never used to hold hands. He didn't like kissing, either."

Dave tried kissing her. It wasn't half bad, even if his lips still hurt a bit. He started to put his arms around her and she moved them back to his sides. "Wait. Don't push things. There's still a lot you haven't figured out. A lot you don't know."

"Like what?"

"Like who I am. Like what's important to me."

"So tell me."

"I'm not sure I even know anymore. I think we all need a little time to sort ourselves out." She put her hand on his cheek. "As my second husband used to say, 'Discontent is the first step in the progress of a man or a nation.' "

He walked her to her car and kissed her again. "That was nice," she said. She handed him a small slip of paper. "Here. This was my second husband's favorite."

It read, "Accept the next proposition you hear."

"Mary?" Dave said.

She started the car and drove away.

Dave was still awake a few hours later when he heard the front door open. He got up to turn on a light at the head of the stairs. It was Bryant C. Whitney, still in his shining silver suit.

"Any luck?" Dave asked him.

Whitney looked up. His smile was radiant. "No. But soon now. You'll see."

AUTHOR'S NOTE

The real Fonthill is in Pennsylvania. The Loompanics Unlimited catalog is available from PO Box 1197, Port Townsend, WA 98368. It includes *How To Start Your Own Country* By Erwin S. Strauss, *Guerrilla Capitalism* by "Adam Cash," and a major inspiration for this novel, *The Abolition of Work* by Bob Black.

ABOUT THE AUTHOR

Lewis Shiner is the author of *Frontera* and *Deserted Cities of the Heart,* both nominated for major awards. His short fiction has appeared in *Omni, RE: AL, The Fiction Magazine, Twilight Zone,* and other markets, and has been reprinted in *Mirrorshades, In the Field of Fire,* and other anthologies. He is the editor of *When the Music's Over* (forthcoming), a benefit anthology concerned with alternatives to violence. He lives in Houston, Texas.